HAVING THE BUILDERS IN

Dame Constance de Clair has a remarkable talent for getting what she wants. And, at this precise moment she wants to transform her beloved yet overly square castle, Vine Regis, by adding an extension. But for once, all is not going according to her plans...

Quite apart from the fact that her builders seem more intent on demolishing the existing castle than they do building the extension, her son's wife-to-be, Susanna (a flirtatious minx with a penchant for drama), has arrived at Vine Regis eager to dislodge her as Lady of the castle; Constance's son, Gervase, appears more interested in going hunting than getting to know his intended; everyone is in a state of mild hysteria as the French threaten to invade England; and to top it all off, there appears to be thievery afoot.

Something is going to have to be done about it all before the estate begins to crumble (quite literally, at this rate) but the question is, what...?

HAVING THE BUILDERS IN

Reay Tannahill

WINDSOR
PARAGON

First published 2006
by
Headline Review
This Large Print edition published 2007
by
BBC Audiobooks Ltd by arrangement with
Headline Publishing Group

Hardcover ISBN: 978 1 405 61706 2
Softcover   ISBN: 978 1 405 61707 9

British Library Cataloguing in Publication Data available

Printed and bound in Great Britain by
Antony Rowe Ltd., Chippenham, Wiltshire

This book is dedicated to Gloria McFarlane,
invaluable critic and best of good friends

CHAPTER ONE

1

Dame Constance de Clair was thirty-nine years old, clever, handsome, assured, and possessed of a strong and sometimes malicious sense of humour which she usually kept under strict control. Though not invariably.

Now . . .

'A troubadour?' she repeated. '*Another* one?' She fixed the man standing before her with a sparkling blue eye and he quailed slightly.

'Yes, Lady. Asking your la'ship for shelter and patronage. The truce in the French wars is bringing them across the Channel in droves.'

'I know that. What I do not know is why you should come to me about it. Finding entertainers to keep the people of the castle amused at mealtimes is one of your responsibilities as household comptroller, is it not?'

'Yes, Lady. But the last three troubadours have been . . .' Master Edward's voice faded. He was a grey, nervous man, with bad teeth and bitten nails, but very good at his job.

She said drily, 'Excruciating. Poor musicians and worse poets. And you feared to risk my wrath by inflicting another one on us? Well, it might come to that, but not quite yet. You have permission. Was there anything else?'

'No, Lady. Thank you, Lady.' Clutching at the rolls of parchment in his arms, which went everywhere with him but which Dame Constance had never seen him refer to, Master Edward bobbed his head a few times, backed away from the table, and scuttled off down the length of the Great Hall, passing on his way Master Robert, the clerk of the kitchen, stout and rosy, who was coming to report that the price of dried fish had soared in the market. And after Master Robert it was Master Nicholas, the chamberlain, plump and fair and loquacious, who thought the Lady might like to know that the cloth for the retainers' new liveries would be arriving any day now.

'Thank you, Master Nicholas,' she said.

She sighed when he had gone, her lips slightly pursed and her hands loosely clasped on the table before her. She had ruled over the castle and estates of Vine Regis since her husband had been killed in the Scottish wars a dozen years before, and found the task of controlling the whole intricate life of a great estate both interesting and absorbing. But despite its superficial variety, there was a certain sameness about it all. Day after day, her senior household officers came to report, one after the other, on matters they themselves were perfectly competent to deal with but which they thought she would wish to know about. As, indeed, she did. Almost as often, there was a procession of receivers and auditors with lists of rents and other dues paid or outstanding on the castle estates; of tenants with petitions; of lawyers and clerks anxious to consult her on leases and contracts. And, always, there were visitors to be entertained—neighbours, and acquaintances, and distinguished personages on their travels.

She enjoyed what she did but there were times

when she thought she would have enjoyed freedom more. She sighed again, and a voice at her side said, 'Dearie me, it's not as bad as that, is it? On a fine, bright day like this, too.'

She had barely noticed, holding her morning consultations, that outside the thick stone walls the sky was blue and the clouds were fresh and white.

Without looking up, she said with a faint smile in her voice, 'And what do *you* want?'

'Do I have to want something?'

Hamish MacLeod was a big, wiry, red-haired Highlander, her most valued and trusted servant, and Dame Constance could feel his pale eyes twinkling at her from under their almost invisible sandy lashes as he went on, 'I came to say ye've a visitor. Abbot Ralph from Stanwelle. Aye, well, it'll help to pass the time till your son's new bride-to-be arrives, will it not?'

She gave a little spurt of laughter as she rose to her feet. 'At whatever hour that may be. Thank you, Hamish. French troubadours, the price of fish, the new liveries, and now Abbot Ralph. What more could one ask?'

2

Surveying her visitor, a man famous for his dislike of fresh air and exercise, she gave in to temptation. 'What a perfect day, Father Abbot, for so early in the year! A gift from heaven. It would be sinful not to show our gratitude. Let us take a stroll outdoors, shall we?'

The abbot was as imperturbable as he was large—just under six and a half feet from the top

3

of his shining tonsure to the soles of his soft leather buskins—and it was hard to tell whether he recognised that she was teasing him. His reply was bland enough. 'If that is your wish, Lady.'

But she was rewarded, when he followed her out on to the stretch of rough grass that surrounded the castle, by the discovery that somewhere on the way down from the Great Hall he had pulled his cowl over his head and his heavy woollen robe more tightly around his substantial middle as if to protect himself against all the hazards of sunshine and spring breezes.

He said nothing at first as they paced around the knoll on which the castle stood, islanded by its wide moat, but after a while he raised a hand to shade his eyes against the light and surveyed the scene spread out before them.

To the north, on the slopes of the vineyard that gave the estate its name, a dozen dark-wimpled, white-aproned women were pruning the branched vines down to heads of three spurs each; to the west, a few village lads were herding pigs into the margins of the Bluebell Wood to root for fodder; to the south, ewes with their new lambs grazed in bright green meadows; and to the east, where the village began, washerwomen spreading their laundry on the river bank to dry were trading insults with a short, fat man idling along the road. The idler, Dame Constance noted resignedly, was Sim Walden, the village's bad character, who was supposed to be spending the day seeding the flax field.

Abbot Ralph nodded. 'Your land is in good heart,' which was another way of saying that it looked well managed and profitable.

The profitability of her land—or, more correctly, her elder son's land—must, she reflected, be relevant to whatever he wanted from her, for he certainly wanted *something*, and something of more value than the small currency of local gossip. So she smiled cooperatively, appearing to accept the compliment at face value, and waited for him to go on.

After a moment, driven to it by her silence, he did. 'And now to the news I bring. You will rejoice, as a devoted daughter of the Church, to know that the abbey has been offered a holy relic of the most profound significance.'

'Indeed? How splendid.'

He glanced down at her, but her expression was perfectly guileless. 'Such gifts,' he went on, 'seldom come without conditions, of course, in this case that we build a separate chapel to house it. This will be costly . . .'

'Ah, ha!' she thought.

'. . . and any contribution, however small, that you feel able to make towards the expense of the enterprise, would be well received. A few jewels, perhaps? Tapestries? Some pieces of gold plate?'

What an optimist he was. If Dame Constance had been the kind of woman who giggled, she would have giggled.

To the best of her knowledge, the abbey of Stanwelle already possessed not only fifteen authentic relics of Our Lord and three of Our Lady, but assorted vestiges of another two hundred and thirty-four blessed martyrs, apostles, patriarchs, prophets and virgins. Interestedly, she enquired, 'And what is the particular virtue of *this* relic, that it should command a whole new chapel in its honour?'

No one else had dared to question Abbot Ralph as he went about extracting gifts and promises from the local gentry. But he concealed his exasperation and addressed himself to a blackbird standing nearby with its head cocked, listening for worms. 'That is something I do not at present feel justified in divulging.' He had to be sure of the chapel before he could be sure of the relic, and he had no wish to reveal all in case something went wrong and he found himself looking foolish. Well, not foolish, perhaps—that was not a trait that could ever be applied to his stately self—but less Olympian than was his wont.

'I am sure you understand.' His voice was exaggeratedly soft. When people had to struggle to hear what he was saying, it always put them at a disadvantage.

But not Dame Constance. 'Oh, dear,' she said. 'Because, without that information, I do not think that at present I would feel—er—justified in contributing.'

The blackbird, as if aware of a chill setting in, flew off.

After a brief meditation, the abbot offered, 'No? Even if, in acknowledgement of your donation, I could grant you Masses and prayers for your soul?'

Dame Constance did no more than raise her elegant eyebrows a fraction.

He tried again. 'Or, since the windows of the chapel will be of painted glass, I might arrange to have your portrait incorporated as a donor.'

The lady was unimpressed by this, too, and turned to direct her steps towards the edge of the moat. There was a kitchen scullion kneeling on the bank, inspecting one of the fish traps, and it was a moment before Abbot Ralph recognised, with disbelief, that she was more interested in the contents of the trap than in his own discourse. He had never known such an infuriating woman.

He made his final bid. 'It might even be possible to have Rome grant a papal indulgence forgiving you for any sins you may have committed in the past, or might commit in the future.'

She turned back to face him, her expression perilously close to winsome. 'I have always led a blameless life, thank you, and expect that I will continue to do so.' Fortunately, he was too absorbed in his fund-raising even to react to this, so she went on, 'But an idea occurs to me. There is one *quid pro quo* which would have much greater appeal for me than portraits or indulgences.'

A faint frown appeared on the abbot's wide, smooth forehead. The words *quid pro quo*, accurately though they described what he had been offering, seemed to him to have an irreligious taint about them. But he was a realist, so he said, 'Yes?'

She had been worrying away at the problem for what felt like months, and now, miraculously, it seemed as if there might be a solution. In an offhand tone, aware that it would be unwise to let him see how much it mattered, she replied, 'I am proposing to build an extension here at the castle, and there is no suitable stone on my son's land. It would be helpful to have permission to take it from the abbey's quarries. Otherwise I will have to send some distance for it, probably to Caen, which, as you must know, would greatly increase my costs.'

She could sense the refusal trembling on his lips, so hesitated only momentarily before going on.

7

'There would be no inconvenience to you, and no loss. I would arrange for the quarrying to be carried out by my own masons, if you prefer, and I am sure we could reach an amicable agreement about the cost of the stone. I believe the present rate to be—ah—in the region of nine shillings a ton?'

He should have expected something of the sort. He had been acquainted with Dame Constance for years, and he knew her to be as clever as she was handsome, with a remarkable talent for getting what she wanted. If she had been a man, he would have admired her for it.

As it was, he was more inclined to admire her for her other attributes and, in consequence, preferred to have as little to do with her as possible. The regrettable fact was that she aroused unsuitable sensations within him. While those sensations were undeniably pleasurable, they meant that he had to do penance for them, and fifty days on bread and water were bad enough for a man who was fond of his food without the added awareness that all the monks in the refectory were pretending not to know about it—while gossiping busily about what their abbot might have been up to, to incur such a penalty.

Now, with Dame Constance waiting for an answer, he folded his lips judiciously. At least she did not seem to expect him to part with the stone for nothing. Perhaps he should? He was a man who enjoyed making the grand gesture, especially when it was easily affordable. The abbey quarries were extensive enough to furnish two or three great cathedrals at the very least.

At last he inclined his head. 'Very well.

Permission is granted. I do not think you need concern yourself about the cost, beyond paying our quarrymen for taking out the stone, of course. We will talk about it at some other time.'

'Thank you.' She smiled. 'I am sure, on that basis, that I can find something to be put towards the cost of the chapel.'

But there was still a question in her voice, and the abbot knew when he was beaten. 'You will not reveal this to anyone else, I trust, but the relic is'— his massive chest swelled with pride—'a true splinter of the Holy Cross, and it is to be given to us by the king himself.'

She had heard that the king was failing in mind and body, a state which was apt to stimulate generosity towards the Church—man's intermediary with God—but she said no more than, 'How gracious.'

'It will bring many pilgrims to Stanwelle.'

'And much profit.'

'So we must hope. In the meantime, I am having plans drawn up. We are having a rib-vaulted roof in the latest style and will be employing not just our sacristan, or even a master mason, but'—he boasted—'a proper architect to supervise the work.'

Her blue eyes narrowed, but before he could discover why, they heard the sound of approaching trumpets and saw the dust of a substantial body of horse.

'That will be the Lady Susanna, Gervase's bride-to-be,' said Dame Constance. 'She seems to have accomplished the journey from her home in the West Country in very good time.'

'A satisfactory match, I trust?'

9

'I believe so. I made the arrangement with her father, who has since died and left her to the care of a guardian. She has spent the last two years in a convent, and will have another year here at Vine Regis before the marriage takes place. She is of the right age—fifteen—and healthy, and brings with her a dowry of three small estates; one in the west, one on the Welsh marches, and another in the north country.'

The abbot said patronisingly, 'A good match, indeed!'

Gervase's first bride had been sweet and spineless. Dame Constance devoutly hoped that his second would be an improvement. One could never tell just from reports.

'The marriage is the reason for the building work I have spoken of.'

'Is it so? Tell me more.'

3

Susanna knew that birds must be singing and the freshness of spring scenting the air. They always did when March gave way to April and the sun began to shine with forgotten brilliance in a pale blue sky. Spring had been her favourite season throughout the fifteen years of her life.

It was a pleasant landscape through which they were passing, gentler than she was accustomed to. In place of the swooping grandeur of the moors in the West Country, rough with bracken and heathers, rocks and mosses, everything here was neat and tidy, the hills—with small hamlets tucked in their folds—sloping smoothly down to flat green

10

valley floors marked out with little stone-walled fields full of sheep or new-sprung crops, and an occasional stream slipping through water meadows. There were blackthorn hedges foaming with blossom, and pale primroses on the grassy banks, and bright yellow dandelions beginning to open their own rays to the sun's.

Charming to look at, certainly, though not exactly dramatic. It was a pity, Susanna thought, because despite two years of the nuns' determination to teach her serenity of spirit, she secretly retained an addiction to the dramatic.

But at least the placid landscape was being much enlivened, however temporarily, by the procession escorting her to her new home. A pageant of purple and scarlet and gold, it wound its slow but spectacular way through the countryside, the dust kicked up by more than fifty horsemen and running footmen smothering the unfurling green of growing things by the wayside and their clamour drowning out the song of wrens and chaffinches.

Always inclined to think in pictures rather than words, Susanna tried to make up her mind what single colour would best represent dust and sweat and shouting and had just decided on a greasy ochre-yellow when she was aware of one of her escort reining in his horse beside her.

'Everything all right?' he enquired. 'Comfortable?'

She had no need to look up. It was her guardian's son, a lanky thirteen-year-old who—at his father's behest—had spent most of the journey trying to persuade her to withdraw her consent to the marriage with Lord Gervase and agree to marry him instead.

It was the silliest idea. They had squabbled with each other, off and on, for most of their lives, she with the advantage of almost two years' seniority in age and he, as he loftily pointed out, with the advantage of many times that in intellect.

'Really, William!' she snapped. 'Of course I'm not comfortable!'

The poles of her litter—a shallow, brightly painted open box—were slotted into the harnesses of one horse in front and another behind, horses whose gait did not match, so that for the last five interminable days, after the first thrill of knowing herself to be the central and most important figure in this gorgeous procession, she had felt, despite her cushions, as if she were being jiggled around like a pea on a drum. When the groom riding the lead horse failed to signal a change of pace to his fellow on the rear horse, there was an impact that jarred every bone in her body. She also had a splitting headache, although that was largely due to the coils of hair pinned tightly over her ears.

As William should have known, she would much have preferred to ride; would have felt not only more comfortable, but safer, too. Although her escort of knights and squires was supposedly armed against attack by one of the bands of brigands that had begun to invade this peaceful countryside, they seemed to be treating their guard duties more as a jaunt than a duty. It would have been reassuring to know that she could set spurs to her horse if she needed to, but the litter had been thought more appropriate, more festive, so her pretty little palfreys were at the end of the procession, being led—which they didn't like at

12

all—by old Tom, her groom from home.

It would have been more festive still, she thought broodingly, nursing the elbow that had just made bruising contact with the frame of the litter, if her husband-to-be had deigned to form one of her entourage. But Lord Gervase, she had been told, was away in Norfolk on business to do with his estates there. He had sent his younger brother, John, to represent him and, at a carefree eighteen, John was too young to impose discipline.

An engaging boy, he seemed to be all arms and legs, his thinness emphasised by the narrow, tight-fitting, slightly old-fashioned tunic that he wore. His sunny smile sat oddly on a face structured round a hooked nose and strong cheekbones, and he was the most rumpled young man Susanna had ever seen. His shirt, instead of being neatly tucked away, peeked out not only at the neck of his tunic, but at the sleeves, even from under the skirt; there were several buttons missing or dangling loose from the long row down the front of the tunic, and his brown hair always stood on end through having his fingers run through it or his hood pushed back from his brow. Susanna, itching to tidy him up, had succeeded in resisting the impulse to ask, 'Do you resemble your brother?' She was not sure that she wanted to know.

Now, William grimaced at her and said, 'Oh, well. If you're going to be like that about it, I'll leave you for more appreciative company.'

What an irritating boy he was!

He hauled on his reins and Susanna turned to watch his progress back to the cheerful rear of the procession, but as she did so she became aware of a burst of shouting ahead of her and of the

13

vanguard of her escort beginning to come to a straggling halt. They were passing along a track in the side of a small rise in the landscape—not quite a hill, but with ambitions in that direction. To the right, the land sloped down towards them, and the slope was suddenly full of rough-looking men armed with knives and pikes.

Her heart turned over. Brigands!

Anna, the elder of her two gentlewomen, riding close behind, exclaimed, 'Mary Mother!' while the younger, Margot, let out an ear-splitting screech— a clear indication, her mistress reflected later, that their attackers were not of the young and handsome type who could have carried Margot off with her goodwill.

Turning to look towards John, she could see him trying to marshal her escort into some kind of order, but the track was narrow and he had allowed them to ride too close together. The crossbowmen were having difficulty positioning themselves to fire. And if the crossbowmen couldn't fire, she realised, it would be a matter of hand-to-hand fighting, with the rest of her escort having to wait until the attackers came within reach, so that they could wield their flails and clubs against them.

She felt desperately exposed in her brightly painted litter. The brigands probably thought that this was a wedding procession laden with valuable gifts, theirs for the taking! How many of them were there? Not more than about a score or so, she thought, but they looked determined and villainous and perfectly capable of overpowering the dressy but disorganised escort behind and before her. How dared they? How dared they!

14

And then, her heart pounding, she wondered what had happened to the Susanna of pre-convent days, who had been as ready to indulge in risky escapades as William or any of her brothers? I'm not afraid, I'm *not*! she told herself. If only she had a horse! Even without any kind of weapon, it was possible to ride down men on foot. But her palfreys were too far away, and too delicately bred. Then the obvious solution occurred to her. Gathering her skirts, she jumped from the litter and shouted to the groom on the lead horse, who was gazing vacantly at their attackers, 'Unhitch her! Now, this instant!'

'Wot, m'lady?' The slack-jawed stare transferred itself to her. 'Whaffor?'

'Don't ask stupid questions. And when you've done that, you can give me a hand up!'

'She'm no horse for a lady. No side-saddle, neither.'

'Never mind that. The rug will do.'

'Better stand back, then. The poles'll drop, and the litter with 'em.'

She was still fidgeting, murmuring, 'Hurry! Hurry!' when William came tearing back along beside the track, bent low in the saddle and wildly brandishing a smallsword she hadn't known he possessed. Turning towards him, she saw that one of the brigands—a surly-faced middle-aged man with a great scar down his cheek and a knife in his fist—was heading straight for the litter as if he expected it to be full of riches. He looked as if he would tear the jewels from her neck and ears without so much as a thought. The greed on his face was horrible, and there was something vicious and personal about it that made her stomach turn

15

over.

William yelled, 'You stupid girl! Get back behind the shelter of the litter,' and although she resented it she knew he was right, because everything was dissolving into chaos, the wild brigands with their knives and pikes striking downhill against the young and inexperienced squires with their flails and clubs, their very *small* smallswords and their nervous excitement. The brigands had purpose; the squires had only their number and a confused sense of duty. The noise of clashing weapons rang sometimes tinny, sometimes harsh, always terrifying.

'Don't call me stupid!'

'Well, you are!'

'I'm not!' But her voice trailed away because, although William was holding the greedy-eyed man at bay with his sword, she became suddenly and shudderingly aware of the reality of the danger. She had just reached the stage of thinking, 'We're going to die! We're all going to die!' when rescue came.

Horsemen.

The brigands, on foot, had been rushing down on the procession from above, but the horsemen came from below, tearing up the hill from the river at its foot, whooping and yelling, riding fast, their mounts completely under control and their swords raised. Their leader came thundering up to leap the track directly in front of Susanna's litter, never glancing aside but intent on the mad-looking, bad-looking villain who had become her personal enemy.

She had an immediate and intense impression of her saviour as the handsomest young man she had

16

ever seen. Not handsome in any well-groomed, conventional way, but dark and dashing and thrilling!

Breathless now with excitement rather than fear, she saw the brigands hesitate as, no longer a gang but a bunch of individuals, they took to their heels, looking round frantically for ways to escape the onslaught. But the newcomers fanned out and pursued them to left and right, laying about them with the flat of their swords until they all disappeared from sight.

Susanna subsided weakly back into the tilted litter among her cushions. She had a last glimpse of her hero, outlined against the sky, as he waved down to John, shouted something cheerful, and then vanished again.

Heroes and villains having alike disappeared, after a heavy-breathing few minutes John rounded up the casualties, whose injuries appeared to be few and superficial, saw the wounds bound up with strips torn from the victims' shirts, and prepared to set the procession in motion again. William bore the bandaged cut on his hand like a trophy, with pride, as he supervised the re-harnessing of Susanna's litter, telling her meantime that she was supposed to be a lady now, not a hoyden. Defensively, she said, 'Well, I had to do *some*thing,' but he was not impressed.

It was several miles before John materialised beside her, by which time, more or less recovered from her fright and as if the question were of no great importance, she was able to ask about the exciting young man. 'Who was our rescuer?'

John said, 'Piers, you mean? A neighbour of ours. He was on his way somewhere in a hurry.

Couldn't stop to be introduced. And I don't know about "rescuer"—we'd have managed perfectly all right without him.'

Slightly offended by her raised eyebrows, he was diverted when the trumpeter at the head of the procession sent an enthusiastic blast heavenwards and she asked, 'Have we much further to go?'

He gave his usual sunny grin—just as if nothing had happened! 'No. The castle lies beyond that wood you can see at the curve of the road; we call it the Bluebell Wood. The trumpeter was announcing our approach.'

Susanna's relief was so enormous that, when they entered the wood with its sweet, cool smell of damp earth and the centuries-old carpet of mouldering leaves muffling the noise made by her escort, she was able to take real pleasure in the light filtering through the high translucent canopy of new greenery and to laugh as the hunting dogs dashed towards the tree trunks and then, their most urgent need satisfied, began leaping at the red squirrels clinging to the bark, just out of their reach and all too obviously sneering at them. It was still too early for bluebells but ahead, where the tall trees diminished into saplings, she could see the sheets of pale growth that hinted at the blue to come. And then spring would truly have arrived.

She could also see some boys herding pigs, boys who stopped larking around when they became aware of the procession and hastily began driving the pigs to the side of the track. *Village* boys. *Village* pigs. It was a reminder that set Susanna's heart fluttering nervously. In a matter of minutes, she would be introduced to her new home, her new family, her new life. She was terrified.

But then they emerged from the wood and she gasped as she saw a wide valley with a river running through it, a river that formed part of the moat surrounding the little island on which the castle stood. Moats were often dull and stagnant, but this one sparkled cleanly in the sun. The castle itself was square and huge—enormous!—with a great gatehouse in the centre of the southern wall and banners flapping on the corner towers. In the fields and orchards beyond the moat there was a scattering of peasants working away busily, and on the far side of the castle she could see what must be the village, a handful of mostly turf-walled cottages dominated by a small church tower.

It was a scene both orderly and fruitful. Susanna knew from John that his mother had managed the estate since his father, the late Lord Nicholas, had been killed some years before. 'She is a marvel,' John had said. 'Gervase wouldn't dream of taking control out of her hands.'

Susanna had done her best not to frown. It seemed to her that Gervase, at twenty-four, should have taken things into his own hands long ago. That was what men were for. She could not feel entirely comfortable at the thought of a future involving a mother-in-law with a managing disposition and a husband who was too weak-willed—or perhaps too uninterested? or too lazy?—to take over the reins. She could not guess which, and it was not a question she could very well ask of his brother. She would just have to wait until she and Gervase met at last and she could judge for herself what sort of man she was marrying.

She remembered her father, when he was arranging the match, telling her that Lord Gervase was a well-thought-of and responsible young man who was making something of a name for himself in the French wars. So he could not be weak-willed or lazy, she supposed. Her father had also said that she was free to choose whether she wanted to be betrothed to him or not, and she had said yes she did. She had wanted to please her father, and Lord Gervase sounded like an excellent match. Her father had been unable to tell her whether he was a pleasant person or not, and in any case considered that to be a matter of no importance. Rank and riches were what counted.

Perhaps, she reassured herself, it didn't matter what kind of man Lord Gervase was.

Her spirits recovering, she told herself that no, it—did—not—matter. Not now that she herself would be elevated, in a few magical months, from being an immature girl into the Lady of the Castle. It was blissful to reflect that nobody would then dare to talk down to her, or reprove her for her failings, or treat her like a child. Fairmindedly, she decided that, although when she was married to Lord Gervase she would outrank her mother-in-law, she would, of course, be unfailingly polite to her, as she had been taught to be. Good manners were *very* important.

There were two figures standing on the grass outside the castle walls, one slender, female and clad in a gown of a striking gentian blue, the other male and towering over her—a churchman, a White Monk. They were deep in conversation and did little more than glance over and raise a hand in greeting to the gaily decked procession that, with cloaks and pennants flying, was rapidly approaching. They didn't stop talking.

20

'Ah, my lady mother,' said John with satisfaction. 'And Abbot Ralph. I wonder what *he* wants.'

4

It was by no means easy to get rid of an abbot who did not wish to be got rid of.

'If you will forgive me . . .' said Dame Constance, but Abbot Ralph was determined to exact the castle's contribution to his new chapel before he left, and all her hints about giving an appropriate welcome to her son's future bride met a wilfully deaf ear. As far as he was concerned, marriageable maidens were ten for a groat; chapel contributions were not. He wanted his jewels, his tapestries, his gold plate, and he wanted them now. Or at least the promise of them.

'Naturally,' she said.

'Yes,' she said.

'Quite,' she said.

'But,' she said.

It had not the slightest effect.

Intent on getting his own back for his personal discomfort, Abbot Ralph dug his heels in, and Dame Constance, in the interests of her building works, did not dare push things too far. She contrived a hasty word with the invaluable Hamish as she and Abbot Ralph returned indoors. 'Find Sir Walter, and tell him to do what he can. At once.'

But Sir Walter, the castle steward, was not immediately to be found, the travellers not having been expected until much later in the day. As a result, there was no formal welcome awaiting Susanna and her escort as they clattered over the drawbridge, through the great gatehouse and into the central courtyard, which was as bustling as a village street on market day, the huge stone-walled enclosure full of men-at-arms gossiping, grooms polishing saddles and trappings, juvenile pages and squires duelling with wooden swords, village women with covered baskets on their arms, and pedlars offering them cheap ribbons and other dubious delights.

Hamish had done his best, but most of the more senior and respectable members of the household were already up in the Great Hall, waiting for their dinner, and he had succeeded in extracting only a handful of the less senior members who had been hanging back, minding their manners, nearest the door. The procession's formal entry into the castle therefore fell well short of ceremonious.

After the first moments of gaping curiosity, a few youthful knights and squires—urged on by Hamish in a sizzling undertone, 'Well, get on with it!'—gathered themselves together sufficiently to run forward and greet their lord's future lady.

Susanna, having been helped out of her litter by a page who looked no more than nine years old, was feeling slightly lost and wondering about the identity of the big sandy man in the grey castle livery whom John was slapping so cheerfully on the back, when the steward belatedly appeared through an archway, a grave and stately figure with silver hair, protruberant pale blue eyes, and the long gown, chain and white staff that signified his office. Bowing deeply to the bride-to-be, he announced that he would lead her to where the

Lady awaited her in the Great Hall.

Mildly seasick from the motion of the litter, and fighting an urgent desire to visit the garderobe, Susanna followed the steward up a wide spiral staircase, lit only by arrow loops in the wall, to the main floor of the castle and the Great Hall.

Like the courtyard, it proved to be very full of people and Susanna recoiled slightly. She was aware, of course, that a castle was like a town in miniature. Designed to withstand siege in dangerous times, it had to accommodate not only family and servants, but soldiers and armourers, craftsmen, cooks, bakers, brewers and physicians, and sometimes sheep and hens and pigs as well. But it was all alarmingly grand, very different from her own home, an ordinary fortified manor house five days' ride to the west, which was sufficiently remote from centres of power and population— and the roads that linked them—to need only the lightest defences.

Scanning the room, which was stone-walled, white-washed, partially hung with tapestries, and as vast as its name implied, she had no more than a general impression of innumerable groups of men standing around gossiping.

They all turned to stare at the blushing Susanna as she and her party followed the stately figure of the steward across the room. Glancing up occasionally as she picked her way across the rush-strewn floor, she decided that most of the older men looked—'workmanlike' was the only word she could think of. Sturdily built, decently dressed, short of hair, lined of face, though middle-aged rather than old. Men accustomed to the outdoors and to deeds rather than words. The younger men, however, were much more stylish, and she recognised that her brothers' friends at home—the only young men, other than William, whom she had ever known—were the merest country bumpkins by comparison. It was an unnerving thought.

John seemed to know everybody, which was understandable enough, but Susanna would have preferred him to pay more attention to her rather than exchanging greetings with all and sundry. She felt very alone and would have given much to have her future husband walking beside her. It would not only have testified to her importance but have given her a comforting arm to lean on.

There was a jester prancing around, with bells on his cap and a tunic blindingly striped in red and yellow, but his witticisms were scarcely raising a smile. Maybe no one was in the mood, or maybe he just wasn't a very good jester. Susanna felt almost sorry for him. A big, ruddy-faced, loud-looking man who was standing slapping his horsewhip against his boots glared at the fellow as if he were thinking of finding another use for the whip, and the jester backed away hurriedly, almost colliding with the steward before diving like a rabbit into the throng.

And then she forgot about him, because she now saw that she was being led towards a small group of people close by the end window, loomed over by the churchman John had identified as Abbot Ralph, but otherwise consisting of the only women in the room. Seated on a stool was a cinnamon-haired girl of about her own age, who appeared to be giving reading lessons to two female infants. Three respectable, middle-aged gentlewomen

24

stood by, so dim of hair, face and gown as to be very nearly invisible. And in the centre, partly obscured from Susanna's view by a chubby, satin-clad gentleman with several lengths of velvet draped over his arm and shoulder, was the lady who must be her future mother-in-law, Dame Constance de Clair.

The abbot was fingering the velvets and saying, 'Those will do nicely,' as the little procession arrived within hearing. 'They should bring a good price at auction among the local gentry.'

But the chubby man objected, indicating the lengths in turn, 'No, Lady! I had intended this for a new doublet for my lord, and this for hangings for our new lady's bed, and that for . . .'

A long-fingered hand waved his complaints away and a crisp, light voice said, 'That will do, Master Nicholas. We have a better use for them.'

And so, at last, having waited impassively for this exchange to end, the steward was bowing before the unexpectedly beautiful Dame Constance and announcing the arrival of the travellers, and the abbot was standing graciously aside, and Susanna was smiling as delightfully as she knew how, given that she was torn between an almost paralysing nervousness and her resentment at being denied the public welcome she was entitled to expect.

5

Dame Constance, arranging a second marriage for her son shortly after the death of his first wife, had, as was customary, taken an entirely practical view

25

of the matter. Gervase's earlier marriage to Felicia had produced only two living daughters, two others having failed to survive infancy, and he needed sons to inherit. So she had sought a bride who would soon be approaching the first fruitfulness of maturity; one who had several brothers—implying fertility and strength in the bloodline—and who was herself physically well fitted for child-bearing. The late Felicia had been of noble lineage but no stamina, and giving birth to little Eleanor had been too much for her.

That Susanna's father had also been able to offer a substantial dowry was a welcome bonus. Two years had passed since the betrothal, years during which Susanna's father had died, leaving her to the care of a guardian, and the girl had been sent to a reputable convent to learn how to conduct herself.

It therefore came as a disagreeable surprise to Dame Constance that, the nunnery notwithstanding, the girl had all the appearance of being a flirtatious little minx. The bodice of her kirtle was far too tightly buttoned over her plump little bosom, and was of a figured apple-blossom-pink taffeta which appeared to have been chosen to draw attention to her pink-and-white complexion. There was a similar sense of calculation about the sleeveless, gold-trimmed surcoat whose colour was of the same innocent baby blue as her eyes. Strands of blonde hair were escaping from the coils above the girl's ears, despite the blue-and-gold mesh caul that was designed to hold them in place, and her long, curling eyelashes fluttered when she smiled.

She was as fluffy and enticing as a kitten begging

26

to be cuddled, which, in a household inhabited by well over a hundred men and only a dozen women, promised nothing but trouble.

Dame Constance sighed inwardly. Then she smiled, cast a minatory glance at her interested audience, which hastily averted its eyes and went back to discussing the French wars, and said, 'Welcome to your new home, Lady Susanna. Let me make my daughter, Isabelle, known to you . . .'

6

Isabelle was the young woman on the stool, lovely, sleek and indolent. It seemed to be as much as she could do to summon up the energy to smile and say, 'Welcome, Susanna,' then wave a limp hand in the direction of the two small girls beside her. 'These are—that is to say, these *will* be—your daughters, Blanche and Eleanor.'

Susanna, gripped by renewed panic, glanced round for support, but John was absorbed in conversation with a dark and striking-looking knight and she could tell that they were talking about her. Sternly, she rebuked herself for being self-conscious—but it would all have been *so* much easier if Lord Gervase had been there. With a sharp intake of breath, she turned back to the little girls, whom she knew to be six and four years old respectively, gave them her brightest smile and said, with all the sweetness at her command, 'You must begin to think of me as your mama. I am sure we will soon learn to love one another.'

The younger stared silently back at her but, dismayingly, the elder tossed her head, shrugged,

27

turned down the corners of her mouth, and went back to studying her ABC.

Dame Constance said, 'Blanche!' reprovingly, and then, her slightly clipped voice smoothing the moment over. 'I trust that your journey went well?'

Before Susanna could reply, John interrupted. 'We had a bit of an adventure earlier on. Brigands. Nothing dangerous. We soon saw them off, scattered them to the four winds. They won't be back.'

Susanna blinked, but she liked John well enough to let him get away with it. After a moment, she said, 'Apart from that, which I cannot say I enjoyed, it was a perfectly pleasant journey.' And then she heard herself, to her own total disbelief, go on, 'Its only disappointment was the lack of your presence.'

Of all the idiotic things to say!

The sapphire eyes under their delicately plucked brows were amused. 'Thank you. But I think you mean the lack of the Lord Gervase's presence, do you not?'

'Yes,' Susanna conceded breathlessly. 'Oh . . . yes.'

'A slip of the tongue, no doubt. I hope you will not misunderstand if I say that no lady of mature years would willingly undertake such a long ride purely for the pleasure of bearing you company?'

'No. No, of course not. Though you could have had the horse litter, with my goodwill!' Even to Susanna's own ears it sounded impertinent, though it had not been intended so. She felt herself beginning to blush again.

If Gervase was twenty-four years old, she deduced that her future mother-in-law must be

28

somewhere in her very late thirties or early forties but, in the matter of 'mature years', anyone less middle-aged it would have been hard to imagine. Susanna's own mother was sturdy and solid, bundled in no-nonsense grey-brown homespun, but Dame Constance's figure was upright and slender in its deep blue gown, while the widow's barbe that she wore—the nun-like white linen headdress shrouding hair and ears and chin, which always made Susanna think of someone peering through a hole cut in a piece of cloth—seemed to enhance her looks. Her mouth was firm and shapely, her eyes wide and well defined, her complexion flawless; only her nose was a little too narrow and arched for beauty.

A juvenile voice broke in on the awkward silence. 'In case you should be wondering,' it said cockily, 'I'm William Burnell.' His voice cracked halfway through, and he tossed his head pettishly.

What an embarrassing boy he was! 'My guardian's son,' Susanna explained, and Dame Constance inclined her head graciously.

The abbot was more successful at bridging the moment with a few majestic words of blessing for the happy couple—or the half of it that happened to be present—and then said, 'I must take my leave, Lady. No, I will not stay to dine with you, but I thank you for your donation.'

Dame Constance smiled. 'You will not forget its price, I hope?'

'There is little likelihood of that.'

As he swept from the room, there came the piercing warble of a flute being blown by a youthful yeoman who had appeared in the doorway, signalling to everyone that the centre of the Hall should be cleared to enable the trestle tables to be set up for midday dinner.

'Now, my dear,' said Dame Constance, giving her full attention to Susanna, 'you will wish to refresh yourself. You have no need to hurry. Sir Walter,' she turned to the steward, 'what arrangements have we made for the Lady Susanna's accommodation?'

'I thought the Lady Felicia's former chamber. It would be the most convenient.'

Felicia's chamber! The Lord Gervase's first—*dead*—wife! Susanna could scarcely believe her ears. Her own mother would never have left such a decision to a servant, not even such a superior servant as Sir Walter. Her own mother was warm and kind and considerate. Susanna did not want to sleep in a dead woman's room. She wanted to go home.

She had been brought up and educated to know all about correct behaviour, what was right and what was wrong, how people should behave, the rules by which they ought to live. But it was almost as if the people at Vine Regis didn't know the rules or—worse—thought they didn't matter.

Dangerously close to tears, she turned to follow the steward upstairs, and heard William's voice raised again behind her. 'And what about me? Where do I go?'

The big sandy man said, with a smile in his voice, 'How about joining the puppies in the stables?'

CHAPTER TWO

1

When, an hour later, Susanna descended again with her two gentlewomen to the Great Hall for dinner, she was confirmed in her view that the people of Vine Regis didn't know anything about correct behaviour. No one paid the slightest attention to her.

She had made urgent use of the garderobe closet and then rinsed the dust and grit of the journey from her face and hands. After that, beginning to feel slightly more charitable, she had surveyed the late Felicia's chamber and discovered it to be bright and airy and pleasant, with pale blue wainscotting painted with dainty golden stars, a handsome, ornately carved hearth in which a fire of some sweet-scented wood was burning, and an arched window looking out over the moat towards the vineyard. Once her clothes chests had been carried up, her lovely new embroidered pink velvet hangings installed round the bed, and her little shrine hung on the wall, it would seem almost homely.

There was to be nothing homely, however, about dinner in the Great Hall, with its deeply embrasured windows, bright tapestry hangings picturing the deeds of ancient heroes, and dressers on which were displayed row upon row of gold and silver dishes, cups, bowls and ewers.

She stood with her ladies at the foot of the stairs

and waited for someone to notice her. No one did.

Chin high, she surveyed the scene. There appeared to be a great deal of coming and going, not to say bowing and scraping, going on. After a few moments, one of her ladies said, 'Madam, shall I go and find out . . .'

'Thank you, Anna, but no. Let us wait.'

Susanna was offended and proposed to stay offended. She would have been tapping her foot except that it would not have been correct behaviour.

She could deduce nothing from the serried ranks of male backs that were almost all she could see. Something was going on, but she had no idea what.

And then William came burrowing a breathless path towards her. 'It's him!' he announced, his eyes popping under the greasy fair fringe of his hair.

'Him?'

'Lord Gervase. He's just got home.'

With a thud, Susanna's heart landed in her stomach. 'Oh?'

'Over there. That big, long thin fellow.'

'Oh?' It was a struggle, but she said, 'Thank you, William.'

'Starchy-looking fellow.'

'I said, "Thank you, William".'

'He's not the dressiest fellow you've ever seen, either.'

'Will you stop calling him a "fellow"! He's Lord Gervase to you.'

'Oh, all right. He's not the dressiest Lord Gervase you've ever seen. Is that better?'

Repressing a powerful desire to shake him, Susanna became aware of the stately figure of Sir

Walter approaching and bowing before her.

Smiling with a faint, carefully cool graciousness, she followed him as requested towards the upper end of the hall and the dais that had been set up to hold the head table. She knew that this was reserved for family and honoured guests, although no one was as yet showing any sign of sitting down.

The same was true of the long tables for lesser mortals that were positioned at right angles to the dais. The lesser mortals were milling around aimlessly, getting in the way of the kitchen servants who appeared to be trying to set extra covers on the tables, presumably to accommodate the newly arrived members of Lord Gervase's riding household. Many of the retainers wore what Susanna knew to be the castle livery, which was in two shades of grey, dark for the thigh-length tunic, light for the hose, with the castle emblem of a bunch of blue-purple grapes embroidered on the left sleeve. Others were clad in countryman's russet.

There was a blue-purple canopy of state at the centre of the head table, a symbol of authority and grandeur under which the lord of Vine Regis would seat himself to dine. Susanna's knees were shaking as Sir Walter led her towards the small group of people standing talking beside it—Dame Constance, John, Lady Isabelle, and the tall, thin, travel-stained young man who must be Lord Gervase.

Her future husband.

He was quite good-looking in a lean and hungry way, a tall, wiry figure with intense eyebrows, a hooked nose, pronounced cheekbones, and a tightly controlled manner that made him appear older than Susanna knew him to be. Much harder in looks than his younger brother, he was not at all what she had expected and she was still struggling to sort out her impressions when Dame Constance said, 'Ah, Lady Susanna, let me make my son known to you.'

Susanna—anxious to make a good impression—lowered her eyes in the approved fashion and sank into a curtsey, while Lord Gervase permitted himself a slight nod of the head that might have meant anything.

2

What it meant, if the truth were told, was that he had a stiff neck from sleeping on an amazingly hard and damp bed the previous night.

But it was also true that he was not in the mood for making conversation with a very young lady who looked as if she had not a thought in her head beyond clothes. Gervase de Clair could never have been described as moody, but he had suffered a trying few weeks, forced to do his duty as lord of his estates by rushing around the countryside when he much preferred soldiering. He had been dissatisfied with the work of his bailiffs in Norfolk and Suffolk, had been comprehensively rained on, and constantly troubled by his leg wound, memento of the French war. And then he had come hurrying home in response to a message from his mother saying that he should make an effort to be at Vine Regis when his bride-to-be arrived, which would be any day now. He knew she was right. She always was. But he could not remember ever having felt so weary and irritable, even at the height of the war.

War, of course, was interesting and stimulating. Estate management and brides were not.

Gervase, like most of the knightly classes, knew only two kinds of women—ladies and whores. The first group was headed by his mother, of course, who was a model for all women of high degree. And Isabelle, his sister, was in the same mould, though her grace and intelligence were shadowed over by her besetting lethargy. And then there had been the late and unlamented Felicia, a young woman so paralysingly refined that she had drained the vitality out of everyone around her. As a wife, she had made no demands on him at all—emotional, physical, even conversational.

Very different were the girls in the better whorehouses, bright and bawdy, ripe for fun and frolic, full of salacious gossip, their only desire to make their customers happy, because happy customers were generous customers. In their company, a man could shed constraint and let his inner self fly free. It was worth every penny of their exorbitant charges. He had sometimes thought it was a pity that one could not possibly marry them.

Called to attention by his mother's quiet, 'Gervase', he summoned up a smile for the pretty little thing in the gaudy clothes who was to be his wife, extended a hand to raise her from her curtsey, and murmured all the approved sentiments. What a pleasure it was . . . meeting at last . . . Vine Regis would soon feel to her like home . . .

It was obvious to Dame Constance that the Lady Susanna was not what he had been expecting, just

35

as the Lord Gervase was not what the Lady Susanna had been expecting.

She sighed to herself. 'Let us be seated,' she said.

3

They sat in a single line strung out along one side of the head table—looking and feeling, as John murmured to Susanna, like a row of giant marrows waiting to be admired—with Gervase under the canopy of state, his mother on his left and Susanna on his right, with Lady Isabelle beyond Dame Constance and John next to Susanna.

The lower orders, called to attention by the stentorian-voiced gentleman who was the Usher of the Hall, distributed themselves according to rank at the three long tables that ran down the length of the hall. Susanna guessed that the table presided over by the stately Sir Walter accommodated the higher-ranking diners, the knights and squires of honour as well as men whom she decided must be the senior household officers—men like the comptroller, the chamberlain, and a learned-looking individual who might perhaps be the receiver or treasurer. Susanna noticed that the handsome knight who had monopolised John earlier was seated at Sir Walter's table.

It struck her, now, that he and Gervase could scarcely have afforded a greater contrast in style. Both were good-looking men, but Gervase looked far older than his twenty-four years while the unknown knight, who was probably nearer Dame Constance's age, appeared brimful of vitality, had patrician features and the most lively eyes Susanna had ever seen.

John, enquired of, replied, 'That's Guy Whiteford. Full title Sir Guy Whiteford of Lanson. He's Piers' father—you remember, we met Piers on the hill earlier?'

Could she ever forget? Did this mean she might see him again? If only, if only . . .

'Guy's a striking-looking fellow, isn't he?' John went on mischievously. 'Cleverer than you might think, too. He's a lawyer and Justice of the Peace for the district, so you'll have to behave yourself. Has his own place—a fortified manor—a few miles to the north of here, but he's interested in breeding and acts as Gervase's Master of the Horse. Has a nice little stud at Lanson.'

'Really?' said Susanna politely. What else could she say? Certainly not, 'And what about his son?'

There were three great stone arches at the far end of the hall, the side ones leading, John said, to the pantry and the buttery, and the larger central one to the kitchen. 'No doors, so cold draughts and cooking smells come sweeping in with the dinner dishes.'

It was the sweeping in of servants and ceremony that startled Susanna. She was perfectly accustomed to formal service, but not to dishes being brought in in procession, with the Usher of the Hall shouting 'By your leave, my masters!' and everyone standing up and taking off their hats and waiting while the server and carver and cupbearer went on bended knee beside their lord who, alone, had a soup bowl to himself and ate from a golden platter. Everyone else shared a soup bowl with his neighbours, and had a thick trencher made of stale bread to do duty for a plate. Susanna knew that the solitary service and the golden platter were a necessary part of any lord's grandeur, but felt that, on an occasion such as this, his future lady might have been permitted to share in that grandeur. She would have liked a golden platter, too.

John said, 'Oh dear. Only green pottage and capon pottage. Not much choice, I'm afraid. I'm told no one was sure when we were arriving, so we're just having to make do with everyday fare.'

Taken aback, she surveyed the other dishes that were being brought in and exclaimed, 'This is just an ordinary dinner, you mean?'

'Well, yes.' He looked at her in mild surprise. 'You could hardly call it a banquet, could you?'

'I suppose not.'

As well as the soups there were roast kid, and roast duck, and spring chickens, and oranges in a sharp sauce. Then crayfish jelly, and loach with a parsley sauce, and young rabbit with a ginger sauce. And then frumenty with venison and, at the lord's table alone, apples with cheese wafers and sweet wafers. Susanna could only feel grateful that she was not expected to do more than transfer to her trencher a spoonful or two from the serving dishes she shared with John. It all seemed shockingly extravagant, although she knew that the leftovers would be given to the deserving poor, already waiting at the gates.

The people at the household tables seemed to be enjoying themselves, particularly the youthful yeomen, grooms and huntsmen seated at the farthest end of the room, as far away as possible from the lord on his dais. Even so, the Usher of the Hall had to shout, occasionally, 'Speak softly, my masters', though the effect did not last long. Susanna envied them. It was very dull having to sit staring out over the hall, looking important. Gervase seemed inclined to talk only to his mother, and John was too busy eating to have any great interest in conversation, so Susanna, very conscious that this was her first public appearance as 'the new Lady' and that she ought to observe all the rules drilled into her by the nuns, retreated into correct behaviour—smiling faintly without showing her teeth, looking down most of the time with her eyelids half closed, and toying with her food. Although she had endeared herself to the nuns by her prettiness and light-heartedness, they had all too often had to reprimand her for laughing and bouncing about. It was not modest behaviour, they said. Now, she was determined to be 'modest' if it killed her.

Her resolution came to momentary grief when she raised her eyes to scan the throng further down the hall, hoping to glimpse the profile of the exciting young man on the hill. But there was no sign of him, so she dropped her eyes again and studied the cheese wafer in her hand as if it were her whole desire and delight. If he were Sir Guy's son, and Sir Guy were a regular guest here in the castle, it was possible—surely it was possible?—that she would see him again.

Her heart might be a little more hopeful, but she was still overwhelmed by the cool formality surrounding her. The convent had had its routines, of course, but they had been routines of a kindly, even cosy nature. Two of the nuns had been delegated to look after her when she first arrived, to make her feel welcome, and she had settled in quickly. Everyone had been approachable. But this was very different. No one was looking after her. It was Gervase's duty to do so, she supposed, but he had said simply, 'We will talk later,' which was no great help.

Hard though she tried to recapture her usual bright outlook on life, by the time dinner drew to its close she had reached the stage of wondering whether it was possible to die of tedium. It was an intolerable thought that she might be fated to sit through two such meals every day for all the remaining days of her existence.

It was mystifying, too, because she knew that the tradition of a hundred or more people eating in the Great Hall under the watchful eyes of their lord was extremely old-fashioned. At her own home, the family ate far more intimately and less formally in the solar, or Great Chamber, which had been her father's combined bedchamber, office and sitting room when he had been alive. Her impression of Dame Constance, so far, was that she was unorthodox in her behaviour—there had certainly been nothing conventional about her welcome for her son's future bride—and it seemed strange that she should cling to such an outmoded custom.

Susanna decided she must ask about it. Tactfully, of course. She did not want to give offence.

4

Meditatively, Dame Constance watched her almoner, once he had pronounced the Grace after meat, march round the Hall with his basket, collecting the bread trenchers, soaked with sauces and drippings from the dishes for which they had done duty as platters, for distribution as alms to the poor. Since Vine Regis was a famously thriving estate, the 'poor' who so regularly congregated on the barbican across the moat were mainly beggars and vagabonds, some of whom had come from a considerable distance, from Amesbury or even Salisbury, by way of the old Roman road. According to the almoner, the beggars were becoming increasingly threatening nowadays, as likely to thank him with a blow from their staves as with any word of gratitude. With the truce in the French wars loosing bands of unemployed soldiers on the countryside, it was becoming an ever more violent place. The attack on Susanna's procession, though John might make light of it, was worrying, and too close to Vine Regis for comfort. Perhaps it was time to stop dispensing the alms that attracted dangerous men into the neighbourhood.

She said something of this to Gervase after the boards had been cleared and stacked to the side. He had been away for several weeks and during that time the problem seemed to have worsened. 'What do you think?' she asked.

'I don't know. Whatever you consider best.' He turned to the castle comptroller who was standing at his elbow and said, 'Let us be entertained with some music and dancing, Master Edward. Who have we?'

'There are a number of strolling singers, my lord. And—er—a new French troubadour. And a band of mummers.' Master Edward's enunciation was poor, largely because he spoke with his lips

41

curled inward as if he were trying to prevent his teeth from falling out, and the word 'mummers' lost itself somewhere in his nasal passages.

'What?'

Briskly, Dame Constance decreed, 'Let us have the singers, Master Edward,' and then, as the man turned away, 'This matter of the beggars, Gervase.'

'Whatever you think wise, mother.'

'Do you have *no* opinion?'

Her son was tall and commanding in appearance but, although he was quite capable of being decisive when he wanted to be, he was not a quick thinker about things that did not engage his attention, so that he was apt to become decisive only after everyone else had lost interest. Dame Constance sometimes wondered if he was a changeling.

'No, not really.'

It was scarcely a good moment for Susanna to appear beside them and interrupt their conversation with a girlish giggle and the world-shaking announcement that she really loved that song, and was it not *so* appropriate? Dame Constance, who had barely noticed that the singers were giving their all to *Sumer is icumen in*, transferred to Susanna the annihilating look she had meant for Gervase. It was unintentional but unfortunate.

Susanna said, 'I am sorry. Did I interrupt?'

Her expression was less conciliatory than her words and, not for the first time, Dame Constance thought, 'Oh, dear.' She had quite enough on her mind without an empty-headed little chit to add to it. She tried to remember what it had been like to be fifteen years old. She herself had been coldly

42

reared in the aristocratic tradition that saw daughters as no more than bargaining counters in the profit-oriented game of marriage alliances. She had had neither the opportunity nor the inclination to be spoilt and petulant. Married at fourteen, she had borne Gervase within the year. Duty had been her watchword then, as it still was. Occasionally, she regretted it and thought what a pleasure it would be to do something scandalous for once. Though the scope for doing something really scandalous in the depths of the English countryside was sadly limited.

She smiled mechanically. 'Yes, but it's not important. Are you fond of music?'

Mistaking Dame Constance's courtesy for condescension, Susanna felt that she was being put in her place. But her, 'Yes, very,' sounded rather abrupt and she struggled to find something to make it less so. 'The nuns,' she went on after a moment, 'used to say it was like having a little lark in the convent, because I was always singing to myself.'

If Dame Constance had been less strong-minded, she would have shuddered. With some regret, however, she noted that her son showed no inclination to pat his betrothed on her neat little bottom and say, 'What a sweetheart you are,' as most men would have done.

In fact, the best Gervase could manage was, 'That's what we need in the castle, is it not, mother? A little lark singing all day.'

'She will be lucky to make herself heard above the general din. Tomorrow, Susanna, you must persuade Gervase to introduce you to your new home, rather than passing his day in hawking or quintain, which he will certainly do, given the opportunity. Though I warn you, it may still take some time before you are able to find your way about without guidance.'

The girl had been standing looking demure but now she glanced up from under her long, curling lashes. 'Will it? I hope not. I have always had a good sense of direction.'

Dame Constance wondered whether she was going to turn out to be one of those young women who, secure in their own ignorance, mistrusted everything they were told by people better informed than they. High on Dame Constance's list of pet aversions were people who did not know what they were talking about, but who held forth as if they did.

With a patience she did not feel, she said, 'The castle was built a hundred years ago by Gervase's great-great-grandfather, Sir Otto, who was a member of the king's household and accompanied him on his crusade to the Holy Land. He saved the king's life at the siege of Acre and, when they returned to England, the king granted him the lands now known as Vine Regis. Sir Otto, being a soldier through and through, built the castle on defensive lines, with no regard for the civilised amenities. Since then, his successors have all tried their hand at improving it without radically altering it, which has resulted in the creation of a great many small rooms set within the roof space of larger ones, not to mention a maze of staircases to service them. We do not even have a walled bailey outside to accommodate bakehouse and brewhouse, stables and pig pens. Everything is crammed into the main building. It is the most

44

inconvenient dwelling imaginable. This is why we have no Great Chamber, and must continue to dine in state here in the Great Hall.'

Susanna said, 'I wondered.'

'I imagine you did. However, the time has come to rectify matters. Gervase needs a Great Chamber, and you will need a more extensive suite for yourself and your household. We also need additional lodgings for guests, and dormitories for the senior knights and squires.'

She turned to her son. 'I have not yet told you, but while you have been away I have consulted a master mason, who recommends building an extension on the east side of the castle. The bailey can come later. There is land enough within the moat and we have settled on the general design. I have contracted with him to begin work as soon as possible. Abbot Ralph this morning agreed to let us take the stone we need from the abbey's quarries.'

Gervase exclaimed, 'Excellently done, mother,' but Susanna's face showed no pleasure. Her colour was heightened and she looked, indeed, almost sulky as she said, 'How lovely.'

Dame Constance thought again, 'Oh, dear.'

5

Susanna was shivering violently, from strain and weariness after her exceedingly trying day rather than from cold, as she sat by the fire in her chamber and waited for Lord Gervase to visit her. He had said they would talk 'later'. How much later she had no idea. So she waited, respectably wrapped in her dressing robe, when she would much rather have been burrowing between her linen sheets and pulling the embroidered coverlet up to her chin in anticipation of sleep.

Her gentlewomen were fussing around, folding her discarded day clothes ready to be put away in the clothes chest, lighting her candles and the cresset that would burn until dawn, arguing over where to place the tray of bread and ale in case she woke hungry or thirsty in the night. Unexpectedly soon, the bell for Compline clanged out from the village church and they all virtuously gabbled three Ave Marias while Anna, the more responsible of the two gentlewomen, made to observe the curfew by placing the metal cover over the fire that would keep it smouldering until morning. But Susanna said, 'No. Not yet.'

When at last he came, Gervase was preceded by a single candle carried by one of his chamber grooms who gave it into the care of Susanna's second gentlewoman, sixteen-year-old Margot. When he departed again, the back of his neck was scarlet and Susanna, deducing that Margot, who had an eye for a good-looking lad, must have given him too warm a smile, frowned at her.

Lord Gervase, it seemed, did not intend to stay long. Refusing the second chair by the fire, he stood, tall and faintly forbidding in his furred chamber robe, looming over his future bride.

She was suddenly grateful that this was not their wedding night. She did not want to go to bed with a stranger and would have expected Gervase to feel the same, had not her mother told her that going to bed with a stranger was something men often did, because they had needs that urgently required

46

to be satisfied. It was different for women, with their more delicate sensibilities and no such needs. And what happened in bed? Well, Susanna had seen farm animals coupling, had she not, and human beings did the same. Women did not find it pleasurable, but it was necessary if they were to achieve the joy of motherhood.

Having been told all this, and knowing that the purpose of marriage was to produce children, preferably sons, Susanna cherished no sentimental illusions. But it was disappointing, just the same, not to find herself in one of those romances of which the poets sang, where love was born in a single flaming glance.

Flaming glances were not, it seemed, Lord Gervase's style. Susanna's tremulously hopeful smile met no response from him. If anything, he looked more harassed than ever. So she abandoned the smile and waited for him to say something.

'I came only to welcome you to Vine Regis and say I hope you will be happy here and that it will soon feel like home.'

Well, if *that's* all you came to say, Susanna thought tartly, you might as well not have troubled yourself. Because you said it all already—exactly that!—when we were first introduced before dinner today.

Aloud, she murmured, 'Thank you,' and added politely, 'I hope to be a good wife to you when the time comes.' It was the correct response, even if her voice carried little conviction.

He was gazing at her fixedly, which made her nervous. It did not occur to her that, small talk not being his forte, he was unable to think of anything more to say.

Never a sparkling conversationalist at the best of times, Gervase was rendered even more laconic by his inability to place his future wife in a wider social context. She was not the kind of young lady with whom he could expect to exchange views on the serious matters that normally concerned him, but neither, despite her style of dress, did she seem likely to speak the language of the *fille de joie*. At least, he hoped not! Certainly, she was not the kind of wife-to-be that he had been expecting. Clever women were the devil, of course, with the notable exception of his mother, but the Lady Susanna did not appear to be clever or to have anything to recommend her beyond her looks—and Gervase preferred quiet elegance to bouncing prettiness. Perhaps she would improve.

'Yes, I am sure you will,' he said at last.

He had taken so long to reply that Susanna had to stop herself from asking, 'Will what?' Had there ever been such a sticky conversation?

As if anxious to escape, he went on, 'You must be tired after these last few days. I'll leave you to sleep. Er—unless you have anything in particular you wish to say to me?'

There were several things she would have liked to say to him, among them that she did not think Dame Constance should have made all the arrangements for adding to the castle without first consulting her son's wife-to-be, who might have her own ideas about the design and what kind of extra accommodation was needed. Also that she, Susanna, should have received a ceremonial welcome when she arrived and should have been introduced to everyone formally as the future Lady of the Castle. She could still hear the nuns clapping their hands and exclaiming, 'You'll be Lady of the Castle! How splendid!' She was *entitled* to be acknowledged as the future Lady of the Castle.

But she had sufficient sense to recognise that this was neither the time nor the place for such complaints. So, in a colourless voice, she responded, 'I hope we will become better acquainted soon. I look forward to it.'

It was an imperfect end to a very imperfect day. When Gervase had gone, Susanna sat seething and looking around for something to throw. Nothing less would relieve her discontent. All she could find was the livery tray of bread and ale, and although it made a satisfying crash when she smashed it to the floor, it did not make her feel any better.

When Anna and Margot came hurrying over, looking concerned, she screamed at them, 'Go away! Go away!' and, throwing herself on her bed, gave herself up to a storm of weeping.

CHAPTER THREE

1

Both Ladies of the Castle passed a disturbed night, Dame Constance partly because she was a natural night owl and partly because her mind was always busy, Susanna because she was overwrought as well as over-tired.

Reviewing the day, Dame Constance found herself reluctantly assessing her son's betrothed. The girl was young for her years and her head had obviously been stuffed full of conventional notions, so that she knew—or thought she knew—who she was *supposed* to be, but didn't know who she *was*. So far, she appeared to be both frivolous and difficult, and Dame Constance was not altogether sure how to handle her. It was exasperating to reflect that it was she who would have to do the handling, because it was she and Isabelle who would have to bear the brunt of living with the girl on a daily basis. Fine to be a man! she thought, to do one's duty in bed and then make one's self scarce.

Susanna, she thought, would be resistant to guidance. But the risky alternative was to leave her to find her own way, hoping that she would grow up in the process and discover the real person within herself. If only Gervase could be relied on to contribute . . .

It was a mystery to Dame Constance that her two elder children, fathered by her endlessly energetic husband, should be so lacking in vitality

50

and strength of character, whereas John, the youngest, had vitality to excess. So, too, against all the laws of probability, had Gervase's elder daughter Blanche, whose naughtiness was an expression of a liveliness that made it difficult for Dame Constance to be stern with her. How would Susanna manage her, she wondered? Time would tell. Dame Constance had the feeling that, if Susanna needed help, it would have to come from the languid Isabelle, who was near to her in age and whose advice, Dame Constance conjectured, would be less unwelcome to the girl than her own. Though Isabelle was perhaps too taken up with thoughts of her own prospective second marriage, which Dame Constance was negotiating for her.

Dame Constance sighed and then smiled at the amount of sighing she had been doing in this last day. She turned over in bed. Long, long ago, when she had wakened from some nightmare, her nurse had always told her, 'Turn over on your other side and think about something else.'

So, now, she gave herself up to dreams of how much more beautiful and practical her beloved Vine Regis would be when there was a gracious extension breaking up the hard, military squareness of the place. Large windows, light, space, oak-panelled walls gilded and painted, a measure of privacy . . .

Over in her chamber in the north-east tower of the castle, Susanna—who normally never had trouble sleeping—spent the night tossing and turning, throwing off the coverlet and pulling it up again, drowsing off and then waking with echoes in her head of what had been said during the past hours—false echoes, some of them, distorted by her sense of having been ignored, unappreciated, even disliked. Awake, she would have remembered that little Blanche, asked to repeat her ABC, had begun perfectly correctly by crossing herself and saying 'Christ's Cross be my speed' before going on 'a, b, c . . .' But in the darkness of Susanna's turbulent night, the childish preface expanded itself to 'Christ's Cross be my speed and I don't like you. I don't want you for my mother.' And when Dame Constance remarked that it would take some time for Susanna to find her way about the castle, the cool echoing voice added, 'because you are such a stupid girl'. And Gervase had obviously thought her to be young and inexperienced, when in fact she had been well taught and knew—in theory, at least—all there was to know about managing a household, however large.

It was all so—so *disappointing*!

In a spell of pre-dawn wakefulness, she lay asking herself, what did she really, truly, honestly want? And found that she didn't know the answer. Did she want romance—or status? Did she want love—or to be Lady of the Castle? The second was achievable without the first. Why did it have to be either/or? Why could it not be both? She would have to *make* people like her—but how? It was not a question to which she had previously given any thought; it had never been necessary. She suspected the nuns would have said, 'Just be yourself, my dear!' but the nuns had never met Dame Constance.

And she would have to *make* Lord Gervase love her. But how?

She woke exhausted when day came at last and,

wearily, crept out of bed and repeated her Paternoster, Ave Maria and Creed, then said the Hours of the Virgin as her women helped her dress. In no mood for facing up to the realities of her new life, she said, 'I think I will spend the day here in my chamber, arranging it to my liking, but we must not forget our manners. Margot, go and make apologies for my absence to Dame Constance and say I am sure she will understand.'

2

Dame Constance was already well into her day— High Mass first, then the routine conferences with her household officers, and now a breakfast of bread, cheese and weak ale in her favourite window alcove in the Great Hall in company with her daughter, younger son, Sir Walter the steward, and the master mason from Normandy who was to build the extension.

Master Emile de Louviers had been highly recommended to her by a cousin in Kent, and she had been told that she was fortunate to catch him between commissions. Knowing Kentishmen to be a hard and demanding race, she was surprised to find that the object of this recommendation was a small, middle-aged man with a stout belly balanced on short stringy legs, thinning salt-and-pepper hair, watery grey-blue eyes, a nasty case of enlarged pores, and features that could never have been described as memorable. Appearances could be deceptive but she suspected that, while he might know all there was to know about masonry, he lacked the force of personality necessary to get things done without being pushed. A master mason was supposed to drive his workers. She hoped that she was not going to have to drive him.

She would find out. In the meantime, he had brought with him a neat little wax model of the extension he proposed building. The design could be altered easily enough, he explained, if the Lady had any special requirements.

The Lady was intrigued, not to say frustrated, to find that the basic design was very much what she had had in mind—a drum tower linked to the main building by a short corridor block. The stonework, carefully marked out in the wax, looked as if it would be a good match for the main part of the castle. The eight-foot-thick walls, said Master Emile, would be constructed with an inner and an outer facing of ashlar, or masoned stone, with rubble filling the space between the two skins.

She had to repress a smile of pure pleasure at the dominant feature of the tower, the almost disproportionately heavy machicolations below the parapet looking like nothing so much as the edging on a good, hearty pastry crust. If she had suspected Master Emile of having any sense of humour, she would have taken it to be an architectural frolic. She loved it.

Hamish, an uninvited but interested spectator, was obviously struck by the same thought. Inhaling blissfully, he remarked, 'Ye can almost smell the steak and kidney. Reminds me of my Aunt Mary. She was a dab hand at pies.'

Dame Constance had become inured to Hamish's frequent references to his extended family in the twenty years since she had known him—the years since he had been taken prisoner

54

by the late Lord Nicholas in a skirmish on the Scottish borders and, having no money to ransom himself, had been brought home by his captor to the square stone castle in the south of England. Lord Nicholas had been amused by the lad's sharp wits and his impudence; amused, too, by the thought of trying to civilise one of those Hielandmen who were widely believed to be no better than savages.

But Hamish had been quick to learn and, as soon as he was fluent in English, had progressed from being a groom of the stable to a groom of the chamber and, in time, a messenger who could be entrusted with any task, however delicate or dangerous. When Dame Constance had given him the role of personal bodyguard a few years earlier, her local acquaintances, to whom the Scots were and always had been the Old Enemy, had thought it very eccentric of her, but they had become used to him, even to his blithe disregard for all the accepted rules of rank and precedence.

Now, she half-frowned and half-smiled at him and said to Master Emile, 'You will discover, as you get to know us better, that Master MacLeod has an astonishing number of relatives, all with their own special talents.' But Master Emile, whose social graces appeared to be sadly underdeveloped, merely stared at her, so she went on, 'In the meantime, tell me about the crenellations? It is, I believe, forbidden to erect a defensive parapet without royal permission.'

Master Emile inclined his head slightly. 'It is a requirement enforced only seldom, but, to be safe, I have already taken the liberty of acquiring permission on your behalf.'

'Have you, indeed? That was well done.'

Master Emile inclined his head again, a man who knew his business, the faintest of self-satisfied smirks marking his undistinguished features. He plucked a stray thread of wax from the model, rubbed it between his fingers and studied it intently. It was a mannerism with which she was to become all too familiar in the months ahead.

'And since I believed you would wish to be truly *à la mode*, I have designed the machicolations in the new French style.'

'It is certainly a change from the usual,' she said.

The size of the tower seemed to Dame Constance to be about right, large but not disproportionately so. Several of the first and second-floor windows had triple lights, the ground and third floors simple arrow loops in the shape of upside-down keyholes.

Isabelle said wistfully, 'I hope we are having traceried heads in the windows? They are *so* elegant.'

'And can't we have some gargoyles?' exclaimed John, not to be outdone. 'Lord Clifford has some splendid ones at Brough. They really make you laugh, and . . .'

His mother raised her voice. 'As you can tell, Master Emile, my children have no idea of the expense of such refinements. Isabelle, just one of those windows will already cost almost twenty shillings and I have no idea how much we would have to pay for gargoyles. As a matter of interest, Master Emile, have you a good stone carver we might call upon?'

The mason, shocked to discover that Dame Constance was taking such an intimate interest in

56

the work, hummed and hawed and then conceded, 'An imager? Yes, Lady. I have a new man who has real talent.'

'How much?' she asked bluntly.

'One pays him a quarter more than the ordinary stone cutter, and there is more time involved. Say three shillings? Perhaps four.'

'For every single gargoyle?' John demanded disbelievingly.

'*Bien sûr*. Though if you wished for heads of St John the Baptist, there is a workshop that turns them out *en masse*, so the costs would be much lower. Inferior workmanship, of course, and lacking in variety.'

Dame Constance, trying to envisage her lovely new tower garlanded with severed heads, shuddered slightly and said, 'Let us forget the gargoyles.' Apart from anything else, she had been through all the costings in detail with her treasurer, who had agreed the terms of the contract with Master Emile, and had no intention of departing from them. She had been warned that even a minor variation in design could lead to a major variation in cost.

'Now—we can see from your model what the outside of the building will look like. Tell me what you propose doing indoors.'

The faint smirk once more in evidence, the mason stretched out a work-scarred hand and lifted the roof and part of the outer wall from the model, all in one piece, revealing the internal layout.

Dame Constance raised an amused eyebrow.

'Storage for flour and ale on the ground floor,' he said. 'Also stables. That is why I have allowed

57

for a doorway to the outside, although in the interests of defence one would prefer to have no such easy means of ingress or egress.'

John chuckled. 'Never mind. With those huge machicolations we could rain down boiling oil and cannonballs by the score on any attackers!'

His mother threw him an exasperated glance. 'I trust that such a situation will never arise. Yes, Master Emile. Please go on.'

'A Great Chamber on the first floor, with a crenellated fireplace, and the chapel, of course, with its arched window and a side chapel or private pew for the family overlooking the altar. Suites for Lord Gervase and his lady on the second floor, with an oratory. And the top floor consisting of separate suites and lodgings for household knights or esquires or children, or whatever purpose you choose.'

'Wooden rather than stone floors on the upper levels, I assume?'

'Yes,' said Master Emile. 'Because of the weight, you understand.'

'And it will be necessary to break through the existing wall to create a passage between the Great Hall and the new Great Chamber.'

'*Bien sûr.* That is to say, of course.'

'And another from the new flour and ale store on the ground floor into the Mill Tower?'

He shrugged dismissively. 'If you are of a mind to pamper your kitchen scullions by enabling them to walk under cover to the stores, instead of going outdoors, yes. Though I see no great virtue in that.'

Dame Constance was biting her lip thoughtfully and meditating on a summer of dust and disruption, when Susanna's gentlewoman

58

appeared with her message.

A trifle absently, Dame Constance said, 'Yes, I imagine her ladyship will wish to arrange things to her liking. Is there anything she requires?'

Margot stammered, 'I think not, Lady. Thank you.'

'Not even breakfast? It will be another three hours before we dine.'

'Oh. Perhaps. I don't know.'

'Go downstairs—over there—and ask the clerk of the kitchen for something to sustain her ladyship until dinner. And tell him her ladyship will dine and probably sup in her chamber.'

As the girl bobbed another curtsey and scuttled off, Isabelle murmured, 'Should I go and see that Susanna is all right?'

Her mother cast her a look of mock astonishment. 'Prepared to make an effort, Isabelle? What is the matter with you? But it is just as well, since I wish you to take her under your wing for the next few months and teach her what she needs to know. In the meantime, let her join us when she is ready. I hope it will not take her more than a day or two to come to terms with her new role as Gervase's future wife.'

Isabelle, who had been married at fourteen and widowed at fifteen, said in her light, breathy voice, 'Oh, I hope not. She really must take charge of the girls. That is what stepmothers are for. I am quite worn out from looking after them.'

'You mean that your gentlewomen are quite worn out,' exclaimed her graceless brother. 'When did *you* ever take an interest in anything but gowns and gossip?'

'Children! Children! And where, by the way, is

Gervase?'

John tossed down the last of his ale and jumped to his feet. 'Gone to inspect the stables with Guy. I'm off to join them. I want to have a look at that new filly Guy was telling me about. Shall I tell Gervase you want him?'

He was already halfway to the door.

'No. No-o-o-o.' Dame Constance exhaled gently as he vanished. 'Three years being trained as a squire in a ducal household and he comes home having changed not at all. Oh, well.' She turned back to the matter in hand. 'Master Emile, it will be necessary for you and Sir Walter here to work closely together. He will be acting on my behalf as superintendent of the works, recording all income and expenditure, supervising the delivery and consumption of materials, and so on . . .'

Sir Walter ran a smoothing hand over his impeccably smooth white hair. He had no illusions about what Dame Constance meant by his acting as superintendent of the works. She meant that she would ruthlessly superintend him, while he was permitted to appear as if he were superintending Master Emile.

3

Wanting to be left alone was all very well, but Susanna soon discovered that she did not enjoy sulking.

Late in the afternoon of the first day, when she was sitting studying the paintings in her little *Book of Hours*, William came bouncing in without so much as a by-your-leave. 'It's a great place, this,' he declared. 'I've been having a wander round. What a pity we're not staying.'

'What do you mean "we"? *You* may not be staying, but I am.'

It was like water off a duck's back. 'The castle's got a real dungeon! Did you know?'

'I wish they would lock you up in it.'

'It's full of chains and things.'

'Rack? Thumbscrews?'

His face fell, though only for a moment. 'I didn't notice. Maybe they were tucked away in an alcove or somewhere. But, oh, I *wish* we had a real dungeon at home. You'd like that, I'm sure you would. I might talk to my father about it.'

Ill-advisedly, she asked, 'And who were you thinking of putting in it?'

He grinned. 'You, of course, if you're a bad wife to me.'

'I am not going to be a wife to you! I am going to be a wife to Lord Gervase. Anyway, nothing in the world would induce me to marry you instead, and I can't imagine why you should think I would. You're just a child!'

'No, I'm not. I'll be fourteen and grown-up soon. And my father says it would be a good alliance, with our estates marching so closely together. He says you don't *have* to marry this fellow.'

'Yes, I do. Your father may be my guardian, but he doesn't know what he's talking about. The pre-contract was set up in full and correct legal form by my own father before he died and it can't be broken. That's all there is to be said. Besides, it's my dowry you want, not me.'

'Of course. That's what any man wants of his

61

wife.'

'Well, you can't have it. Now, go away. I am busy.'

Characteristically, he glanced round her impeccably tidy chamber and said, 'You don't look it,' then hopped up into the window embrasure. 'Oh, you can see the moat from here. That's nice. They've put me in the tack room above the stables. Can't see anything from there.'

'William! Go away!'

'All right, I'll go and have a look at the mews,' he said obligingly. 'The falconer's offered to show me the hawks.'

It was one of the most trying things about William, Susanna thought when he had gone. He was inquisitive about *everything*.

4

On the following morning, a knock at her door heralded Gervase's two daughters, with their nurse in attendance, one hand on Blanche's shoulder and one on Eleanor's. The children stared at her wide-eyed for a moment, until the nurse gave Eleanor a slight shake and said, 'Remember what the Lady told you!'

Taking a deep breath, Eleanor faltered, 'Good morning, Lady Susanna.' She was a pretty but rather anonymous-looking child with refined features, hazel eyes, honey-coloured hair parted in the centre and curled over the ears, and a seemingly placid disposition. Like her elder sister, whom she superficially resembled, she wore a long, plainly cut pink kirtle embroidered with rosebuds.

As nervous as she, Susanna could at first do no more than smile encouragingly, aware of still being in her chamber robe and with her hair tumbling down her back. Not a figure of authority! She tried to smile at Blanche, too, but the older child was staring round the rearranged chamber and refusing to catch her eye. Susanna was reminded that this had once been their mother's room—but Eleanor had never known her mother, while Blanche, at six, was surely too young to remember her.

'Good morning, my pets,' she essayed, just as Eleanor hurried on, 'Our grandmother says we are to ask if you are well, and if there is anything you need, and if you will be able to come downstairs and join us soon.'

'Your grandmother is very kind. I had a great many bruises after my journey in the litter, but my women have been applying poultices of comfrey and the aches are beginning to fade and I am feeling much better, thank you.'

Suddenly, she had Blanche's attention. Scornfully, the child exclaimed, 'I'm *always* hurting myself, but *my* bruises get better without poultices!'

'How lucky you are!'

The nurse scooped the girls closer to her. 'We must not trouble her ladyship longer. Bid her good day—politely, mind!'

Susanna was just about to call after them, 'Wait! I have some gifts for you!' when Blanche's voice drifted back from the staircase. 'Why do we have to be polite to her? I don't see why we have to be . . .'

She gave the children their dolls that afternoon, in the Great Hall after dinner. They were pretty dolls, their bodies stuffed with rags and their heads carved out of wood, the faces and hands painted by Susanna herself in as lifelike a fashion as she could contrive. She had also stitched modish, grown-up clothes for them, cutting up a favourite old blue velvet cloak for the purpose. It had been a sacrifice, but she had thought it worthwhile. Now, she was not so sure. She was not even sure that the girls knew what dolls were for.

'They are to play with,' she offered helpfully.

'Oh,' said Eleanor. 'Are they?' Holding her doll gingerly round its middle, she went on after a moment, 'How do we play with them?'

'Well, you—you pretend they are alive, and cuddle them, and make them do things like sit or stand or walk about, and hold pretend conversations with them,' replied Susanna weakly.

'That doesn't sound like much fun. *We* play with spinning tops!' exclaimed Blanche.

Coolly, Dame Constance intervened. 'That will do, Blanche. The dolls are charming, Susanna. The girls will soon come to love them.'

Only Isabelle showed a proper appreciation and interest. 'That is an unusually pretty blue. I have some tiny pearls which we could sew down the front, and if I can find a length or two of gold thread, we could weave some hair for them to go under the veils. What do you think, Susanna?'

'Oh, what a lovely idea! I had nothing like that in my own needlework chest!'

And so the ice was at least partially broken, and

Susanna went off with Isabelle in pursuit of trimmings.

She knew from John that Isabelle had been widowed after only a year of marriage and was curious as to why she should be back at Vine Regis instead of remaining with her new family. Unable to think of a way of phrasing her curiosity tactfully, however, she forced herself to watch Isabelle going through her stitchery chest and was rewarded when the other girl pulled out a man's woven belt and said, 'Ah, that should do. It is clean enough, since my husband rarely wore it, and the gold threads should unpick quite easily.'

Susanna asked, very correctly, 'But don't you wish to keep it as a memento?'

Isabelle's lovely amber eyes widened. 'Of what? Of a year sharing a bed with an old man, who had already had two wives before me?'

'Er . . .'

'Well, he was not old, precisely,' Isabelle conceded, 'otherwise my mother would never have permitted the match. But I was fourteen and he was almost three times my age, and already had two grown-up sons. When he died, they inherited, and since they dislike me as much as I dislike them, I chose not to stay but to come home to Vine Regis.'

'Oh.'

'Yes, oh,' said Isabelle amusedly. 'When I marry again, I hope to do better.'

'When you . . . ?'

'My mother is at present negotiating a settlement with a gentleman closer to my own age.'

'How splendid. Is he nice? Do you like him?'

'I don't know yet. I am not well acquainted with

65

him, but yes, I think so. He has a very easy, friendly manner.' Her lips were slightly pursed, as if a little less ease would have suited her better. 'Which makes me extremely fortunate, you will agree,' she resumed. In languid triumph, she drew several fine silver pins from among the hanks of thread in her chest, each with twenty or more tiny embroidery pearls impaled on it. 'There we are! I knew I had them somewhere. Let us go and relieve the girls of the dolls, shall we? I wonder if they have discovered how to play with them yet?'

They found the girls in Susanna's chamber, with Anna crossly telling them that was *not* how they were supposed to play with dolls.

Little Eleanor was backed up against the wall, her doll clutched to her, while Blanche had a firm grip on her own doll's arms and was using them to punch and pummel Eleanor's doll with the greatest enthusiasm.

Isabelle said in a weary voice, 'Really, Blanche!' while Susanna hesitated for a moment and then laid firm hands on the older child and tried to loosen her grip. There was a nasty, tearing sound as one of the seams parted. Blanche let out a loud wail. Susanna, sorely tempted to slap her, managed to refrain.

Even so, it was not a good augury.

6

Next day, prodded by his mother into finding a free couple of hours, Lord Gervase offered to show the Lady Susanna round the castle.

They were astoundingly polite to each other. It

required no more than the sight of two or three stairs for Lord Gervase to warn the Lady Susanna to take care in case she fell, and the Lady Susanna unfailingly thanked him for his advice and trod with such delicacy that, more than once, she very nearly missed her step altogether and went flying.

It proved something of a trial to her that Gervase was nothing if not systematic. Beginning in the wine cellar at the foot of the Buttery Tower, they worked their way up past the sweltering kitchens, through the Great Hall, up again and along to cast a glance into various small offices, and then to retreat downstairs once more to the courtyard, from which they entered the west range of the castle and saw the carpenter's shop, the armourer's workshop—where Susanna had to stop her ears against the noise—and the tailors' cubbyhole. Then it was back to the courtyard and the north-west tower, with the castle archives in the cellar and the treasurer's office above, then Lord Gervase's private rooms, and then the chapel and the chaplain's lodging which, Lord Gervase told her, would be moved to the new extension when it was completed. 'As will my private suite, and yours,' he added. 'In the model, they look very fine.'

'Do they? I haven't seen the model,' Susanna remarked. No one had offered to show it to her, and nothing would have induced her to ask. Briefly hopeful, she looked up at him, but he wasn't embarrassed—and didn't offer.

'Oh, you should. Gives you a really good idea of what it will all look like.'

By the time they reached the physician's eyrie, Susanna was completely lost. With the north range, the north-east tower, the east range and the Mill Tower still to go she also began to feel ready to faint with exhaustion. Everywhere was very full of people and very full of noise.

Trying not to be overawed, or to allow her ignorance to show, she stood by, saying—or breathlessly gasping—almost nothing beyond a dutiful yes, no, how interesting, while Gervase exchanged a knowledgeable word or two with the only workers who seemed to matter to him, those associated with the warlike or sporting side of life, the armourers, the master of the henchmen who taught the squires and pages of honour how to bear arms, the stable grooms and the falconers. In the end, she had to attract his attention by laying her hand on his arm and saying, 'Perhaps we could postpone the rest of our tour until another day?'

'Are you tired?' He was surprised. 'Never mind. You have seen everything you need, and you will now be able to find your way around to all the places that matter.'

'I will certainly know where to go,' she murmured, 'if I need the dents beaten out of my armour.'

Fortunately, her voice was lost in the general clamour.

7

In the days that followed, Susanna did her best to recapture her normal self, bright and interested and inquisitive. Silly she might sometimes be, but she was not stupid. Behaving well when other people were behaving badly endowed one, she knew, with moral virtue, a virtue in no way diminished by the self-congratulation that accompanied it. Or so the nuns had assured her.

So she put her inner uneasiness aside and took her demure and submissive place in the life of the castle as Gervase's wife-to-be. Not a word did she utter in Dame Constance's hearing without first reviewing it carefully in her mind, though Gervase was another matter. Susanna had no need to guard her tongue in his presence, because after their tour of the castle he seemed to feel that his duty was done and rarely even ventured within hearing distance of her. For several days, a 'Good morning' or 'Good evening' was the sum total of their communication. Susanna sensed a few times that he was watching her, as if he were trying to assess her, and she was unexpectedly reminded of a puppy she had once had, which had resisted all attempts at petting until it had made up its own mind as to whether she could be trusted. But Lord Gervase wasn't a puppy.

The castle inhabitants watched and gossiped, but their interest faded as the arrival of the future Lady Gervase was overshadowed by the arrival of the builders. The procession was less colourful than Susanna's had been but no less impressive in its way. Master Emile was in the lead, mounted on a pony laden with huge saddlebags. After him came several ox carts with their top-heavy burdens shrouded in cloth that had been waterproofed with a coating of mutton fat—which was smellable, according to William, from a mile off. And bringing up the rear, on foot, was a small army of journeymen and apprentices, scaffolders and carpenters—Master Emile's team, who travelled with him and were accustomed to work with him on all his contracts.

These fifty men were only the nucleus, he explained loftily to Dame Constance. Other crafts would arrive when required, and he would find common labourers locally, when he needed them.

'Er—yes,' said Dame Constance weakly. It was astonishing how much space fifty strangers, with their baggage and tools, seemed to take up; how untidy they were, and how much noise they made, shouting in such a variety of languages—English, French, Spanish and Dutch being only the most recognisable.

'Talk of confusion of tongues! It's like the Tower of Babel,' she sighed to Sir Guy, her son's Master of Horse, who grinned and replied, 'And you know what happened there!'

Surveying him suspiciously, she said, 'What?'

'Everyone knows that, surely? The building industry is a distillation of all human foibles, which is to say all human error. The Tower of Babel fell down because they brought the builders in.'

She laughed back at him. 'Thank you! I can always rely on you to make me feel better, can't I?' Then, 'No, Guy! I haven't time to be kissed. I have too many other things to do. Guy, I said *no*!'

8

If Dame Constance had, in general, been less preoccupied with the building works, not to mention all the estate matters that Gervase should have been attending to, she would have found time to try and put Susanna at ease but, as it was, she

70

did no more than say to her son that he should try to impress upon the girl that his mother was not a tyrant.

'I'm not so very frightening, am I? But she acts as if I am. It would be a relief to see her behaving naturally.'

'I think,' replied her son judiciously, 'that it is just that she is trying very hard to control her natural frivolity, so that you will recognise her as being quite sensible and capable of taking responsibility as future Lady of the Castle.'

Well, well! thought Dame Constance. She could—just—understand Susanna's desire to enjoy the distinction of being future Lady of the Castle, and the lustre and esteem that went with it, but she suspected that the girl's ambitions did not see beyond the title to the very real burdens that it entailed.

'Is that what it is?' she said. 'I had no idea that you had come to know her so well.' He was one of the least perceptive of young men, but perhaps there was hope for him yet if he had taken the trouble to discover how his future wife might be feeling. She would have been less surprised by the truth, which was that Gervase had culled his information from John, who had been cornered by the garrulous William with complaints that Susanna had become very stuffy all of a sudden and theories as to why this might be.

Gervase himself was still trying to make up his mind about her. She had made no real impression on him, and it did not occur to him that he had given her very little opportunity to do so.

Dame Constance said no more, adding only, 'I should have thought that giving the girls their

71

lessons, and playing games with them, and teaching them songs, would be as much responsibility as she can handle for the time being.'

True to form, Gervase replied, as he unfailingly did when something was of little or no interest to him, 'Yes, mother, I am sure you are right.'

He had no way of knowing how much it irritated her or, indeed, that Susanna, sitting beside him at the lord's table and afforded no more than an occasional remark from him—mostly on the lines of 'This is excellent mutton, is it not?'—could overhear enough of his conversations with Dame Constance to be driven to distraction by his constant repetition of that selfsame phrase.

Did he never—ever!—say, '*No*, mother'?

She knew that, by the very fact of his being a man, Lord Gervase was a superior being and that, accordingly, she ought never to criticise him. But it was hard. Harder, still, the sense of being ignored. She felt a little spurt of temper.

She would *make* him take notice of her. The question was—how?

CHAPTER FOUR

1

Susanna soon discovered that she did indeed have her hands full with the two little girls. They adored their grandmother, stern though she could be, and behaved astonishingly well in her presence, sensing—as small children so often did—the precise limits of her tolerance. Even when Blanche's occasional impertinence was met with a reprimand, it was rarely a crushing one, as if the child's liveliness was to be encouraged. Susanna found it very frustrating. It undermined all her efforts to teach the child to behave more like her placid sister Eleanor. Since the episode of the doll fight, when Blanche had seen the flash of anger in Susanna's eyes, the child had been wary of her and Susanna found it irritating that it was she, not Blanche, who was having to make an effort to improve their relationship.

Since Susanna could not always have the girls trailing around at her heels, her gentlewomen were very soon complaining of being overworked. Anna, the elder, wondered whether Lady Susanna might permit her to take on an assistant, a chamberer. She had discovered that there was a girl in the village, the second of the local weaver's seven daughters, who was bright and presentable and seemed anxious to better herself. Her name was Alice.

'Of course,' Susanna agreed, and then began

fretting. Should she mention it to Dame Constance? The girl would be a member of Susanna's own household, so it was none of the Lady's business. On the other hand, perhaps it would be tactful. Best to mention it casually, when the opportunity presented itself.

From her window that afternoon, she could see Dame Constance stalking round the edge of the moat with the master mason in attendance and Sir Walter, the steward, trailing behind. So, taking the children by the hand, she said, 'Let's go and see what is happening. It all looks very exciting!'

Where, only a day or two before, there had been a peaceful and pleasant vista of rough grass, cropped by one or two sheep, now there was chaos. Ordered chaos, perhaps, to people familiar with building sites, but something of a shock to the uninitiated.

Blanche, for once, was amenable. Trying to run ahead of Susanna, tugging on her arm, she demanded, 'Who are all these strange men? What are those bundles of grass and twigs for? What is the blacksmith doing? Why are they sawing wood over there when the 'xtension is going to be made of stone? What a lot of noise they're making! And what a mess! My goodness, grandmother isn't going to like this! Where's Hamish? He'll know what's going on.'

Susanna had been brought up in the belief that servants should be kept firmly in their place, lest they try to take advantage. So she said repressively, 'You mean MacLeod. I believe he has ridden over to Stanwelle on an errand for the Lady. But I can tell you most of what you are asking about.' She knew just enough, she hoped, to guess at the

74

answers. 'What they are doing is building a special lodge for the masons and workmen. It's only temporary—temp-o-ra-ry—*there's* a new word for you. It means just for a short time.'

Tossing her head, Blanche repeated, 'Tempry.'

'So it's only built on a wooden framework, with walls made of wattle—that's woven hazel twigs, plastered over—and a thatched roof. It will be where the men store their tools, and have their dinner when it rains, and perhaps sleep if there are no beds for them in the village. The men in white aprons are probably Master Emile's assistants—the ones with experience are called journeymen and the others, the ones wearing headbands, must be learners or apprentices. I have no idea what the blacksmith is doing. Take care, Blanche! You might trip and fall over!'

Trailing her already battered doll by one arm, Blanche insisted, 'Let's go and ask grandmother!'

Dame Constance was telling Master Emile, 'Yes, I appreciate that the lime kilns will be required when building begins in earnest, but that we should suffer the fumes from the kilns for any longer than necessary simply to enable you to limewash the walls of your lodge does not seem to me justifiable. And lime is a dangerous material, is it not? Could we not buy it in, rather than making it here on site?'

Master Emile was not used to having to explain things to clients, and certainly not to females. Patronisingly, his attention on the hazel twig he was rubbing between his fingers, he said, 'If you are prepared for the extra costs and possibly inferior quality, yes. As for limewashing the lodge walls, it seals the surface . . .'

'. . . and makes the lodge look smarter. I see that, but . . .'

'Grandmother! Grandmother!'

'Yes, Blanche?'

'Why is the blacksmith hammering away, when there aren't any horses needing to be shod?'

In response to the Lady's questioning glance, Master Emile sighed again. 'He is making nails from lengths of wire to fix the timbers. And he sharpens my workmen's tools, and sometimes makes new ones for them.' He turned to the journeyman beside him. 'Show the little lady, Hal.'

Grinning, Hal opened his goatskin bag and produced a well sharpened chisel, and then a hammer with a huge head which he teasingly pretended to be about to drop on Blanche's toe.

The child squealed happily, but her elders turned a unanimously disapproving eye on the young journeyman, whose cheeks coloured slightly under their powdering of stone dust as he put the tools back in his bag.

Blandly, Sir Walter made his contribution by gesturing towards a large tent that was being erected on the edge of the moat, just where the river fed into it. 'I, too, have a lodge, Lady Blanche,' he said. 'We do not want workmen marching in and out of the castle, spreading dust and dirt everywhere, do we? So as superintendent of the works I am setting up my office out here. Our village weaver has made the special linen for it, and I consider that it looks very handsome.'

As everyone turned to admire the tent, Susanna thought she would never have a better opening. 'Oh,' she said brightly, 'the weaver? I have just decided to employ his second daughter to act as chamberer to one of my gentlewomen. What a coincidence!'

'You—have—what?' said Dame Constance.

Susanna gulped. 'I have just decided to employ . . .'

'Never mind. I heard. Perhaps you are not aware that Vine Regis has a rule . . .' Dame Constance stopped. A public reprimand to Susanna could do nothing but harm. 'We will discuss this at some other time. In the meanwhile, Sir Walter, let us go and admire your tent.'

And so off they went, an erect Dame Constance leading, Susanna seething behind the little group, with four-year-old Eleanor looking as uninterested as she had looked throughout, and Blanche tugging so hard on Susanna's hand that, just as they reached the river bank, Susanna had to give her a sharp jerk and say, 'Walk properly!'

Almost as if it were deliberate, a moment later Blanche tripped hard over the handle of a pallet that had been left lying on the ground. Susanna felt the child's hand jolt free of hers and glanced down sharply to see her stumble, stagger, and fling out her arms, her doll flying through the air. Then, even as Susanna reached out to her, she tripped again and went straight into the river.

Susanna screamed, 'Help, someone! Help!' and, falling to her knees, feeling oddly dizzy and disorientated, stretched out towards what was no longer a naughty child but just a struggling pink bundle in the water. She had to shake her head frantically to clear it and bring her eyes and her mind back into focus.

The child was already beyond her reach. Passing the inlet into the moat, the current picked up speed, and by the time the others present had seen what was happening the little face, its mouth opening in a scream before it vanished under water again, had been carried well out from the bank.

Dame Constance, turning to see her granddaughter in imminent danger of drowning, felt her heart turn to ice. Picking up her skirts, she ran along the river bank, gasping for breath and from fear, stumbling over bits of wood and other rubble, gesturing to one of the workmen to follow her. 'Young man, push that ladder out towards her. She needs something to take hold of.'

'Blanche! Blanche! Reach for the ladder!' But she could hear her own voice breaking in her throat and knew suddenly that wailing and moaning would never penetrate the child's consciousness. Only the familiar grandmotherly discipline might—just might—do that.

She tried again, sharply. 'Blanche! Blanche! Reach for the ladder!' But it was too late and, arms flailing wildly, Blanche went under again.

There was a dreadful, helpless moment of silence and inaction before Dame Constance screamed towards Master Emile. 'Can any of your men swim?'

But even as Master Emile shrugged in a very French way, the young journeyman, Hal, was stripping off the leather gloves and white leather apron that were the badges of his craft, and slipping off the bank into the river. With the way the current was running, a few strokes were enough to carry him level with Blanche, and he turned over on his back, pulled her—no longer struggling—on to his chest, and fought his way over to a smooth stretch of the bank. By now, there were many hands to lift her onto dry land.

Dame Constance sank down beside her. Was she still living? Breathing? With a gasp, she cradled the child to her—cold, so cold!—and then, holding her by the shoulders, tried to shake the life back into her.

But Master Hal, getting his breath back, said, 'No, Lady. That's not the way. Let me.'

She stared at him with intensity, and then nodded. 'A cloak,' he said, and Susanna whisked hers off and gave it to him. Kicking aside some bits of wood and rubble, he laid down the pretty sheet of blue velvet and placed Blanche on top of it. Then he began pumping the life back into her with his hands flat on her chest beneath her throat. A dozen steady light pressures, then a pause, and another dozen. Aeons seemed to pass before she spluttered of her own accord and uttered a choking wail. Then Master Hal turned her over on her stomach and nodded to Dame Constance. 'She should be all right now. Leave her for a bit.'

At last, still choking and spluttering, Blanche tried to sit up. Her grandmother, her face colourless but her gown darkened where she had held the child to her, helped her.

Many minutes passed and the workmen began drifting away, the excitement over, while Dame Constance and Susanna still knelt hovering over the distraught child, feeling almost as weak as she did, Dame Constance making soothing noises and Susanna wondering how soon she might decently get up and ease the ache in her knees. Glancing up, she saw Eleanor standing to one side, forlorn and neglected, not altogether sure what the fuss was about. She had her own doll under one arm, and Blanche's hanging from the other hand. Susanna smiled at her reassuringly and she smiled limply back.

After a while, the tone of Blanche's crying changed and the erratic gulping and choking gave way to a succession of steady sobs that sounded as if they would never stop. 'It was all swirling round, and round, and round, and I couldn't breathe, and . . .'

Susanna thought, 'She's playing up. She's all right.'

In the end, Dame Constance recognised it, too. The child would probably have caught a chill and might feel sick for several days; certainly, she had to be attended by the apothecary, then put to bed and kept warm and cosseted and nourished. But, herself faint from the shock of it all, she knew that restoring Blanche to some sense of normality was of the first importance.

So, her arms still around the child, she said, 'Enough, Blanche. I know you were frightened, but we are all frightened sometimes and we must learn to overcome it. And where are your manners? You must thank Master Hal for saving you.'

The child took a deep, shaky breath. 'Thank you.'

Susanna was just thinking that a little more warmth and sympathy were what Blanche needed when, her breath still coming in gusts, the child raised a shaking hand to point at Susanna and shrilled, 'It was her fault. *Her* fault. *She* pushed me in.'

Dame Constance said, 'Nonsense, Blanche,' and, sending for her nurse, gave the woman strict instructions and despatched the child to be dried off and put to bed to recover from her ordeal. Then she turned to Master Hal, and thanked him, and said, 'Tell me something about yourself.'

'I'm Master Emile's head journeyman, Lady.'

'Yes?' She waited, but he said no more, which was interesting in its way. Both his face and voice hinted at unexpectedly good breeding.

Dame Constance might wonder about Master Hal's background but she respected his reticence, so she smiled mechnically and said, 'Now, Master Emile, life must go on. Shall we resume our inspection?'

Just as if nothing had happened! reflected a simmering Susanna. It was like John after the brigand attack. The crisis was over, and there was no more to be said. What a strange family this was!

She herself had no one to talk to, was given no opportunity to explain what had occurred. Even the unspeakable William had gone off that morning with Lord Gervase, John and Sir Guy to exercise some horses, and did not reappear until halfway through supper. So Susanna spent what remained of the day going over and over the terrifying little drama in her mind, sending for news to the nursery every half hour—Blanche was peacefully asleep—justifying herself to herself and becoming more overwrought by the minute.

As a result, when for the first time she found herself having a real conversation with her husband-to-be, it was not the kind of conversation either of them would have wished.

Preceded by a page sent to announce that he proposed visiting her, Gervase arrived in her chamber after supper. Failing to observe the tightening of her pretty pink lips when he began with the usual meaningless, 'I hope you are well?' he launched straight into what he had come to say.

Which was, 'My lady mother is displeased.'

After the kind of day she had had, it was too much. '*She* is displeased?' Susanna shrieked. 'And am I supposed to be *pleased* at your horrid little daughter accusing me of pushing her into the river?'

Gervase was not accustomed to being shrieked at. Needing a moment to readjust his mind, he replied automatically, 'She is not horrid. She's a lovely child. It is just that she is not yet of an age to have attained moral reasoning.'

'Oh? And you think she will suddenly attain moral reasoning when she reaches her seventh birthday? It seems highly unlikely to me.'

'The Church says she will. No doubt we shall see.'

His tone, now, was sufficiently chill to bring Susanna at least partly to her senses. She knew perfectly well that her future husband had every right to expect humility and obedience from her, and here she was, behaving like a shrew. A few days ago, she had thought, 'I will *make* him take notice of me,' but she had not intended to do it this way.

Gervase continued to stare at her, shocked by the revelation that his future wife was not the rather negative little thing he had supposed. He himself, never having felt the kind of emotional pressure that demanded instant release, completely failed to understand her spurt of temper, her shameful lack of self-control. Nor did it occur to him that, on this occasion, Susanna's rage might be fanned by guilt. It was a guilt that she knew to be unreasonable, but that didn't help. She had been in charge of the child and the child had nearly drowned.

He tried to reassure himself that she was young yet; that she would learn. He hoped so, because scenes made him deeply uncomfortable.

Frowning, he resumed, 'In any case, that is not what has displeased my mother. As it happens, she does not think you pushed the child.'

Susanna's eyes widened. 'Not?'

'No. Eleanor confirmed that it was Blanche's own fault. My mother has also spoken strongly to Master Emile about the dangerous clutter on the site, like the pallet which apparently caused Blanche to trip. She says it is an invitation to accidents. It is fortunate that Blanche is recovering well.'

'Yes, I know.'

3

Just how well was not immediately obvious to the adults at Vine Regis, in whose presence Blanche continued to appear subdued and sniffly.

William, however, on his return to the castle, was unable to resist joining the end of the queue of wellwishers visiting the invalid and found her bouncing up and down in her bed despite all the efforts of her nurse to quieten her.

'What a horrible brat you are,' he said. 'You're supposed to be poorly.'

'I nearly drownded,' she boasted.

'Pity you didn't.'

'Have you ever nearly drownded?'

' 'Course not. I have more sense.'

'Oh, pooh. I wouldn't be here any more if I'd drownded! I'd be in heaven. Grandmother said so. She was *crying*. She'd have missed me. She *likes* me.'

'Well, that's a matter of taste.'

'Whassat mean?'

'Some people like you, some people don't.'

'Why?'

'Dame Constance is your grandmother. That's why she likes you.'

Blanche thought for a moment, her mouth turning down at the corners. 'Susanna's my stepmother but *she* doesn't like me!'

'She's not your stepmother yet, and if she doesn't like you that's because you're naughty. You're not nice to her.'

'She's not nice to me!' She stopped suddenly. 'Ooh, I feel sick!'

William, who had never been sick in his life, didn't believe her. 'Serve you right.'

Blanche said. *'You're* not nice to me either! Nurse, nurse! I feel sick. I'm full of water. I don't like water. Go away, William!'

People were always telling William to go away. It didn't bother him. He knew that it was because he had an enquiring mind which others found tiring, and made some, even brats like Blanche, feel less clever than they thought they were.

So, 'All right,' he said obligingly as the nurse

84

hurried across with a bowl. As he went, he felt rather sorry for little Eleanor, sitting quietly to one side as usual, while Blanche demanded all the attention.

4

'Apart from the state of the site,' Lord Gervase was saying, 'it is the matter of the weaver's daughter that concerns my lady mother.'

Susanna tossed her head. What now?

'She says that you must learn to think beyond your own convenience . . .'

Dame Constance, trying to divert her mind from its absorption with Blanche, had put the problem more bluntly than she might otherwise have done. Subtlety was wasted on Gervase.

Susanna's 'Ooooh!' was a gasp of outrage. '*My* convenience! And who in this castle, other than I, gives the slightest thought to *my* convenience? Who in this castle . . .'

He held up a hand. 'I may have expressed myself badly. I—er—was endeavouring to explain the situation to you in a way that would not offend your sensibilities.'

'Well, you can't be said to have succeeded, can you?' She flung away towards the window, adding with a quaver in her voice, 'Perhaps you should just say what you mean and forget about my sensibilities.'

She felt both hurt and indignant. *Everything* was going wrong. She didn't care what he thought of her. She didn't care what anyone thought of her. She had been trying so hard to be good and no one appreciated it. She hated it here. She wanted to go home to her mother. She sniffled, on the verge of tears.

Gervase, Lord de Clair, was in general a patient man, almost inhumanly so, but even he had his limits. Having been snapped at by his overwrought mother, he was not prepared to be snapped at by his future wife.

He strode over to the window and grasped her hard by the wrists. 'Very well. It is a rule of Vine Regis that village girls may be employed as field workers or laundry maids, but *not* within the castle. For one thing, it is wrong to give them ideas above their station, but, more importantly, in this castle, when I am at home with my household, there are in general close on two hundred men. And only ten women. Men have certain appetites, and any unprotected woman is bound to be in danger. My lady mother, my sister, and you are protected by your relationship to me. Your gentlewomen are also to some extent protected by it.'

Dame Constance had said, 'That second woman of Susanna's—Margot, is it?—is a wanton little hussy. She should be sent away and we will find someone more suitable.'

One thing at a time, he thought. 'But the risk for a village girl who is no more than the servant of a servant, especially if she is pretty, as I understand Alice to be, is not acceptable to my mother, and should not be to you. If you think about it for a moment, you must see the sense in what she says.'

His mother's precise words had been, 'If the girl is pretty and presentable, the result is bound to be bastard babies! And I won't have it.'

In conversations with her son, Dame Constance

86

was apt to go to the heart of the matter, without wasting breath on refinements that would probably pass him by. She might otherwise have pointed out that Susanna was an innocent, but that even a moment's reflection should have sufficed to show the girl the difficulties inherent in living in such a male-oriented society as Vine Regis. Knowing very little about Susanna's personal background or her early life at home, it was not easy to judge what, in her personality, was innate and what a product of her upbringing. Perhaps, Dame Constance thought, she might be persuaded to confide in Isabelle. She certainly would never confide in Dame Constance.

Susanna, made to feel foolish and ignorant, tossed her gleaming curls at Gervase. 'You make the place sound like a den of wild beasts. Can you not order your men to behave themselves?'

He hadn't guessed that anyone could be so naïve. 'No,' he said.

'Well, I could tell Alice to . . .'

'No. It has nothing to do with Alice herself. You have seen dogs on heat? Men can be like that, and a girl's virtue offers her no protection.'

She went pink with embarrassment. She remembered her mother telling her that men often went to bed with women who were not their wives because they had needs that urgently required to be met. Was this what Lord Gervase meant? After a moment, surveying him doubtfully, she said, 'What should I do, then?'

'Do? *I* don't know. Let her stay for a few days, maybe, under your first gentlewoman's supervision, while you find someone older and plainer?'

She was diverted, the shrewishness gone as if it had never been. 'Older and plainer? Is *that* why your mother's and sister's gentlewomen are so—so—invisible?'

'I would guess so.' He laughed with relief.

Susanna was looking at him oddly, her mouth pouting a little and her eyes wide.

He could not know how his laughter transformed him, softening the hard bones of his face and relaxing the saturnine brows. Susanna realised that, when he dropped his guard, he could be quite an attractive man.

Even so, she found herself thinking of the dashing Sir Guy Whiteford. She couldn't imagine *him* ever saying, 'Yes, mother . . . Yes, mother . . . Yes, mother . . .'

Or his son Piers, whom she had seen once on her first day at Vine Regis, but never since.

5

A few days later, a messenger arrived summoning Gervase to Westminster and a conference of the barons. It had been common knowledge for some time that the health of King Edward, third of that name, had been failing, as had his wits, and it was clear that discussion of the succession could no longer be postponed. The natural heir was his orphaned grandson, Richard, but Richard at ten years old was too young to rule. The question was, how should the country be governed during his minority.

A regency was the preferred answer in such a case, with some senior member of the royal family ruling on the boy's behalf and in his name. The only problem was that the obvious candidate—the boy's uncle, John of Gaunt, Duke of Lancaster—was haughty, harsh, and quarrelsome, with a fine natural talent for making enemies among his inferiors, notably the all-important merchants of the City of London.

'A handsome man,' remarked Dame Constance reflectively. 'I was presented to him once.'

'Mother!' exclaimed her son, shocked by the gleam in her eye, and even more shocked when she smiled coquettishly at him and fluttered her eyelashes.

'Looks,' he pointed out, 'have nothing whatever to do with it. His arrogance has made him dangerously unpopular with everyone, lords and commons alike.'

Airily, she responded, 'Heigh ho. Oh well, I am sure the barons will succeed in resolving the situation in God's good time. Before you leave, you will, I hope, find the opportunity to ride round some of your lands and remind the manor holders what their lord actually looks like? And I trust that you do not propose taking your full riding household to the conference? I cannot spare Sir Walter from superintending the building works, and I need Sir Guy for—ah—what do I need you for, Guy?'

He was startled, but there was a decided twinkle in his eye as he replied, 'To conjure up all the horses, mules and carts we need for bringing the stone and timber and limestone to the site.'

'Yes, I knew there was something. So you will have to make do with their deputies, Gervase.'

Gervase sighed heavily.

Susanna, sitting virtuously to one side with her embroidery, looked up sharply, aware of an undercurrent of laughter that she didn't understand, one from which Gervase and she were excluded but in which Dame Constance and Sir Guy and even Hamish MacLeod—a mere servant who, in Susanna's view, was allowed far too much latitude—were all participants. Isabelle was off in a dream, as usual, while John seemed to be, as she was herself, aware but mystified. It was all very peculiar.

Sir Guy grinned. 'In any case, I, for one, have too many other things on my mind at present, Gervase, including presiding over the quarter sessions next week. There's an interesting case coming up. The village ale-wife is accused of trying to poison her husband.'

Susanna realised that she didn't even know the village possessed an ale-wife, far less one who was murderously inclined.

Later that afternoon, she summoned Alice to her chamber and said, 'Tell me about the people in the village.'

The weaver's daughter was pretty, rather shy, and having difficulty in finding her bearings. Although she was expected to sleep in the room allotted to the Lady Susanna's gentlewomen, her mistress had no objection to her paying occasional visits to her family in the village. But there was no question of her going or returning alone, said her ladyship. Mindful of Dame Constance's strictures, Susanna insisted that she be responsibly escorted, usually by Hamish MacLeod when he was available—for no one, Susanna reflected cattishly, could be more responsible than he!

On this particular afternoon, Alice's escort had been augmented by Master Hal, on an errand to the village, and young Master William Burnell, 'just having a look round'. Alice told Susanna that Master Burnell had discovered Master Hal to be a West Countryman like himself, and had amused everybody by arguing the respective beauties of their two home regions. But since neither Alice nor Master MacLeod had ever been to the West Country, their amusement had soon palled. Master MacLeod, remarked Alice in passing, was a very kind gentleman, and so considerate!

'Hmmm,' Susanna said. 'Now, tell me about the people in the village.'

Alice was already smitten by her pretty young mistress, whom she found wonderfully easy to talk to, and Susanna soon found herself with far more information than she could absorb. There was Father Hoby—who, priest or not, was A Bad Man—and Sim Walden, who never did a hand's turn, and drunken Will Knapp the thatcher who was going to fall off a roof one day and hurt himself, and any number of others.

No mention of the ale-wife, so Susanna was forced to ask, 'And the ale-wife who is accused of poisoning her husband?'

Alice's pretty dark eyes opened wide. 'He's a dreadful man! He *deserves* to be poisoned!'

'Alice!'

'Well, he does, my lady. And everyone knows it. Luckily, the tythemen on the jury will know it, too, so they'll be bound to let her off.'

'But that's wrong!'

It was a sharp reminder to Alice of one of the fundamental laws of peasant life, that one should never tell important people anything other than what they wanted to hear. She tried to put things right. 'Well, I don't think she was trying to *murder* him. She only used henbane, which made him feel strange and fuzzy and as if his legs and arms were falling off.'

'That sounds quite bad enough. I am shocked!'

Alice looked suitably downcast. 'Yes, my lady.' She wondered how noble ladies like her mistress dealt with the problem of hateful husbands. From what little she had seen of life in the castle, poisoning them would be very difficult indeed, what with official tasters and shared dishes and so on. She supposed the ladies must simply wait and hope that they would be killed in battle. Though if the ladies were noble, they must also be rich and could afford just to run away.

CHAPTER FIVE

1

The weather had suddenly turned very warm, but that was not the reason why Susanna found herself blushing furiously after dinner the following day.

While she knew, in theory, about the troubadorial habit of addressing love songs and poems to some Unattainable Highborn Lady in the audience, she had no personal experience of it and found it very embarrassing to have a handsome— well, moderately handsome—stranger gazing into her eyes and addressing her as his 'dear heart's queen'. And in front of her future husband and mother-in-law, too!

> '. . . think it an honour her to serve
> A thousand times more than he deserve.'

Susanna scarcely knew where to look, so she tried smiling graciously down at the hands folded in her lap and then stole a glance at Gervase, who didn't seem to mind, while Dame Constance's face was completely devoid of expression.

Dame Constance, in fact, was hoping that this new man, Alain de Niort, the third troubadour to have presented himself at Vine Regis in as many weeks, would move on as rapidly as his predecessors had done. Although he was a superficially presentable young man, there was something that struck her as faintly seedy about him and her brief conversations with him had shown him to be an intellectual *poseur* of the most disagreeable and patronising type. He had smooth and shining brown hair, hazel eyes that never changed expression, a prim mouth, very round pink cheeks and an inflated opinion of his own talents. Dame Constance did not like him, which would not have mattered in the least if he had been a better musician. But the songs to his lute with which he had previously regaled the company had been very ordinary indeed and his light tenor voice, though pleasant enough, scarcely carried halfway down the Great Hall.

It was little better when he abandoned his lute in favour of recitation. The after-dinner company became restive and talkative, so that Gervase had to raise his voice to remark all too audibly to his mother, 'At least he's a better poet than he is a singer, praise be to God.'

Young M. Alain could not help hearing, and his small, rather rose-buddish mouth tightened and the roundness of his cheeks became more pronounced as he persevered with his recitation. Trying to suppress a giggle, Susanna was aware of John, at her side, murmuring, 'Looks as if he'd like to break his lute over Ger's head, doesn't he?' It was too much, and she laughed outright.

But there seemed to be no stopping the young man, and his poem was very long, so that the company in the Great Hall had stopped even pretending to listen when there came a sudden and startling noise that put an end to the after-dinner entertainment—a deep, loud, booming, crumping sound followed by a rattle of stones over by one of the windows. And powerful enough for the vibrations to be felt.

Gervase and Sir Guy leapt to their feet, exclaiming, 'Cannonball!' and rushed to the window alcove, followed by almost every other male in the Hall—dozens of them. Even John, his eyes screwed up in puzzlement, vanished from Susanna's side into the mêlée.

Cannonball? It could only mean one thing. The French truce must have ended and the war had begun again. Susanna, half frightened and half thrilled, sat with her hand to her throat, wondering, was it possible? Had the French landed on the coast and made their way inland without anyone knowing? Was the castle really being attacked? Were they all in danger?

The shock was so sudden, the mixture of emotions so unfamiliar, that it was several moments before she gathered herself together sufficiently to glance across at Isabelle, who was sitting there looking no more than faintly intrigued, and Dame Constance, her elegant brows drawn in a slight frown. Typical! thought Susanna irritably. Let us on no account make a fuss! What is another drama, here or there?

Well, she could play that game, too, now that she was learning the rules. She smiled faintly and tucked an errant curl behind her ear.

After a minute or two, Gervase's voice rose above the general clamour. 'Stop that at once!' he was shouting. 'At once. Do you hear me?'

Susanna had no experience of warfare, but it seemed a very odd thing to say in the circumstances. Surely one didn't just tell enemy cannoneers to 'stop it' and expect them to obey?

And then Gervase was elbowing his way back

through the throng, sighing explosively as he came to a halt before his mother.

'Yes?' said Dame Constance interestedly.

'*Your builders!*' Much to the surprise of his betrothed, he seemed to be in a thunderous temper. Was it possible that, for once, he was not going to say, 'Yes, mother'? She stared at the pair of them, enthralled.

'*My* builders?'

'Well, you were the one who wanted an extension built!'

Dame Constance let it pass. 'And what are *my* builders doing to offend you?'

'Trying to demolish the Great Hall, that's what they are doing!'

The mild surprise on his mother's face, although he did not know it, had little to do with what he had said, but much to do with how he had said it. For the first time in the twenty-four years of his life, he reminded her forcibly of his father, the late Lord Nicholas. Just so had Nicholas reacted to the unexpected; just so had his weatherbeaten skin coloured up with fury; just so had he taken every minor mishap or misjudgement on the part of others as a personal affront. Although it had made Lord Nicholas somewhat trying to live with, it was gratifying to discover that somewhere deep down in Gervase's normally controlled self there burned an inherited spark.

Rising to her feet and smoothing down her graceful skirts, she said, 'Explain, please.'

'They are outside on some scaffolding with a great maul hammer, knocking out the window sill.'

'Well, that is preferable to a cannon bombardment, I suppose,' she replied provocatively.

Hands on hips, Gervase continued to stand and glare at her.

'Where,' she asked, 'is Sir Walter?'

Gervase bellowed, 'Walter!' and the steward emerged from the throng, stateliness personified and not a hair out of place.

'Explain, please,' said Dame Constance.

'I believe, Lady, that Master Emile would be better equipped than I to do so.'

'Then send for him, if you would be so kind.'

'Yes, Lady.'

Sir Walter was annoyed, though there was no question of letting it show. The Lady did not value him as she should. Somehow, indefinably, Dame Constance had conveyed that, as superintendent of the works, he *should* have been able to explain what the builders were up to—and why. This was not Sir Walter's own view, which was that his role was simply to ensure that everything ran smoothly. *What* was running smoothly had nothing to do with him.

It took some little time before Master Emile presented himself, grey of skin as always, before Dame Constance. Even his new robes to the value of sixteen shillings, provided by Dame Constance as part of his contract, looked as if he had been cleaning his tools with them.

She, casting a reproving glance at the knights and squires who were congregating inquisitively around her chair, waited until they had backed away before she said, 'Unless I am mistaken, Master Emile, you are still at the preparatory stage of the building work for which you are contracted. You are organising your lodge, and your workers, and some of your materials, but you are not quite ready to start on the actual labour.'

Stating the obvious gave her no pleasure, but she had discovered that it was necessary to reassure Master Emile that, female though she was, she was a rational being, and had eyes in her head.

'*D'accord*,' he agreed.

'May I ask why, then, at this stage, you are opening up what will be the corridor from the new Great Chamber into the Great Hall? Because that is what you are doing, is it not?'

The master mason's tone was as deferential as any paying customer had the right to expect, but his words were designed to put the laity in its place. He was not accustomed to being questioned about his work, and certainly not by a woman, Lady or no. 'A structural requirement,' he said.

Gervase, still angry, opened his mouth but his mother waved him to silence. 'Yes?' she said. 'Tell me more.'

After a moment during which he appeared to be struggling with some inner demon, Master Emile muttered an almost inaudible '*Zut alors!*' and then, aloud, 'It is a matter of the number and size of the—ah—ashlar blocks for the extension.'

Encouragingly, Dame Constance said, 'Yes?'

Another pause, then, 'We wish the stonework of the new tower to run in even courses, do we not?'

'Yes.'

'I am at present engaged in estimating the materials needed, the number and size of the stone blocks required. In order so to do, I must know *précisément* where the entrance from the new extension into the existing Great Hall will be. The floor level as it now is, you understand? Otherwise, we will have either courses of uneven size or many more steps up or down from old to new than you would wish.'

Dame Constance stared at him. 'I see. It is a matter of the floor level. Could you not simply take measurements?'

'But how can we measure the height of the floor *inside*,' Master Emile enquired condescendingly, 'when from the outside we cannot see it? That is why we must demolish the window sill down to floor level.'

'I have never heard anything so stupid!' Gervase exploded. 'You are saying that we are to have a gaping void in this wall until the extension is completed? For months, and months, and months?'

'We will, *naturellement*, cover the opening with a canvas while work is in progress.'

'Perhaps,' offered Dame Constance after a careful interval, 'you might measure the distance outside from the sill to the ground, and then here, indoors, measure from the sill to the floor, and subtract the inside from the outside measurement? You could then mark the correct level on the outside wall with tar or limewash, or something of the sort.'

With bated breath, everyone waited while Master Emile studied the fragment of stone he was rubbing between his fingers and struggled to avoid admitting that he hadn't thought of that. 'I suppose we might essay that,' he said grudgingly at last. 'But it is a method that lacks precision, and I am accustomed to precision in all things.'

'The blame will not be yours,' Dame Constance

assured him, 'if things go wrong. In the meantime, perhaps you will be good enough to abandon your demolition of the window sill. Thank you for enlightening us, Master Emile. I will not keep you any longer from your work.'

After he had gone, Gervase demanded, 'And who is to rebuild what they have already knocked down?'

'One thing at a time,' replied his mother through gritted teeth.

2

Gervase rapidly recovered his temper, but not his calm. It was, Susanna thought, watching him, as if some celestial hand had given him such a good shaking that it would take time for him to settle back to normal.

She was surprised to find him at her side.

'Well, that was fun, wasn't it?' he said cheerfully.

'I—er—yes—was it?'

'Yes, of course. A little excitement never comes amiss, always makes me feel better. I was wondering . . . My mother wants me to ride round and inspect some of the manors, and I thought I could start this afternoon. Would you care to join me? I've shown you round the castle and it would be good for you to learn something about the estate as well.'

It was an olive branch of sorts. She had been feeling cooped up and welcomed the idea, and her pleasure showed when she said, 'I would like that!'

His smile was attractive, and when old Tom led her favourite palfrey from the stable, he was suitably admiring. 'What is her name?'

'Angel, because she behaves like one.'

Susanna felt quite in charity with him, especially when it became clear that, for him, riding and talking were mutually exclusive occupations. Spring was in full flood now and she was able to take delight in the lushness of the countryside and the warmth of the sun as they rode through the park, stocked with deer and game, towards the outlying manors. She sat her mare peaceably while Gervase spoke to the holders of the charming houses they visited and introduced her to the tenants as their future Lady. The years ahead began to look much more appealing.

They were approaching the furthest point of their tour when they observed a small party of horsemen heading in the direction from which they had come. Gervase exclaimed, 'Robert Salvin! I had forgotten my mother had summoned him.'

Young Mr Salvin returned his hail in the friendliest way, and the two parties came together, the grooms and attendants holding back.

Gervase and Mr Salvin having agreed that, yes, the weather was fine and, yes, the spring planting had gone well and, yes, they were both in excellent health and, yes, the news from Westminster was tantalising, it occurred to Gervase to introduce Susanna, whom Mr Salvin had been studying attentively. That she turned out to be Gervase's future lady did not diminish the young man's interest in the least. It was clear from the warmth in his crinkling gaze that he thought her very fetching.

She had become familiar with appreciative looks from some of the knights and squires at Vine Regis but was learning to ignore them, to look through the men as if they didn't exist. This, however, was more direct, more personal, and something inside her gave an odd little tweak of satisfaction.

Susanna surveyed Mr Salvin in return from under her eyelashes. He seemed a pleasant enough person, fashionable in his dress, brown-haired, brown-eyed, and good-looking in a way that threatened to become plump. His manner was smooth and his smile admiring.

Susanna had no fault to find with that, but Gervase, from being amiable became unexpectedly curt. 'How long will you be staying?' he asked, and when Mr Salvin, his eyes still on Susanna, replied, 'A few days, I should think,' he said only, 'Indeed?' He suddenly looked—what?—sour.

Susanna couldn't understand it, and then a thought struck her with the force of a thunderbolt. Was he—could he possibly be—jealous? There might have been any number of reasons for his reaction to Mr Salvin, but to Susanna there was only one possibility that appealed.

She had been wondering how to make Gervase take notice of her and now she thought she knew.

She smiled blindingly back at Mr Salvin and said, 'How delightful. We shall see more of you.'

Gervase, who had been holding her reins, twitched on them sharply. 'We must be getting on. We will see you later, Robert.'

'I look forward to it.'

As they rode on, even the cooing doves and strolling peacocks of Woodcote and Amerscote failed to divert Susanna from consideration of how to make Gervase properly jealous, so that he would appreciate her as she wanted him to do. So that she would awake the romance in his soul. He must have *some* romance in his soul, surely?

At the moment, he was not at all romantic. He was cross. It was a good sign.

3

The sun had not yet soaked through the massive walls of Vine Regis and Susanna found herself shivering later in the day as she began to make her way down to supper in the Great Hall. Then she heard a light footfall on the stairs behind her, and there was a male arm round her shoulders, and a voice murmuring, 'Are you chilled, my pretty one?' and she felt a surprisingly soft male cheek laid against hers.

It had the strangest effect on her. Only when years and experience came to her was she to remember how this, her first direct physical contact with a handsome young man, had been responsible for arousing in her the earliest stirrings of adult awareness. At the time, she thought only how queer and delicious was the melting sensation down in the small of her back.

It was no more than a momentary encounter, Mr Salvin recognising, even if Susanna did not, that castle corridors were altogether too public to be safe for kissing. Removing his arm from her shoulder, he accompanied her down the stairs, talking of the weather and the excellent hospitality of Vine Regis. He always enjoyed coming here.

'Yes,' she said. And did he come here often?

'Now and then, on business of one kind or another.'

Throughout supper, with Mr Salvin seated next to Isabelle and giving most of his attention to her, Susanna fluttered her eyelashes at him whenever she thought no one but Gervase was looking, but although Gervase's expression became steadily more frozen, Mr Salvin failed to respond, his attention all on Isabelle. Which was just as it should be, Susanna told herself. He had excellent manners and Isabelle was, after all, the daughter of the house.

At one point, catching William's disapproving eye from the far end of the pages' table, Susanna smiled angelically at him, causing his frown to intensify. How she behaved was no business of his. She must remember to tell him so—not for the first time.

Young Mr Salvin had come out of the blue, and he returned to the blue two days later, taking a courteous farewell of the ladies and promising to visit Vine Regis again soon. Not that there was anything unusual there, Susanna was slowly discovering. There was a steady stream of visitors at the castle—receivers and auditors, superior tenants, lawyers, neighbours with their wives and families, senior churchmen, and occasional courtiers on their travels. Fleeting acquaintances. In most cases, Susanna doubted whether she would even recognise them again. But she would certainly recognise Mr Salvin, and hoped to be given the opportunity.

It made Susanna feel very important to hand his helmet up to her mounted husband-to-be when he was ready to ride off to Westminster after a week of virtual invisibility during which, on his mother's orders, he had been reestablishing his lordly presence among his affinity. It was an occupation he found dull beyond bearing. Setting off for the outside world, therefore, where there was some promise of action—even if not the bellicose action his soul craved—put him in an excellent humour. He even beamed down upon his two little daughters—Blanche fully recovered from her ordeal—and on his bride-to-be who, overcome, smiled brilliantly back up at him.

'What a pretty picture they make,' murmured Susanna's chamberer, Alice, to Master William, who had just come down from the Great Hall and happened to be standing beside her watching, though she was beginning to learn that 'happened to be' was not an apt phrase where he was concerned. Wherever he was, it was usually by intent. He didn't like to miss anything.

Now, all he did was frown and mutter, 'I suppose so,' almost as if he disliked seeing everyone looking so friendly and cheerful. But it couldn't be that, Alice thought. She glanced up at Master MacLeod, standing on her other side, and caught a glimmer of amusement in his eye. What a lovely man he was! She smiled shyly back at him.

To Susanna, as Lord Gervase clattered away with his household over the drawbridge, it seemed almost as if he were going to war. Fortunately, he wasn't, so she had no need to worry about him.

Or not until Dame Constance said, 'Well, let us hope he casts his vote wisely,' and John laughed. 'You mean let us hope that he has the sense to side with the most powerful of the barons?'

'Of course. Enemies are no less enemies even when one makes them by default.'

Susanna exclaimed, 'But Gervase won't, will he?'

'Probably not.' Dame Constance's shapely brows were raised as she went on, 'I think, Susanna, that it is high time you and I had a talk. In my chamber, in about an hour, if that is convenient?'

What, Susanna wondered, would happen if she said it was inconvenient? But she didn't dare. Dame Constance always threw her into a state of confusion, so that she became immediately and intensely self-conscious.

There were no gold stars painted on the walls of the Lady's austerely elegant chamber, and the top of the clothes chest bore an alarming number of parchments and what looked to Susanna like accounts rolls. But Dame Constance's manner was relaxed and smiling as she waved Susanna to a cushioned stool.

Not that she relinquished the initiative. For the intervening hour, Susanna had been considering what she should say to the Lady, but she was gracefully forestalled. It did not occur to her that Dame Constance was looking forward to their conversation as little as she.

'I will not ask if you are happy here in your new life,' Dame Constance began. 'It would surprise me if you were. The leap from being a girl to being a woman is more abrupt than from boy to man, because a girl's life is much more sheltered. But it

106

seems to me that we would be well advised to discuss life at Vine Regis and your role here.'

'The nuns,' Susanna interrupted defensively, 'taught me . . .'

'A great deal, I have no doubt, but most of it theoretical. When you take up your role as wife and helpmeet, you will enter the realm of practicality. Knowing how to keep house is not the same as knowing how to keep *this* house.'

'But the principles . . .'

'Are the same. Yes, indeed they are. But principles do not instruct you in the names and backgrounds, the personal eccentricities of the people you daily have to deal with—people whose loyalty depends on how you treat them, which in turn depends on how well you know them. Tell me, for example, what you have learned about Sir Walter Woolston in the weeks since you have been here.'

The steward. 'He is a very superior gentleman,' Susanna said hesitantly, 'about forty years of age, with a courteous manner and—er—the habit of addressing people rather than talking to them. He is an efficient administrator, I suppose, otherwise he would not be the steward of Vine Regis.'

'And?'

'And—er . . .'

'And he has his own estate nearby, which is looked after in his absence by his wife, who is a dreadful shrew of a woman, a real harridan. They have two sons and three daughters, all between the ages of ten and twenty, and his besetting sin is vanity. He is by no means as clever as he thinks he is. I find it necessary to keep a close eye on everything he does, and he believes I do not value him as I should. But in general he is, as you have deduced, a competent administrator and *I* am able to take his failings into account, while *he* is prepared to put up with a good deal for the honour of being steward of Vine Regis.'

Susanna said, 'Yes, well, you have known him for a long time.'

Dame Constance laughed. 'Shall I go on?'

'I *know* that I will have a lot to learn about the people on the estate.' Even to her own ears, her voice was decidedly petulant.

Dame Constance restrained herself from saying, 'It is high time you began.' Instead, she went on, controlling her irritation at having to teach Susanna what she ought to have enough sense to recognise for herself, 'More than that, my dear. I am sure you know that Gervase, like all men of rank, spends little time at home. Fighting, attending the royal court, travelling, these are the three primary duties of a lord, and it is for his wife to represent him at home when he is away. He is served by bailiffs, provosts, rent collectors, land managers, and she must govern them all. She must be as well informed as they are about what they do and how they do it. Otherwise she cannot be sure that they are performing their duties to the best advantage. In your case, this applies not only to the people here at Vine Regis, but to those on Gervase's other and more distant estates. You will have to be awake to local usages, rights and customs. You will have to be autocratic, circumspect or kindly as the situation requires. You will have to know everything about the management of his affairs . . .'

'In fact,' intervened Susanna without stopping to

think, 'I will have to know a great deal more than *he* does!'

Dame Constance's mouth twitched. 'Yes, that is true, within limits. As it happens, Gervase is well informed about most such matters—I have made sure of that—but he is not interested. You will find, as you gain experience, that few men are prepared to bestir themselves in what does not interest them.'

Susanna didn't see why women should have to do it for them. Especially mothers!

She did not say so, however. She wanted to say, 'And when I am married to Gervase and have learned all this, will I be acknowledged as the Lady of the Castle? Will you hand the keys over to me?' but again she didn't dare. Instead, she asked very correctly, 'But how can I learn all this?'

'Listen. Watch. Ask.'

At that moment, one of Dame Constance's gentlewomen came into the room. Susanna had not yet learned to distinguish which of them was which; they all three looked so alike, so staid, so drab. Dame Constance said, 'Yes, Matilda?'

Learn about the people of the castle . . .

Matilda, Matilda, Matilda. Brown hair, thick eyebrows. Matilda is the one with the eyebrows, Susanna told herself. Remember, remember.

Her interview with Dame Constance was clearly over. As Susanna left the room, the gentlewoman stood aside to let her pass and Susanna smiled graciously. 'Thank you, Matilda.'

She did not see the eyebrows rise expressively as the woman caught her mistress's ironical eye.

There was something Susanna wanted to know, but the only way she could see of working round to it was to lose the question in a more general conversation.

Sitting at her stitchery with Isabelle next day, she held the linen away from her at arm's length to study the effect of the doves she was embroidering. They didn't look much like doves, more like fluttering kerchiefs.

'Perhaps you should do them perched rather than flying,' Isabelle suggested.

'I should ride over to Amerscote or Woodcote and study them more carefully,' Susanna sighed. 'The dovecotes there are lovely. The manors are lovely, too. So friendly and cared for. At home—I mean, where I come from—most of the dwellings are rather stern and—and—disciplined.'

Isabelle was not interested but her mother, she knew, was. So, seizing her opportunity, she asked, 'Like the people within them?'

'I suppose so. We are all very strictly brought up to believe in obedience and duty, to hold by what is right and what is wrong.'

'That doesn't sound very comfortable.'

'No.'

With a faint smile, Isabelle remarked, 'How did you manage to become so bright and bubbly in spite of it?'

Susanna, her embroidery sunk in her lap, blushed slightly and reflected for a moment. 'I *do* believe in obedience and duty, and holding by what's right and what's wrong, but my mother is a very warm and loving person and I am her only daughter. I'm spoilt, I suppose. She always wanted me to have fine clothes, and to look my prettiest.'

'In contrast with your surroundings?'

'I suppose so. Cold, damp, grey houses . . . Life is a constant struggle against the weather—the rain and the wind—so that even the houses have to be strong-minded! But you mustn't think I don't love the West Country. The sea coasts, the moors and the mountains—you should see them. They're magnificent.'

'But harsh.'

'It depends how you look at them.' Susanna was defensive. 'They're dramatic, and I like that. But I do see the charm of the land around Vine Regis. And the manors are so kind and welcoming.'

She plunged. 'Does the Lady have some favourite manor on Vine Regis? Or on one of Gervase's other estates?'

Mystified by the sudden intrusion of Dame Constance into the conversation, Isabelle replied, 'I don't think so. Why?'

'I just wondered.'

Annoyed and depressed after Dame Constance's lecture, Susanna had been unable to imagine continuing to share the castle with her after she and Gervase were married. There had been no hint of the Lady abandoning Vine Regis to the newlyweds and going off to live elsewhere. Indeed, Susanna had the feeling that, unless something were done, Dame Constance would be with them for ever, keeping an eye on things, perpetually analysing and criticising.

There must be *some* way of persuading her to go

away.

An hour or two later, erupting uninvited into Susanna's chamber, William found himself listening with the greatest interest to Susanna talking to herself.

After a while, chin on fist, he said, 'Well, if she won't go, you can.'

'What do you mean?'

'I keep telling you, you don't have to marry the fellow. No Lord Gervase, no Dame Constance. Simple.'

'Really, William! Not that again. I *am* going to marry Lord Gervase.' If only it were Piers Whiteford, about whom she dreamed night after night! 'I am beginning to feel quite attached to him, and I think he is developing some feeling for me. He is just reserved by nature and doesn't show it.'

'Humph!'

'And, as you well know, nothing on this earth would induce me to marry you, even if there were some legal way of breaking off my pre-contract with Lord Gervase. Think how embarrassing it would be for everyone.'

William's eyebrows rose exaggeratedly and his mouth turned down at the corners. 'I don't see why. All you'd have to say was that you didn't like him and you didn't want to share your home with his mother.'

'That's all, is it? And no one would be embarrassed? Anyway, it's not a possibility. I don't *not* like him, and there must be *some* way to persuade Dame Constance to go and live somewhere else!'

'How about finding another husband for her?

Or there are other possibilities I can think of. What about a convent?'

She scowled at him. 'William, will you *go away*! Whatever happens, I would never, ever marry *you*. Go back home to Cernwell and tell your father so.'

'No. I'm enjoying myself here. It's much more entertaining than it is at home. I'll stay,' he gave his familiar, cocky grin, 'until you decide to come home to Cernwell, too. And then I can escort you.'

He was still grinning as he ducked out of the door to escape the jug she threw at him.

6

When he descended into the Great Hall a few minutes later, looking for mischief, he was immediately aware of what he mentally categorised as Something Going On.

It was a queer place, the Great Hall, sometimes bursting at the seams with people, at other times empty and echoing. At night, although the falconers slept in the mews with their hawks and the grooms in the stables with their horses, everyone else bedded down on the hard floor of the Great Hall, using their rolled-up cloaks for pillows. It was all very different from Cernwell, where most of the servants and retainers were local and slept at home in the village at night.

Now, certainly, there *was* something going on, but he couldn't find out what. There were three or four small groups of men standing around talking earnestly—household officers surrounded by their minions—and Dame Constance was sitting looking concerned at her favourite table, discussing something with the inevitable Hamish. William, trying to look as if he had developed an interest in the tapestries on the walls, drifted around with his ears cocked, but everyone glanced at him irritably and fell silent at his approach. It was very frustrating.

If they wanted him out of the way, he thought, they only had to say so! After a while, it occurred to him to wander off and vanish behind one of the great pillars.

They didn't know him well enough to check that he had actually gone and, when he reappeared, Hamish was over by the cannonball window—its sill not yet rebuilt—studying the floor intently, and Sir Walter was staring at the dressers holding the gold plate equally intently.

Hamish said, 'No, nothing!' and, raising his head to look at Dame Constance, discovered William's inquisitive face peering at him.

'Away ye go, laddie!' he said sharply. 'This is none of your business.'

But William was perfectly capable of putting two and two together, especially when he knew the answer. 'You think someone might have come in off the scaffolding and stolen some of the cups and plates?'

Coolly, Dame Constance said, 'We believe there has been a theft, yes, and we must investigate all the possibilities. Theft is unheard of at Vine Regis, and I will not have it!'

'Ho, ho,' thought William. He had the greatest admiration for Dame Constance, but felt she was a bit too authoritarian at times. It couldn't be good for her. Anyway, in the matter of theft, there was no point in saying, 'I will not have it!' unless you could be sure any potential thieves were dutifully gathered around, paying attention.

'I wish it to be kept quiet for the present,' continued Dame Constance. 'Any hint of such a thing, and everyone in the castle will feel themselves contaminated by suspicion. Do you understand?'

'Oh, yes,' said William cheerily. Should he tell them? It would have to be now, because it would seem very odd if he left it till later.

'But you don't need to worry,' he went on. 'I know where the stuff is.'

Dame Constance said, 'You . . . ?'

'Lord Gervase took it with him yesterday.'

Dame Constance sat back limply, her hands dropping to her lap. 'Explain, please.'

'Just before he left for Westminster, one of his grooms came rushing up here with a saddlebag. He said my lord would be staying in lodgings in the City and had no fancy for drinking out of a wooden cup or eating off a bread trencher. So he wanted to take one or two cups and platters and bowls with him. The fellow stuffed them in the saddlebag and off he went. I thought someone would have told you.'

'Thank you, Master William.'

Hamish laughed. 'Reminds me of my cousin Jamie, who failed to tell anybody he was moving the beasts up to the shielings—the high pastures—and got chased for his life as a cattle reiver.'

'I hope he survived?'

'Oh, aye.'

'It is more than my son would do if he were here at this moment. As if we did not have enough worries without his thoughtlessness! Thank you,

115

Master William. You have been very helpful.'

'Delighted,' he said. 'But have you *really* never had any thefts at Vine Regis?'

'Never.'

He resisted the temptation to say, 'Some day your luck will run out.'

CHAPTER SIX

1

Dame Constance said, 'Must we?'

'Yes, Lady.'

She sighed. More bells! First, there had been the mournful day-long jangling of the passing bells rung by the acolytes who had come to carry her dying castle chaplain—an old man, who had long been sick—to the abbey of Stanwelle, there to spend his last remaining hours in the company of his spiritual brothers. He had been a kindly soul, and she had always liked him even when she doubted his store of wisdom.

And after that, news had come, if somewhat belatedly, that the king was dead, which had entailed twenty-four unbroken hours of ringing out the death knell from the church tower. As if in compensation, silence reigned over the building site for the next week, the workmen having allotted themselves an unauthorised holiday and vanished in the general direction of Salisbury, with its taverns and whorehouses. Dame Constance's tight-lipped remonstrances had no effect on Master Emile, who merely shrugged and said it was customary, and happily they did not have to be paid for unofficial days off.

'If they absent themselves now, before work has even begun, what is it going to be like in future?' she demanded of Sir Guy, to whom she unfailingly turned for sanity when things began to get out of hand.

Unable to resist, he quoted Gervase at her. 'Well, you are the one who wanted the extension built.'

After an ominous moment, she remembered. 'And you are the one who can't tell a maul hammer from a cannonball!'

He laughed. '*Touché!* But you can't control everything, my dearest love, however much you might like to.'

'I suppose not.' She wrinkled her elegant nose. 'Perhaps you should make a note to remind me of it—on the first Tuesday of every month, say?'

2

When the men had wandered back at last, they had brought dramatic news. Three days after the king's death, the French truce had expired. Everyone had known this was due to happen, but no one had expected the French to take such swift advantage.

After Sir Guy had weeded out the more unlikely fancies from the builders' barely coherent gossip— cannonballs with wings, arrows that could fly round corners, ships as navigable on land as at sea—he was able to deduce that, while England's royal council was engaged in arguing about young Richard II's coronation protocol, Charles V of France had despatched a fleet to devastate the Channel ports. Rye, Weymouth, Plymouth, and then Southampton and Poole had all suffered within days of the ending of the truce.

Gravely, Sir Guy reported to the breakfast table, 'It seems there is already invasion hysteria, not

118

only around the coast but inland.'

Dame Constance's fingers were spread over her eyes. 'At least Vine Regis is fortunate in being well away from the sea, but—oh dear—I suppose Gervase will be off again!'

'Not immediately. Though there is talk of Thomas of Woodstock gathering a force, and from what I know of Gervase he will be unable to resist joining it.'

Susanna exclaimed, 'No, surely not!' She was perfectly prepared to think of herself as Gervase's wife-to-be, but not as his widow-to-be. 'Oh, how awful!'

She was ignored.

'Why?' demanded Dame Constance irritably. 'Why do we have to hear this from builders' gossip? Why can my son not take the trouble to send a messenger?' Sir Guy quirked an eyebrow, and she went on, 'I know. I know. Show him the chance of a fight and everything else vanishes from his mind!'

'Are you remembering Nicholas?' he asked abruptly.

She stared at him. 'You should know better than that.'

'One can never be altogether sure.'

'Oblige me by not talking nonsense and tell me, what did I do to deserve such a son? Thank goodness John has no martial ambitions.'

'And neither has Piers,' said Sir Guy with a faint smile. 'I've often thought that is why he and Gervase are such good friends. Complementary rather than competing personalities.'

Susanna's brain reeled. A husband-to-be who wanted to get himself killed? A dream lover who

119

didn't?

'Yes. Well, I suppose the world must go on,' said Dame Constance prosaically. 'There are foundations to be laid.'

3

And so the subsoil had been tested, the line of the new building marked out, and the foundation trench dug by an untrustworthy-looking crew of casual labourers whom Master Emile had recruited from among the vagrants wandering the countryside, it being beneath the dignity of his own men to undertake such unskilled work. Dame Constance could not tell whether the casual labourers' slow progress was due to a simple reluctance to exert themselves or the desire to go on being paid a wage for as long as possible, with the additional benefit of being fed from the castle kitchens. At least it had resolved the problem of the undeserving poor who had formerly congregated on the barbican, waiting for distribution of the trenchers from the dinner tables. The trenchers now went to the labourers, although Dame Constance's clerk of the kitchen maintained irritably that half the 'labourers' were in fact former beggars posing as workmen when feeding time came round. Master Emile, applied to, merely replied that casual labour was impossible to monitor. Dame Constance was beginning to find his *'C'est la vie'* attitude profoundly annoying.

But now, at last, the trench was completed and Dame Constance was sighing, 'More bells!'

because Master Emile was insisting that the foundations be laid with full ceremony—church bells, priestly blessings, holy water. At least there was no mention of the traditional blood sacrifice.

'My craftsmen would be uneasy in the knowledge that evil spirits have not been dispelled before work begins. The demons who live underground and in the air about us derive pleasure from causing damage to buildings and those who build them. The proper rites must be carried out in order to reassure my men that they are protected against the malice of faeries, fiends, and demons.'

Dame Constance, unimpressed by the thought of faeries at the bottom of her garden, nevertheless recognised that it was necessary to soothe the craftsmen's traditional fears, pagan though they were. So she invited Abbot Ralph, the most readily available senior churchman, to lay the foundation stone and vanquish any evil spirits.

She held out a hand in welcome when he turned up, at his most majestic, to perform the rites.

'Lady,' he responded, inclining his head as he returned her grip. But he seemed a little on edge, and his hand trembled very slightly, which tempted her to mischief. So she continued to hold his hand while she said, 'How kind of you to come. I do not expect you, of course, to "lay" the foundation stone which, as you can see, is already in position, but simply to tap it with this special little golden hammer and say a blessing over it.'

Then she took pity on him. She had never been so sharply aware of the disturbing effect she had on him, and the laughter bubbled up inside her as she released his hand and gestured towards the hammer whose handle had been wrapped in gold leaf for the occasion. He would like that, she knew, and he did.

Accepting the hammer from six-year-old Blanche, who had demanded to be entrusted with it, he said, 'Thank you, my child. Now, shall we begin?'

'If you please.'

Bending, a movement for which his ample frame was not designed, he tapped the foundation stone briskly, once, then returned the hammer to Blanche, straightened up, raised his hands in blessing, and began, '*Pater de coelis deus, spiritus sancte . . .*'

The workmen all looked suitably impressed, even if they could only guess at what was being said. This was even more true when it came to the turn of the village priest, Father Hoby, who gabbled his way through a Latin exorcism of which he himself understood barely a word, while from the village church the Vox Domini bell rang out to deafening effect. Then, his stringy yellow hair flying wildly, the priest dipped his asperser in the bowl of holy water and waved it over the foundation trench. Dame Constance, familiar with Father Hoby's approach to the casting of aspersions, took care to stand well back, but Abbot Ralph, listening to the gabbling with closed eyes and a pained expression, was not so fortunate. Neither was Robert Salvin, who had arrived the previous evening on his promised return visit to Vine Regis. He was standing next to Isabelle and, turning in surprise to find her retreating from his side, received the full benefit of the holy water.

His expression lost something of its customary

122

affability as John, laughing merrily the while, helped him brush the droplets off his velvets. Nor was he amused as the labourers busily began shovelling rubble into the foundation trench while Father Hoby pranced alongside, distributing more holy water over every shovelful, his protruberant pale blue eyes popping. 'It makes him feel like God,' John murmured. Mr Salvin said no more than, 'Hmmm', but Susanna overheard and was shocked. And then John transferred his attentions to her and she saw that the droplets of water on her own surcoat were attracting a fine film of mortar dust and exclaimed, 'No, John. Stop. You'll rub the dust in.'

It was with genuine gratitude that she heard Dame Constance say, 'I think we might be forgiven for retreating indoors, don't you, Susanna? Before your gown is quite ruined.'

'Oh, yes. Yes, please.'

Abbot Ralph consented to join them in the Great Hall for a cup of wine, and Susanna was able to observe him closely. When his eyes merely flitted over her, she decided it would not do. He must be made to recognise her. After all, she might need him some day, for some at present undefinable reason.

Although he was conversing with Dame Constance, he was standing well away from her, so Susanna was able to join them without, she hoped, any appearance of interrupting.

Dame Constance said, 'I think you have met my future daughter-in-law?'

'Ahhh. Yes.'

Her eyes modestly lowered, Susanna said, 'I am honoured that you should remember me.'

123

Abbot Ralph clearly didn't. He was a very elevated personage, so, feeling that she ought to say something reasonably intelligent, she went on, 'I am most interested in Stanwelle. Do you have a convent attached? I should very much like to visit it.'

The abbot gave a perceptible shudder. 'No. There are a number of convents in the Cistercian order nowadays, but not at Stanwelle.'

'A pity,' said Susanna.

Dame Constance, catching an exchange of glances between Susanna and Master William, hovering around as always, was faintly puzzled. Had there been something behind Susanna's superficially innocent enquiry? Or was it nothing more than a desire to justify her ill-mannered intrusion into the conversation?

4

Generous though Father Hoby had been with his holy water, he had not been generous enough to explain why the foundation trench, bone dry at sundown, proved to be full to the brim of water next morning. The swans were not paddling in it, but it was a near thing.

Master Emile was unaccustomed to such misadventures on sites where he was master, and said so in no uncertain terms to his head journeyman. 'I gave you the responsibility of testing the subsoil,' he shouted. 'And you have failed me. How did you not see that the water table was high?'

'I did not see that it was high because it wasn't,'

124

Master Hal snapped back.

'It must be!'

'No, it mustn't!'

Work on the site came to a halt as everyone drifted towards the two men inquisitively. One or two of the scaffolders made suggestive punching gestures, but the master mason and head journeyman had their dignity to consider and merely went on shouting. After a while, Sir Walter emerged from his superintendent's tent, his smooth white brows raised, and glanced up towards the castle windows. The Lady Susanna and Master John were staring out interestedly but there was no sign of Dame Constance, although Sir Walter would not have wagered a groat that she was unaware of the rumpus taking place below. Establishing his presence by rapping sharply on a convenient outcrop of rock with his staff of office, he declared such noisy altercation unseemly in view of the recent death of the king. In any case, the argument was surely easy enough to settle. 'A test hole. Over there, I suggest,' and he pointed to the opposite side of the trench from his tent.

Master Hal grabbed a spade from one of the bystanders and dug into the soil where Sir Walter was pointing, about a yard away from the trench. Arms akimbo, Master Emile stood by his side, glowering.

When he had dug down two feet, with no sign of the water table, Master Hal said, 'You see?'

'Continue.'

Master Hal went on digging, gradually disappearing into the pit. The scaffolders were sniggering loudly, and Sir Walter was smiling patronisingly when Master Emile finally admitted defeat.

'*Pfui!* Where then does the water come from?'

Master Emile, Master Hal, and all the other journeymen—encouraged by advice and assistance from the indefatigable William—spent the entire day hammering stakes into the ground at random locations and pulling them out again, bone dry. Sir Walter having declared a headache from the noise, they considerately avoided the immediate surroundings of his tent, but nowhere else escaped.

The water table was not unduly high, nor was the river, and the basic limestone showed no sign of being particularly porous. Master Emile could not understand it.

His face grew longer by the minute, his slack mouth slacker. He began muttering to himself. William, sidling up to him to eavesdrop, discovered that he was repeating the word, 'Gerhard,' time after time. Considerately, William refrained from asking Master Emile who Gerhard might be, but addressed the question to Master Hal instead.

Master Hal went on hammering. 'Ha!' he snorted. Then he stopped and leaned on the long handle of his hammer, saying thoughtfully, 'I wonder? I'd guess he's thinking of Gerhard of Amiens who laid out the ground plan of the cathedral at Cologne. The Devil didn't like the idea of a cathedral and threatened to stop Gerhard from completing the work by causing a canal to emerge from the foundations . . .'

'No!' William exclaimed.

'. . . but Gerhard thought he alone knew the secret of how canals were built, and the Devil didn't, so he wagered his soul on it. But he told his wife the secret and Satan teased it out of her. Next thing, a canal began to flow from the foundations and Master Gerhard realised that he had sold his soul to the Devil. So he threw himself from the scaffolding into the void and was never seen again.'

'Is that true?'

'Oh, yes.' Master Hal took a firmer grip on his hammer and chuckled. 'But I can't think that Master Emile has sold *his* soul to the Devil. I doubt if Satan would even find it worth bargaining for.'

In the end, Master Emile gave up muttering and decided that the only solution was to have a small conduit dug to drain the water from the trench into the river. It was all drying off nicely when everyone went to bed.

But in the morning, the conduit was clogged with rubble and the foundation trench was full of water again. And also on the third morning.

John said, 'I've never seen anyone literally tearing his hair before.'

Isabelle extended a beckoning finger and, unthinkingly, he leaned forward, only to have the exposed edges of his shirt tweaked back inside his tunic, and his own hair smoothed down by sisterly hands. 'Oh, very droll,' he said, and promptly restored his hair to disorder by running his fingers through it. 'This obsession with appearances!'

Susanna, who had been dying to tidy him up for weeks, smiled beatifically.

But his mother merely said, 'Don't be foolish. You may do something useful by riding over to Stanwelle and telling Abbot Ralph that I wish to borrow his architect. And don't come back without him.'

Abbot Ralph was annoyed, and so was Master

Emile when the very superior person who dignified himself with the new title of architect duly appeared, bearing the measuring rod that symbolised his professional status. M. Bernard of Dol, though much less French than Master Emile, felt that it enhanced his dignity to be known as Monsieur. He would have preferred to be addressed simply by the title of Magister, with no name attached, but this tended to cause confusion in the mind of the average ignoramus, so Monsieur it had to be. Fortunately, Dame Constance and the architect took to each other at once. Here, she thought, was a man who knew what he was talking about, and one who had the air of authority which Master Emile so conspicuously lacked.

Not that M. Bernard was able to come up with any ideas which Master Emile had not already tested. River high, water table high, porous limestone? No. Hmmm. There was the remote possibility of an underground spring, but close inspection showed no sign of water movement within the trench. Hmmm. Dirty water thrown out from the kitchen? No more than a couple of bucketsful. Hmmm.

The workmen, unacquainted with the saga of Master Gerhard, had nevertheless begun reviewing all the tales they had heard of otherworldly beings who, living underground where a building was proposed, did everything they could to hold up the work. Meanwhile, Sir Walter stood by his tent smirking. He had never seen any need for a master mason, far less an architect. He himself was perfectly competent to handle everything.

The water was drained off again through the cleared conduit, Father Hoby waved his asperser again, and everyone went to bed.

In the morning, the trench was dry. The architect preened himself, as if his presence alone had achieved the miracle, and so did Father Hoby. Master Emile said dismissively that it was no doubt some pocket of underground water that had now drained away naturally.

5

Where such a pocket of water might have come from was a mystery. There had been no rain for weeks, and the weather had become increasingly hot—much too hot for Dame Constance. It made her feel ill, and being woken by the summer dawn in what according to the clock should have been the middle of the night did not improve matters. Neither did the succession of problems on the building site, or the workmen muddying the moat by cooling off there rather than in the free-flowing river, as instructed. Her normally calm and controlled temper began to fray slightly at the edges.

She would not otherwise have visited the schoolroom and reprimanded Susanna, she thought gently, although it did not sound so to Susanna, for rushing out at daybreak to inspect the trench; it was unladylike behaviour. Especially— although Dame Constance refrained from saying so—when Susanna's tumbled hair showed all too invitingly to every male within sight that, despite being fully dressed, she was probably still warm from her bed.

'Grandmother doesn't like hot weather. It

always makes her grumpy,' said Blanche.

Susanna was resentful. Why should she be made to suffer just because Dame Constance didn't like being hot?

'At least it's stopped you smiling,' said little Blanche, with annihilating frankness. 'Why do you always smile? You can't feel smiley all the time!'

Susanna hadn't been aware of the perpetual smile. 'Well, if you'd rather I looked cross, I will! Now, come and look at the pictures in my *Bestiary*, my book of animals, and tell me what they show. What is that?'

'A sheep, of course,' said Blanche scornfully. 'As if we didn't know *that*!'

'Then, if you are so clever, what is this one?'

Eleanor said doubtfully, 'A horse?'

'Have you ever seen a horse with such a long neck, and a bump on its back?'

'No-o-o-o, but perhaps the artist isn't very good at drawing.'

Susanna began to smile, and then stopped herself. 'It's a foreign animal. It's called a camel. It lives in countries where food is scarce, and when it has more food than it needs it stores the extra in the hump on its back. Just like people with fat tummies.'

'We don't want to know about foreign animals,' Blanche declared. '*We* want to go down and see what the builders are up to *now*!'

So did Susanna. 'Oh, very well. And we can take a walk in the woods one day soon and learn about animals and birds closer to home.'

What the builders were up to was tamping down the rubble in the trench and preparing to pour lime mortar over it.

To Master Emile, restored to his accustomed state of self-satisfaction, Dame Constance had said, 'You do not feel that perhaps we should wait for another dawn just to be sure the trench remains dry?'

'No, no. *Tout va bien.*'

She hoped he was right. 'Excellent. Then perhaps you would now arrange to have the ground tidied up so that it is possible for us to move about without tripping over something? I asked you to do so before, I believe, after little Lady Blanche's accident.'

There was not an inch of the island on which the castle stood that was not a clutter of tools and materials, of planks and trimming axes, of braces and handsaws and mallets, of ramps and wheelbarrows, hods and hoists, scaffolding poles and ropes to lash them, piles of stone rubble for the core of the new walls, and piles of ashlar blocks for the facings. It was also Dame Constance's impression that, every time a workman moved something out of his way, he moved it to where it would inconvenience him all over again five minutes later.

Only Master Emile could deal with the general lack of orderliness, but something also needed to be done, and swiftly, about the way the site was carpeted with stone chips, wood shavings, and the oyster shells destined to prevent the lime mortar from squeezing out of the joints while it was drying.

Gentle hints had no effect, and neither did outright requests. Master Emile's invariable response was a gesture signalling, 'Don't bother me with such trivial details'. In the end, Dame Constance summoned her steward and said, 'Sir Walter, see to it that all that mortar grit is cleared away and all those carpenters' shavings swept up. This untidiness is intolerable. And I want a path to be kept clear at all times between the drawbridge and the Barbican Rise, so that people coming and going do not have to weave their way through the present succession of obstacles. It is quite unacceptable.'

Arrange for the sweeping up, indeed! Sir Walter's dignity was insulted, but before he could say more than, 'Yes, Lady,' he was granted a reprieve by the appearance of the disreputable figure of one of the shepherds struggling towards them from the barbican. One of the ewes gone dry? Sir Walter wondered. A lamb failing to thrive? A fence needing repair? He had missed his regular inspection because of all this building nonsense.

The shepherd, at sight of the Lady, was bobbing his head respectfully, while at the same time unhitching the tunic tucked up in his belt, so that it dropped to hide the gap between his thighs.

Dame Constance, ignoring this byplay, said pleasantly, 'Good day, Will. What brings you here from the meadows?'

Head still bent, the shepherd addressed the empty air somewhere around his middle.

'Speak up, Will. I cannot hear you with all this noise going on.'

'Sheep, Lady. Sheared.'

Dame Constance frowned. 'So soon? We usually wait until the middle of the month.'

'Not me, Lady. Strangers.'

'What do you mean, "strangers"?'

'Prize ewes in t'south meadow sheared in the night. Fleeces gone.'

She stared at him. 'But the sheep themselves are still there?'

'Aye, Lady.'

Dame Constance let out a little puff of disbelief. 'Let me be quite clear about this. You are saying that during the night someone sheared all the prize ewes in the south meadow, and made off with the fleeces?'

'Aye, Lady.'

'Did you see them? Hear them?'

'Nay, Lady. Didn' hear nothing. Was sleeping in t'west meadow. Found sheep in t'south meadow bare this morn.'

'*All* of them?'

'Aye, Lady.'

There was a sudden outburst of swearing from Master Emile's workmen and Dame Constance threw up her hands. 'All this noise is beginning to addle my brain. Sir Walter, you had better go down to the meadow with Will and investigate. In the meantime—ah, here is Sir Guy. Just the man we want.' Imperiously, she beckoned the Master of Horse who was dismounting at the gatehouse.

'Crisis?' enquired that gentleman, raising an ironic eyebrow. 'How can I help?'

'Come indoors and I will tell you.'

133

'Not vagabonds,' said Sir Guy firmly. 'Not the ordinary bands of ruffians that infest the countryside.'

'No?'

'No. They're too noisy and undisciplined. And most of them are unemployed soldiers, probably townsmen who would have no idea how to shear a sheep, far less identify the pick of your flocks.'

'I suppose not. And casual thieves would think the meadow too close to the castle for safety, even though in the absence of Gervase and his men the fields are unguarded.' She ran smoothing fingers over her forehead, and sighed. 'But surely it would have been much easier simply to drive the flock away—steal the fleeces on the hoof, so to speak!'

'No, it wouldn't!' piped Blanche, an interested audience at this discussion. 'Just think of a band of rough men driving a flock of prize ewes away. Sir Guy would have caught them in no time!'

'Thank you, Blanche. But I seem to recall telling you that you might stay only if you were quiet.'

'Yes, Grandmother.'

Susanna said, 'Come here and sit by me,' and for once the child obeyed.

After a moment, as if she were reluctant to face up to the question, Dame Constance resumed, 'Someone local, then?'

Sir Guy said, 'You have no reason to doubt the shepherd's own honesty?'

'He has been honest for fifteen years. Why should he stop now?'

'Then who?'

They both spoke at once. 'Sim Walden!'

Every village had its bad character, and Sim was Vine Regis's.

Dame Constance said, 'Guy, as justice of the peace, you . . .'

His gaze held hers. 'Can and should raid his house in search of evidence? At once, before he has time to be rid of it? Yes, of course.'

Blanche gave a gasp of excitement, but Sir Guy grinned at her and then at Susanna. 'No, you can't come! This is man's work.'

He had the most astonishingly smiling eyes. He radiated all the life and vigour that Susanna had seen in his son. She felt as if she were going to faint.

8

'I want to go and watch. Why can't we go and watch? We could pretend we were going into the village for something else . . .'

Firmly, Susanna said, 'No.'

'Why not? You never let us do things we want to do. Why can't we?'

'Because we can't.'

'That's a silly answer. What you mean is, "because I say so".'

The child's resistance grumbled on for most of the morning, until even her grandmother allowed her exasperation to show. 'Blanche, you are reaching the limit. Be quiet, please, or go back to the schoolroom.'

Sir Guy returned to report no success. 'Not a trace of anything. Even his sheep shears were as clean as a whistle. They don't look as if they have been used for months.'

'A little too clean, perhaps?'

'Perhaps.'

Sir Walter reappeared in time for dinner, reporting that he had nothing to report. The shearing had been competently done, although there were still one or two ewes—the bad-tempered ones, according to Will—who seemed to have fought free of the thieves and were still trailing half-sheared fleeces behind them. No, there was no sign of the grass having been trodden by many feet. And no, there was no trail leading out of the meadow.

After dinner, when young M. Alain was performing with voice and lute against a low rumble of talk, his eyes embarrassingly fixed on his Unattainable Highborn Lady, Susanna sat trying to divert her mind by reflecting on Dame Constance's advice to her about getting to know all about local people and local affairs. In this instance, it was pleasing to discover that the Lady seemed to have failed to meet her own high standards. How lovely it would be if she, Susanna, were able to come up with the solution. Listen, watch and ask, she had been told. So she would!

The more she thought about it, the more convinced she became that she herself was in an advantageous position when it came to finding out. Listening to gossip was a very bad habit, she knew, but it could be useful. Men didn't indulge in the right kind of gossip, she suspected, and Dame Constance would never gossip with anyone. Even Matilda of the Eyebrows and the other two gentlewomen were not local and had very little to do with the lower orders in the village. Whereas she, Susanna, had an excellent source.

She found Alice in the garderobe, mending a tear in Blanche's favourite pink dress. Because of Dame Constance's preoccupation with the building works, she had not yet done anything about finding an older, plainer replacement for Susanna's young chamberer and Susanna herself had not even tried.

Now, she said, 'Your stitchery is very neat, Alice. That tear will be almost invisible when you have finished.'

Alice glanced up. 'Thank you, my lady.' But her smile was strained.

Brightly, Susanna went on, 'What an exciting day we have been having. Were you down in the village this morning? What is everyone saying about this mystery of the sheep shearing?'

'I don't know, my lady.'

'Oh, surely they must be talking about it?'

'Well, yes. But . . .'

'Poor Sim Walden always gets the blame for these things, doesn't he? But this time he seems to be innocent.'

'Him!' There was a world of contempt in the girl's voice.

'Alice?'

'Sim Walden is never innocent.'

'Never?'

'Never.'

'Not even this time?'

'No. He . . .' She stopped abruptly.

'So you *do* know something?' Susanna said carefully.

Alice flushed, and briefly shook the dark head still bent over her sewing.

137

Her voice full of sympathy and understanding, Susanna said, 'You can tell me, you know.'

The girl shook her head again and gulped, on the verge of tears.

Susanna had a flash of insight. 'Is it something to do with your father?'

At last, Alice looked up. 'Oh, my lady, I don't know what to do! He wouldn't let me in to the carding shed, but he was soaked to the shoulders and there was a strong smell of wet wool in the house. He would never have stolen the fleeces, but . . .'

With a sigh, Susanna said, 'I think you must come and tell Dame Constance what you know. She will not be angry with *you*, though I can't promise that she will not be angry with your father.'

9

The truth emerged easily enough next morning. Alice's father, along with Sim Walden and two of the latter's cronies, all of them clad in rough brown tunics, the weaver identifiable by the green apron of his trade, stood lined up before a table in the Great Hall where sat Dame Constance, wearing a violet-blue kirtle and cote-hardie with long tippets to the sleeves, Sir Guy in a short, high-necked crimson doublet and the fashionable parti-coloured hose, one leg white and one scarlet, and Sir Walter—as if immune to the heat—in his usual long fur-trimmed grey robe.

Susanna, sitting unobtrusively to one side, could see that the villagers were intimidated by their

138

grand company and even grander surroundings, but soon recognised that Sim Walden—who had thought himself cleared after Sir Guy's raid on his home—was a man whom defensiveness made surly. It was very stupid of him, she thought. Even if it didn't seem to him to be worth denying his guilt, surely he must see that it would be wise to appear obsequious or, at the very least, apologetic.

His judges, better acquainted than Susanna with the vagaries of human nature, ignored his manner and were resigned to his motives.

Sir Guy, in particular, was not only familiar with how the villagers' minds worked but adept at putting two and two together. He said, 'So I take it that, needing some good stout cloth, you stole the fleeces and bartered them with the weaver for cloth?'

After a momentary hesitation, Sim muttered, 'Aye.'

'And weaver John, you agreed the deal without question?'

Susanna wondered how such a plain and surly man could have fathered the bright and pretty Alice.

'Didn' know where he got the fleeces. Could ha' been anywhere.'

'But you must have guessed, when you heard what had happened in the south meadow.'

Sir Guy's eyes were stern and penetrating, his voice hard, and Susanna was taken aback to discover that there was a very different facet to his personality from the one with which she had become familiar. From being tolerant and humorous, he had become rather frightening, and she almost felt sorry for the sinners. It was just as well that she had told Alice to stay upstairs with the children.

'Might've,' the man conceded grudgingly.

'But by then you were in too deep?' Sir Guy said, 'I want the truth. This is not a court of law and, as you know, the Lady's justice is always merciful.'

Sir Walter raised his smug voice. 'I would advise, in this case, that it should not be too merciful. We are all aware that Sim Walden is an habitual criminal and deserves to be punished accordingly.'

The scruffy little fat man on the other side of the table glared at him, and snarled—Susanna could think of no other word for it—'Oh, you think so, do you? And you think your furred robes make you an honest man? Well, we know better, don't we, lads?'

The weaver looked startled, but Sim's two cronies nodded agreement. Sir Walter spluttered with fury. 'How dare you!'

'We knows what you been up to. Don' know why, but we knows what. Spoiling the Lady's plans, that's what.'

'Rubbish!'

'Then what was them two boys of yours doing in their skiff on the river? Saw them when we was taking a squint at the south meadow a couple o' nights back. Full moon. Something to do with that flooding in the trench we've all heard about, I'd guess.'

'Rubbish!' said Sir Walter again, but his lips were as pale as his face.

Sir Guy intervened. 'That will do, Sim. You have to be punished, and you may think yourself lucky that I am giving you only two days in the stocks.

140

You and your friends. Weaver John has only been foolish, and we will let him go in the hope that he has learned his lesson. Now, take yourselves off.'

When they had gone, Sir Walter huffed, 'I cannot imagine what . . .'

But neither Sir Guy nor Dame Constance was paying attention.

10

'I don't understand what this is all about,' she murmured to Sir Guy as they made their way down from the Great Hall to the building site. 'It seems highly unlikely that Walter and his sons should have anything to do with the flooding. How could they—and why should they? There is no sense in it. I wouldn't trust Sim Walden's word on anything!'

Sir Guy had his own view of the matter, but said nothing other than, 'Even so, I wouldn't have thought Sim to be so inventive. We must investigate now, at once. The question has to be resolved one way or the other.'

'I suppose so. But I can't believe in such disloyalty!'

'You mean you don't want to.'

He knew her too well. 'Perhaps,' she said.

How to approach it? she was wondering when they emerged into the open again, but Sir Guy took the problem out of her hands.

'I was not myself present throughout the proceedings, so pray correct me if I am wrong, Master Emile,' he began, 'but I believe that, when you were taking soundings to discover the source of the water penetrating the foundation trench, the only area you did not test was the vicinity of Sir Walter's tent on the river bank.'

'Yes.'

'Perhaps you should test there now, although the trench is dry and has been filled in. *If* you have no objection, Sir Walter? But it might help to resolve the mystery.'

Sir Walter shrugged as if there were no reason in the world why he should object, while Master Emile, only mildly interested now that everything was under control again, was prepared to be amenable, especially if it confirmed that the problem had been no fault of his.

Master Hal was summoned, with a couple of the most muscular labourers armed with stakes and mallets. They drove the first stake in hard and staggered and very nearly fell over when it met no resistance. 'Ground's soft,' one of them muttered. 'Not long since it been turned.'

'Spades, then, my lads,' decreed Master Hal.

With the spades they did meet resistance, less than two feet down, and after much scraping and many cries of, 'Careful, lads,' discovered the top of a narrow pipe running from the trench in the direction of the river. It disappeared under Sir Walter's tent.

'How strange,' Sir Walter volunteered. 'I wonder how that came to be there.'

Dame Constance was beginning to understand, and nodded at Master Hal. That young man's mind, it seemed, was running on the same lines as hers. A few minutes' more digging between tent and river bank revealed a continuation of the pipe, and Master Hal, stripping off his leather apron and gloves, slipped into the water and vanished from

142

sight.

When he emerged, tossing back his head of sun-streaked fair hair, it was to report, 'There's a gated opening in the bank below water level. It's shut now, but when it's open it would fill the pipe with water.'

So they tracked the rest of the pipe more precisely, although there was no need, and discovered that it entered the foundation trench no more than an inch or two below its lowest level.

'Ha!' said Master Emile with satisfaction. 'The water would soak in during the night, but with the gate closed in the day there would be no sign of movement at the point of entry. That is why all our inspections did not find it.'

Every eye was on Sir Walter. Dame Constance said, 'Sir Walter, why?'

'I know nothing of it,' he replied with unimpaired calm. 'Now, Master Emile, the Lady requires me to tell you to instruct the carpenters to clear up all those wood splinters and shavings, so that people may walk about in a civilised manner.'

Unintentionally, Master Emile helped him out. He snorted, 'If you wish that done, then it is *you* who must order the chief carpenter to do it! I know better than to try. Wood shavings are being created all the time, and he will tell you that he cannot spare a boy to sweep up every few minutes. And having told you that,' he gave a pettish twitch to his shoulders, 'he will ignore you.'

'I am the superintendent. He cannot ignore me.'

'You think so?'

Dame Constance said, 'I will leave you to argue it out. Sir Guy, I would be obliged if you would join me indoors.' And she swept off, the hem of her

143

elegant blue gown attracting a pale golden border of wood shavings as she went.

11

Dame Constance's invitation was obviously directed at Sir Guy alone and the rest of the audience began to disperse. Susanna was left standing there thinking, 'Well, really!' Not a word of thanks! Not so much as a glance! When *she* had solved the mystery of the sheared sheep and, more important, of the flooded trench as well. Accidentally, perhaps, in the latter case, but what had that to do with anything? Another wave of homesickness overcame her. How she disliked this place! And her future mother-in-law, too!

A voice beside her said, 'Never mind, lassie. The Lady's just a bit upset. You can understand it.'

Lassie! And what did the Lady have to be upset about? Susanna was not in the least mollified.

Directing a haughty glance at the over-familiar servant and uttering a repressive, 'Thank you, MacLeod,' she turned away and said to Margot, 'Please take the girls indoors and tell Anna that they have my permission to play with their spinning tops for a while.'

Blanche, as she might have foreseen, demanded, 'Why? Where are you going?' but Susanna's look silenced her.

When the children were out of sight, Susanna picked up her skirts and almost ran across the drawbridge and past the Barbican Rise to the privacy of the wood.

Hamish, hesitating briefly about following her,

144

reflected that she would come to no harm there. And his presence, besides being unwelcome, would deprive her of what looked like a much-needed opportunity to throw a tantrum. He wished she would grow up. The Lady had enough problems without a self-centred little madam for a daughter-in-law. Instead, he turned to Alice, lingering worriedly nearby, and told her that no one held her responsible for her father's doings. Smiling at him gratefully, she thought again how kind he was.

Susanna succeeded in holding back her tears until she was safely out of sight of the castle and into the heart of the wood, a cool and sweet-smelling refuge from the enervating heat that had settled on the countryside in the last few weeks and seemed as if it would never lift. Careless of her figured pink skirts, she subsided breathlessly on to the soft carpet of moss and humus and gave herself up to her misery.

It began with a sniffle, which developed into a sob, and then a succession of sobs, and then into a wail, and finally into a torrent of tears. In the time since she had been at Vine Regis she had begun to feel a little more settled, less unhappy, but suddenly she felt as sorry for herself as she had done right back at the beginning. She had been trying so hard to fit in to the life of the castle and her position as Gervase's future wife, but no one acknowledged it. There had not been a word of appreciation for her efforts, not even today. Worst of all, there was no one she could really talk to. She could make polite conversation with Isabelle, yes, and discuss routine matters with her gentlewomen, but no more than that. She remembered how the nuns had encouraged her to

145

talk about her feelings—but how simple those feelings had been, then! Now, she had no one to look to for advice or understanding.

Then, gradually, as the tears wore off, she remembered the Lady's pet Highlander saying that Dame Constance was upset. Why should she be? What right had *she* to be upset? Susanna was just beginning to puzzle over the mystery when a slightly drawling voice spoke from behind her. 'My lady?'

She had been aware of the faint rustle of fallen leaves but had been too absorbed to read any meaning into it other than some errant whisper of a breeze. She gasped, and her hand flew to her throat.

The voice turned out to belong to Alain de Niort, the troubadour, and she was not at all pleased to see him. They had barely exchanged a dozen words in the weeks since his arrival at Vine Regis, and she had been wishing very much that he would transfer his troubadorial attentions to Isabelle, who would simply ignore him in a way that she herself had not yet learned to do. It was all *so* artificial and meaningless, this 'dear heart's queen' nonsense! There was only one man in the world whom she wanted to gaze romantically into her eyes, and of him she could but dream. The dreams should have begun to fade over the weeks, she knew, but they were revived every time her hero's father tossed a smile in her direction.

And then M. Alain said in a wonderfully sympathetic tone, 'You are distressed. We can't have that. I am at your service, as you know.' She stared up uncertainly into his boyish face with its round pink cheeks, 'And I am a very good listener,' he added.

It was a particular talent of wandering troubadours to be good listeners and to carry gossip as well as poetry and song from castle to castle—it was what made them acceptable even when their music was inferior. Susanna knew this perfectly well, but it did not occur to her that M. Alain might find her own troubled waters worth fishing in. More than anything, she needed to pour out her problems into a friendly ear, and there was something safe and reassuring about talking to a complete outsider.

So she talked to him, and talked, and talked, while he nodded and murmured, 'Oh, my poor lady,' at appropriate intervals.

But in the end he made a mistake. He had sat down beside her on the soft, resilient, sweet-smelling ground and, after a while, from the eminence of his ten years' seniority and a less than innocent desire to comfort an unhappy girl, he put his arm around her shoulders, his hand drooping against the bare flesh of her throat, and murmured, 'And you have been so very, very good, not allowing your unhappiness to show.'

The patronising remark as much as the physical contact reminded her abruptly of who she was and where she was. She jerked sharply and gave a small screech, immediately regretting it—not because she didn't feel like jerking and screeching but because it was a juvenile reaction and *quite* undignified.

He froze for a moment and then languidly withdrew his arm. Susanna discovered that she did not like him. Not at all.

It wasn't only that he had dared to touch her,

who had never felt a man's touch before—or none beyond the softness of Robert Salvin's cheek against hers. It was that M. de Niort was an unpleasant person and she couldn't imagine why she had been so foolish as to pour her troubles out to him. The sympathy gone from his face and voice, she recognised that his hazel eyes had never changed their expression. She remembered, too, what Gervase had said about men being a danger to unprotected women.

She couldn't imagine Dame Constance finding herself in such a situation but she tilted her chin and, doing her best to reproduce the Lady's cool arrogance, said, 'You are impertinent, sir. You may go.'

He hesitated for a moment, and then rose to his feet, his resentment almost tangible. 'As you wish, my lady.' Whereupon he strolled off, in no hurry. It was insulting.

She was just reflecting that she should have added, 'And please stop addressing me as your "dear heart's queen" when you are entertaining the company after dinner!' when, disbelievingly, she heard the faint crackle of footsteps again. He *could* not be coming back? Could he?

It was a relief to recognise that the steps, this time, were approaching directly along the path from the castle, rather than from the southern margins of the wood.

And this intruder proved to be less unwelcome. Someone she liked. Someone who liked her. Someone she had flirted with in the hope of making Gervase more aware of her. Someone who visited Vine Regis frequently to discuss business with Dame Constance.

Susanna said, 'Have you just arrived? I didn't know you were expected.'

Shrugging lightly in reply, Robert Salvin glanced around. 'So this is where you escape to when life in the castle becomes too much for you? An excellent refuge, if I may say so.'

It was necessary to deny that life in the castle was ever too much for her, but to make it sound convincing was difficult. She stammered, 'No, it's not like that.'

Although most of her tears had dried, there were one or two drops still clinging to her lashes as she looked up at him. One of those rare and fortunate females whose features remained unblemished by weeping, she looked both woebegone and alluring. He dropped to the ground beside her, smiling. Shyly, she smiled back, and without warning found his arms around her and his lips on hers.

She might have thought, 'Oh, no! Not again!' but although it came as a shock it was also oddly blissful, and after the first moment of surprise she nestled into his embrace, sighing, feeling warm and comforted.

'What a pretty little thing you are,' he murmured, gazing down at her. Then he kissed her again, the smile in his eyes the same but his lips less gentle.

She took fright.

Her response was as instinctive as it had been with M. Alain, the sense of comfort vanishing abruptly in face of an acute unease. It was all too intimate, too dangerous. Confusedly, she remembered that she had first set about attracting Master Salvin in order to make Gervase jealous,

149

and had succeeded. But Gervase was no longer here and she had no such excuse. She could not doubt that she was doing something very wrong, *morally* wrong according to all the standards by which she had been raised and educated.

With a sharp, 'No!' she struggled upright and pushed him away, and when he tried to force more kisses on her she resisted. She couldn't think what else to do, so, in the end, she slapped him hard across the face. And then sat back and thought, terrified, 'What have I done?'

He grasped her hard by the upper arms, staring into her eyes. Then he released her as if he were tossing her aside and moved away from her, though not very far, his pleasant features becoming very much less pleasant. His breathing was erratic as he said, 'I see. So you are just a shameless little hussy. You lead a man on, you tease him with promises, and then you refuse what you have invited him to expect.'

She didn't understand what he was talking about.

Leaning back, propped on his hands, he enlightened her, his voice contemptuous. 'I wonder, does Gervase know the kind of wench he is marrying? He told me off very severely for showing I thought you attractive. Most improper, he said, when I was here to court Isabelle. He held *me* entirely to blame, unobservant fellow that he is . . .'

She stared at him blankly. 'Here to court Isabelle?'

After a moment, 'Don't pretend you didn't know.'

'I didn't! I didn't!'

It was awful, dreadful, shaming. Admittedly, she had chosen to try and attract him, but that he should respond, in the circumstances, was surely far more shaming? Did Isabelle know that he was not to be trusted? Isabelle, who was so languid and detached that she showed no sign of anything other than common courtesy when she sat beside him at table or talked to him in company.

'I don't believe you. You're horrible, hateful,' she gasped.

'You are, of course, entitled to your opinion, as I am to mine.' He rose to his feet and bowed mockingly. 'May I escort you back to the castle, my lady?'

'No, thank you. I will find my own way.'

Only after he had gone, when she had sat for a while miserably scanning the history of their encounters, did she realise that she had not, in fact, achieved her original aim of making Gervase jealous. It seemed he had been angry only because Master Salvin was not being sufficiently attentive towards his sister.

It was too bad!

Her misery this time beyond tears, Susanna vented it instead by reviewing the denizens of her world and deciding there was no one—no one at all—even remotely worthy of her liking.

CHAPTER SEVEN

1

That evening, she was painstakingly polite towards Master Salvin who was, after all, a guest of Vine Regis. In the case of M. Alain, however, rather than gazing down at her hands while he went through his paces, she stared straight ahead, coldly.

Everyone noticed, though no one remarked on it. Or not then. But the men, particularly the youthful squires, speculated and gossiped afterwards, and the gossip inevitably spread outdoors to the labourers who were daily tantalised by the sight of the plump and pretty little lady in the low-necked gown whose husband-to-be was away at Court. By such routes, it returned to Sir Guy, who took it up with Dame Constance.

'The most popular theory,' he reported, 'is that the fellow tried to force his attentions on her, and was rejected. Perhaps you should have a word with her?'

The Lady's response was trenchant. 'Oh, how I *wish* I were a man! Then, at least, I could relieve my feelings by swearing. If something of the sort happened, why has she said nothing? No, no, Guy, don't tell me. What a foolish girl she is! She must be aware of the effect she creates.'

'She *is* very innocent.'

'Yes, I know she is,' rapped Dame Constance, in

no way pacified. 'That is the trouble. But if only she would dress more soberly! Isabelle says she thinks that Susanna, in her mother's eyes, could do nothing wrong—hence her immature taste in colours and clothes. Every little girl loves pink and blue, and regards the increasing depth of a neckline as an index of adulthood. Unfortunately, I know Susanna would take a word from me as criticism, and I do not want her to go to the opposite extreme. I will have to think about how to deal with her.'

'While you are also thinking about how to deal with Sir Walter?' he asked provocatively.

'How fortunate it is,' she said, 'that I like you. As it happens, I have decided not to confront him with the business of the trench. I know too well that I will get nowhere. He will continue to deny the whole thing.'

'So?'

'So, I will go on wondering why he wanted to make things difficult for me. But he knows, I think, that if anything else goes wrong suspicion will immediately fall on him. So he will, I hope, have the sense to embark on no more such foolish enterprises.'

Reflectively, Sir Guy remarked, 'I am inclined to suspect that he may have been trying to make things difficult for Master Emile rather than for you. It is my impression that he believes he himself could supervise the works as well as any master mason.'

'Do you really think so?'

'He has a very high opinion of himself.'

'Yes, but . . . Oh, how I wish I had never embarked on all this.'

153

'Give me your hand,' he said and, when she did, he kissed it. Still holding it, he told her smilingly, 'It will be worth it when it is finished.'

She grimaced back at him. 'It had better be!'

2

Susanna, indignant though she was over the behaviour of M. Alain and Master Salvin, had decided to say nothing because she knew that both episodes would reflect badly on her. She should not have gone rushing off into the wood on her own. She should have taken one of her gentlewomen with her. But she had wanted to be alone, to savour her misery in peace, and it was only afterwards, as she had trudged back to the castle, picking her way through all the building clutter and keeping her head down in case the evidence of her tears still showed, that she had recognised her own foolishness. She would be more careful in future.

But she was resilient by nature and M. Alain and Master Salvin had only annoyed her, not alarmed her, so that she anticipated no further trouble from either of them. When she ventured into the wood again a few days later, therefore, she did no more than glance around to reassure herself that there was nothing and no one to worry about. She would have brought Margot for company, but Margot was an impatient companion at best, always looking for distractions and having no interest whatsoever in Susanna's current preoccupation with natural history.

There were a couple of sawyers in the wood,

sawing away at a tall birch, but Susanna dismissed them from her mind. They were only workmen, and harmless.

It never occurred to her that they might be far from harmless. They were not only bored but dangerously drunk on a strong brew from the village ale-wife—the one who had been found Not Guilty of trying to poison her husband. Seated on the ground on either side of the birch, their legs stretched out before them, they pulled the double saw back and forth, back and forth, with mind-numbing monotony, the subject of their desultory conversation, as always, women.

'Wouldn' mind 'aving a go at *'er,*' said one, and his fellow, in no doubt about the identity of the 'her', agreed fervently.

'Man's away. Missing 'im. Think she's ripe for it?'

'Mebbe.'

'Nah. Not mebbe. Sure sartain. Kissing them fellows day 'r two back. Want to wager? I mean, look at 'er.'

With perfect timing, Susanna drifted into sight at that moment, her *Bestiary* in her hand and a search for hedgehogs on her mind. There was a sweet little painting of them in her book, in the bright colours that rejoiced her soul. They were shown rolling on the ground under some grapevines, with fallen grapes impaled on their spines. The book said they were very fond of grapes and, having cleverly collected them by this means, took them back to their burrows to feed their young. It didn't say where their burrows were to be found, but Susanna had seen no signs of hedgehogs, burrows or, indeed, fallen grapes in the

155

Vine Regis vineyard and thought the hedgehogs might prefer to dig their burrows in the uncultivated soil of the woods. If she could find traces, it would enable her to give the girls a nature lesson about them.

Where were the burrows? Between the roots of the trees, perhaps? Would there be infant hedgehogs in them at this time of year? Her *Bestiary* did not tell her. Suddenly, it occurred to her that the sawyers might know. They spent much of their time in the woods and, unless they were completely unobservant, must have some knowledge of the wildlife around them.

Glancing over at them, she saw them only as two workmen doing the work they were paid for, the kind of workmen who habitually tugged their forelocks when confronted by their betters. She had been brought up to keep her inferiors at a distance while being polite even to the peasantry—the nuns had said that all were the children of God—so she walked over to them and asked with cool courtesy, 'I wonder whether you have seen any hedgehogs here in the woods? I am looking for their burrows.'

To the man who had been speculating about her virtue, it seemed an unlikely story. After a moment's slack-mouthed silence, he cast a meaning glance at his fellow, and rose to his feet. If the little lady wanted to play games . . .

'Mebbe 'ere,' he told her, leading her over to the edge of the glade. 'Down atween the roots. See?'

She looked, but saw nothing. 'What? Where?'

And then his voice said, 'Uh-huh!' and she felt his heavy arm around her waist, pulling her backwards against his bare-legged, wiry body, and there was a smelly breath against her cheek, and a slurred voice growling, 'Wot a pretty lady.'

It was so unexpected that she started violently, letting out a scream that was more of fury than of fright. But then a sweaty hand was clamped over her mouth and the fright predominated.

Tossing her head against the suffocating grip, she tried to tear away from the man, jerking with her elbows and pulling at his wrists, but he only gripped her more tightly. Nothing broke the stillness of the wood except the sound of his breathing and the rustle of her struggling skirts. Her frantic eyes saw no sign of the aid she so desperately needed. She would have screamed for help if she could, but no one would have heard.

It seemed to last for all eternity. The man was strong and she choked against the hand over her mouth, feeling sick at the smell of him. She was beginning to tire when, unexpectedly, miraculously, childhood memories came to her aid, and her brothers were playing rough games with the little sister who had offended them in some juvenile way, and she remembered scratching and kicking and biting until they had wearied of their fun and let her go. Instinctively, she employed the same tactics now, reaching up and back to pull at the man's hair and scratch at his eyes, while biting at the pad of flesh on the filthy sweaty palm covering her mouth and turning her ankle to scrape down his bare leg with the buckle of her short walking boots.

He let out a yowl, partly of pain and partly, as she later realised, of surprise at the unladylike nature of the pretty lady's response. Suddenly, she was free.

Stumbling at first, she ran, only slightly hampered by her skirts, as fast as she could towards the open air beyond the wood, where there were people and safety. Even as she ran, she was aware of not being followed, but dared not take even a moment to look back.

Pink and flustered, trying to control her breathing, she left the wood and slowed down as she made for the drawbridge. All she wanted was for someone she loved to hug and reassure her. She wanted her mother. Or the man of her dreams, who would have protected her from it all.

The panic was fading, but she was still too emotional to think what to do. This, on top of the encounters with M. Alain and Master Salvin just days before! She must take time to get her mental breath back. She should report the men, who were clearly a danger to any woman who came within their reach, but . . .

She threaded her way, head down, through the encroaching jungle of men and materials towards the drawbridge and then into the courtyard, where Hamish MacLeod came over to her, frowning a little. 'Is everything all right, my lady?'

Automatically, she tossed her head. Automatically, she replied, 'Yes, of course, MacLeod. Why should it not be?'

3

When she entered the Great Hall for supper a few hours later, she discovered that Dame Constance wished to speak to her privately, afterwards.

It was too much. Susanna felt as if every

mouthful of food was lodging in her throat, even as she tried to listen to the gossip going on around her—gossip either about the coronation of the new boy king, or about an accident that had happened on the building site earlier in the afternoon.

The first half-dozen courses of stone had been laid and it seemed that two hod carriers had been taking rubble up a ramp to fill in the space between the outer and inner facings of the wall when one of them had slipped, the hod had tilted sharply, and all the rubble had gone flying through the air—showering down on the unfortunate Sir Walter, who had happened to be passing at the time. He had a nasty lump on his forehead as a result and was reputed to be threatening Master Emile with the direst retribution for his incompetence.

'It was quite funny,' William reported. 'Both kinds of funny, in fact.'

'I don't understand.'

'It was funny-ha-ha to see His Stateliness jumping out of his skin, and funny-queer that the hod-man should have slipped.'

'I suppose so.'

William eyed her suspiciously. 'Are you all right?'

'Yes, of course.'

'Well, think about it! Barefoot on a wooden plank. How could he slip?'

'You're going to tell me, I suppose.'

'I nipped up to have a look while all the fuss was going on, and there was a splodge of wet mortar on the plank. He'd trodden in it and gone skating.'

'Oh, is that all?'

'What do you mean "all"? How did the mortar

159

get there? The mortar comes after the rubble, not before, and they haven't got as high as that yet.'

She sighed. 'You're making a mystery where there probably isn't one. What does Master Hal say?'

'Accidental splash.'

'Well, there you are. And you're not being very sympathetic towards Sir Walter, poor man.'

William frowned heavily. 'He's made himself unpopular with the builders, with that superior air of his. It might almost be deliberate, but I can't work out how it was managed.'

'William, you're trying to make a mountain out of a molehill. I'm sure it was just an accident.'

'You're not interested, are you?'

'Not terribly. I have other things on my mind.'

The last time she had been bidden to Dame Constance's private chamber, it had been to submit to a lecture on what she would need to learn if she were ever to be worthy of being Lady of the Castle. It was a memory that failed to console her when, this evening, she presented herself, as requested, in the calm, elegant chamber, its pale wood panelling warmly lit by the rays of the descending sun, and found Dame Constance in a loose, dark blue velvet robe, the crisp white widow's barbe discarded and her hair, glossy black save for a graceful wing of silver, flowing to her shoulders. It did not occur to Susanna that this informality was designed to put her at her ease; rather, she took it as a hint that the Lady was preparing for bed and intended their interview to be brief. So she smiled politely, as if she had not a care in the world, and waited.

Then Dame Constance picked up a small book

from among the parchment rolls on her clothes chest and held it out to Susanna. 'I think this is yours?'

Deep inside, somewhere under her breastbone, Susanna's heart gave a hollow thud. 'Oh. So it is. I dropped it—er—in the wood. I am so glad someone found it.'

'Yes. It's a pretty little book. It would have been a pity to lose it.'

There was a moment's silence, while Susanna tried to cover her confusion by leafing through the pages until she came to the ones about the hedgehogs. She held it out to Dame Constance. 'I was in the wood looking for hedgehogs, you see, so that I could teach the girls about them.'

'And M. Alain was helping you?' Dame Constance's tone was casual. There was the general gossip reported by Sir Guy, and Hamish, when asked, had remarked that a day or two back he had happened to notice the troubadour strolling off in the direction of the wood soon after the Lady Susanna, and had hesitated briefly about following but been diverted by more immediate calls on his attention.

'Who?' Susanna faltered. 'No! What are you talking about? I don't understand.'

Dame Constance looked at her consideringly. The girl was genuinely surprised, she thought, but the colour had drained from her cheeks and there was something about the quivering lips and fluttering eyelashes that was not quite right. Something had happened. The question was—what?

She said, 'Sit down, my dear. Is there anything you want to tell me?'

161

It was too direct a question for the unprepared Susanna. How could she possibly admit to the terrifyingly self-disciplined Dame Constance what a mess she had been making of things? Though *none* of it was her fault!

She sat down and, smoothing out her figured pink skirts, repeated, 'Anything I want to tell you? No, I don't think so.'

'Or anything you want to ask me?'

'No, I don't think so.'

'Not even who found your *Bestiary* and brought it back?'

It would have been a natural question for Susanna to ask, and she might have added, 'Should I give them a reward, do you think?' But she only pouted as if the matter were of no interest.

Lacking any cooperation from her future daughter-in-law, Dame Constance was forced to come to the point. 'I would prefer not to have to say any more, but it is unavoidable. You should, I fear, know the gossip so that you can correct it. I myself cannot help put an end to it unless I know the truth. But put an end to it we must.'

Susanna gulped. 'Gossip?'

'It was Father Hoby who brought your *Bestiary* to me this afternoon. He had been given it by two of the men who were sawing down trees in the wood. He demanded to know how they had come by such a valuable thing and they hesitated, then said . . .'

The sawyers! Susanna's brain went numb. 'What?'

'They said they felt it their moral duty to report that they had seen you lying under a tree in the arms of a gentleman and found the book after the two of you had gone.'

Susanna's pretty pink lips opened in astonishment. 'It isn't true! Not a word of it! And that was days ago, anyway!'

Dame Constance dropped her eyes to hide the exasperated amusement in them. Trying to remember whether she herself had ever been so naïve, she thought not. Her instinct had always been to guard her emotions and her tongue—something, she supposed, to do with having been reared in a thoroughly undemonstrative family. She had never found it easy to make a display of emotion, not even to hug her children when they had been adorable, huggable babies. It was a fault in her, she knew, but a fault which had helped to give her the strength of character necessary to survive in a harsh and unforgiving world.

Carefully, she asked, '*What* was "days ago"?'

Lips quivering, eyes wide, Susanna wailed, 'Oh, I suppose I had better tell you!'

She couldn't possibly confess what had happened with Master Salvin, but the sawyers seemed to have spoken of only 'a gentleman', so M. Alain would have to take the blame, since Dame Constance seemed to assume he was the gentleman in question. The episode concerning him came out in fits and starts as Susanna studied each word before she uttered it, reducing all the complaints which she had confided in him to no more than a slight attack of homesickness. And she had most certainly not lain in his arms!

Dame Constance, perfectly capable of recognising an edited version of the truth when she heard it, said, 'I see.' Then, after a moment, 'It could have been worse, it seems. Apart from the

163

initial error of letting yourself be alone with a young man, you seem to have handled the situation quite well. And you will know better in future.'

Susanna breathed more easily for a moment, until Dame Constance went on, 'But the sawyers? I am, of course, entertained by their talk of "moral duty", which is not something one would immediately associate with the drunken ruffians whom Father Hoby describes. But your *Bestiary* is a valuable little book which they might have sold at a considerable profit next time they found themselves in a town.'

Her tone was questioning and she obviously expected some answer. Susanna began worriedly, 'I suppose they . . . It wasn't like what they say at all. They found it only because I dropped it when *they* assaulted me! What happened was this!' She hesitated and then the story came out in a rush. 'Oh, it was horrible!' she concluded shakily. 'Truly horrible!'

Dame Constance felt sorry for the girl, even while she sighed internally over her ridiculous innocence. Guy was right. She was not to be trusted out on her own.

'Horrible? I imagine it must have been. I hope you succeeded in really hurting him?'

Susanna could not believe that the Lady was looking and sounding almost sympathetic. 'I think so, but he was more shocked than anything else.'

Then Dame Constance went on reflectively, 'Now comes the question, why should they have made your encounter with M. Alain sound so much more—damaging—than you tell me it was?'

'I don't know!'

'Think about it for a moment.'

164

Susanna hoped she did not look as blank as she felt, but Dame Constance seemed to expect some kind of sensible answer. 'Perhaps they were hoping for a reward?'

'Then why invent the tale about M. Alain?'

She tried again. 'I have no idea. They could have had a reward without that. Perhaps they felt they had to explain how—why—they found the *Bestiary*? Or—no! They must have known I was bound to report them for attacking me. Might they have been trying to protect themselves? Trying to forestall me by making *me* appear as bad as they were?'

Dame Constance nodded approvingly. 'That is perceptive of you. It seems the likeliest answer. And it shows the kind of low cunning one might expect of them.'

'Do you think so?'

'We will question them in the morning. Now go to bed and try to get some sleep.'

'Yes, Lady. Thank you.'

4

When a keyed-up Susanna entered the Great Hall next morning, she discovered that her presence was not required.

'It would be painful for you,' said Dame Constance, once more attired in the front-laced kirtle and white barbe which made her look so formidable. 'Sir Guy is experienced in interrogation and will soon get at the truth of the matter. I have summoned a small jury from among the castle staff.'

'But I've told you the truth!'

'Yes, of course. But it is better that they convict themselves out of their own mouths. Leave it to Sir Guy.'

As it transpired, the two sawyers stuck to their story like limpets. Sir Guy took them through it again and again, together and separately, but they failed to weaken. The lady had lain under a tree in the arms of a gentleman whom they knew not to be her husband, for they had watched the Lord ride away to Court some weeks earlier. She had been wearing a pink gown, which they described accurately, but they could not identify the gentleman, who had been partly obscured from their sight by the lady herself. They had talked for a few minutes, and then the gentleman had bent to kiss her—at which point the sawyers had modestly looked away.

Sir Guy gave a snort of laughter. 'You are to be commended on your delicacy of mind. Now, I will have one of you alone again.'

When Hamish had escorted the second sawyer out of earshot, Sir Guy asked the first, 'For how long did you watch them?'

'Wurn't rightly *watching* them. We wus working.'

'Were they not aware of your presence? Embarrassed, perhaps?'

'Dunno.'

'What kind of tree were they lying under?'

'Dunno.'

'Come on! Timber is your business. You must have noticed.'

'It were an ash.'

'And how long did they lie there?'

'Dunno. We wus in an' out o' the trees, looking

for a good strong beech to make the centering for the arches and vaults.'

'So you only glimpsed them a few times?'

'Aarh.'

'Mostly when they were sitting talking.'

'Lying talking. She wur in 'is arms.'

'Mmmm. Take this fellow away, Hamish, and bring back the other one.'

'Aye, aye,' said Hamish. 'Will ye be wanting this one again, or should I just tip him in the moat and be done with it?'

Dame Constance exclaimed, 'Hamish!' and his pale eyes twinkled back at her.

'Aye, weel,' he said. 'Come on, laddie. It's off to the dunce's corner for you.'

The second sawyer was the cocky one. He had seen enough and for long enough, he claimed, to have no doubts as to what had been going on. As for the kind of tree the erring couple had been lying under? A birch.

'Not an ash?'

'Birch.'

'Sure?

'Aarh.'

It wasn't decisive, of course, but it confirmed the unreliability of witnesses whom no one would have trusted to squash a flea. The Vine Regis jury, indeed, was beginning to suffer itch by association and, unobtrusively backing away, swiftly and unanimously declared the sawyers guilty of slander against the Lady Susanna.

That one of the sawyers had laid lascivious hands on the said lady was not mentioned. The gossip about the troubadour had already gone the rounds, but Dame Constance had been adamant that the second episode should not be disclosed, for Susanna's own sake.

'I could hang you,' Sir Guy told the two men, 'for your slanders and other crimes I am aware of.' They knew what he meant; the cocky one's eyes shifted under the fringe of filthy mouse-brown hair. 'But the gallows are too clean for you. You will therefore spend five days and nights in the pillory and after that you will leave the district for ever. If you show your faces here again, you will be arrested and hanged without need for further trial. Do you understand me?'

Sober now, after their night in the castle dungeon, they had not expected to be let off with their miserable lives. Sir Guy almost felt sorry for them until the cocky one opened his mouth and it was clear from his sneering expression that what he was about to say was likely to be something inconvenient.

But before he could speak, Hamish had an arm round his throat, his hands clamped behind his back, and was dragging him off to the pillory.

The villagers, who had taken a hearty dislike to the building fraternity—thieves and bullies, every one of them, and all with an eye to the women— enjoyed themselves greatly in the days that followed. They pelted the men with everything that came to hand and as the days passed their aim improved, so that the sawyers learned not to scream and swear, as they did to begin with, because an open mouth was promptly filled with stones, or rotting cabbage, or cow dung.

They were a sorry sight when, bruised, black-eyed and retching, they were given the opportunity to collect their few belongings and then helped on their way by the flat of their escort's swords, and abandoned in empty countryside a long twenty miles from Vine Regis.

Susanna prayed that that was the end of the affair, and for her it was. But the repercussions at Vine Regis were far from ended.

5

Subdued and miserable, she would have kept to her chamber throughout these events, but Dame Constance would not permit it. Susanna must learn strength of mind, she said. More than that, she added a few days later, she would have to learn to see herself as others saw her, and mend her ways accordingly. Her gowns, for example. She dressed more appropriately for a Court banquet than for a country estate.

'My mother thought my gowns were very pretty and suited me very well!' Susanna exclaimed.

'No doubt. But at home, and indeed at the convent, you were a cherished girl protected from the world. Now you are an adult, and must look out for yourself. I suggest you consult Isabelle about the style of your kirtles and surcoats, and Master Nicholas will be able to find some suitable fabrics. In the meantime you should, I think, drape some pretty scarves over those low necklines of yours. And don't, in future, go wandering around the countryside without a bodyguard. That is inviting trouble. You may borrow Hamish to accompany you at any time.'

Susanna had no wish to borrow the big Highlander. Not only did she consider him over-

169

familiar, she disliked the way he regarded the world as designed for his personal entertainment. She was not accustomed to being laughed at. 'Very well,' she said. 'Thank you.'

'My child, I am trying to *help* you!'

Susanna knew that her sulkiness was unbecoming, and that Dame Constance was probably right, but she could not do other than resent the implication that her taste in clothes had anything to do with what had happened.

'Yes,' she said. 'I know. Thank you.'

'There is another thing.'

Susanna was wondering what else there could possibly be, when the familiar clamour floating up from the building site resolved itself into voices crying, 'Fire! Fire!'

Dame Constance snapped, 'Builders! I suppose it is too much to hope that someone has set a light to Master Emile's shirt tails! Come, Susanna.'

They met Hamish MacLeod on the stairs down to the Great Hall. 'It's the scaffolding, Lady. It's all the poles stacked against the wall waiting for use. Greenwood. Smouldering. Nothing tae worry about. I mind when the same thing happened tae our Cissie when she was building her wee house at Mellon Udrigle.'

'Our Cissie?' Dame Constance stopped abruptly. 'Sister? Niece? Cousin?'

'Second cousin twice removed.'

'Even after twenty years,' Dame Constance remarked to Susanna, resuming her downward progress, 'Hamish is still able to produce family members of whom I have never heard. I hope, Hamish, that Cissie's house survived?'

'Oh, aye. Nice wee place.'

'Good.'

When they reached the outdoors, they discovered that the fir scaffolding poles stacked against the Mill Tower were glowing brightly along much of their length, sending off showers of sparks and a slow resinous smoke.

Master Emile was standing there looking annoyed, while Master Hal had organised a chain of men with leather buckets who appeared to be having some success in dousing the fire with water from the moat. 'How fortunate,' Dame Constance remarked, 'that it is past the children's bedtime, otherwise Blanche would be giving Master Hal a helping hand.'

Master Hal, overhearing this—as Dame Constance had intended he should—grinned at her cheerfully. 'Once we've got the fire out, we'll rake everything away from the wall and maybe find out what started it.'

'Yes, that would certainly be of interest. Please keep me informed,' said Dame Constance. Then, 'Come, Susanna, we are nothing but a hindrance here. Let us return to my chamber and resume our discussion.'

Susanna would much have preferred to stay and watch, but she followed the Lady dutifully.

Ignoring the faint smell of smoke that had penetrated upstairs, Dame Constance remarked thoughtfully, 'Master Hal seems an excellent young man, does he not?' Then, 'As I was about to say when we were interrupted, the sawyers have, as you know, been punished for laying hands on you, although Sir Guy took care that the truth of that episode did not come out. I hope you have thanked him for it?'

171

Susanna struggled to readjust her mind. 'Not yet,' she faltered. 'But I will.'

'Good. However, the problem of M. Alain remains. Although most people now believe the gossip to have been false—for which again you must thank Sir Guy—the truth of what happened makes it necessary that he should leave.'

'Oh, yes!'

'I am relieved that you agree. So you will tell him that he is no longer welcome at Vine Regis . . .'

'Me? Oh no, I couldn't!'

'Not just at once, which would look suspicious. In a week or two, perhaps.'

'I couldn't! What would I say? Couldn't someone else do it?'

But although Dame Constance was able and prepared to be tolerant for considerably longer than most people, her patience was approaching its limit. Susanna thought her unremittingly even-tempered, and had no idea that her patience might snap.

Though not quite yet. Dame Constance took a deep breath. 'Normally, such a task would fall to the household comptroller, but I understood that you wished some day to be mistress of Vine Regis. If you cannot face such a minor unpleasantness as dismissing an unsatisfactory minstrel, you can hardly think yourself equipped to rule over it.'

Susanna had just sufficient self-respect left to save her from dissolving into tears. 'No,' she murmured. 'Of course not.'

6

The Lady's word being everyone else's command, the men fussed over the scaffolding while Isabelle, languid to the core, found herself required to take charge of Susanna's wardrobe. Since clothes were her only passion, she did not object; indeed, she almost welcomed the task, always having been repelled by Susanna's fondness for pinks and blues. She herself, her colouring inherited from her father, had tawny hair and played up to it by dressing in apricots and ambers so that she made Susanna think of the lazy-looking lioness in her fateful *Bestiary*.

She and Gervase's chamberlain, Master Nicholas—the cherubic gentleman who had been so reluctant to part with his best velvets to Abbot Ralph on Susanna's first day—were great allies, and when the pair of them took Susanna's wardrobe in hand she became quite unable to complain that no one paid her the attention she craved. Morning, noon and night, or so it seemed, they were discussing possibilities.

'A thin kirtle and sideless surcoat, with deep armholes, for what remains of the summer?'

'Yes, and a warmer kirtle and close-fitting cotehardie for when the cooler weather comes.'

'Colours?' asked Master Nicholas. 'I have a length of sarcenet in deep rose which would do very well for the summer kirtle.'

Susanna, who had thought she was to be deprived of pink forever, gave a sigh of relief.

'And for the surcoat?'

Master Nicholas eyed Susanna measuringly. 'I believe the Lady Susanna would look well in green.

173

A myrtle green for the summer surcoat, perhaps? I have some linen from Rennes . . .'

Susanna said, 'I don't like green,' but was ignored.

'Yes, with an embroidered border round the armholes. Excellent,' agreed Isabelle. 'I believe you are right about the green, Master Nicholas. And a darker shade for the cooler weather would be excellent.'

Susanna said, 'But . . .'

'It will give you authority,' Isabelle told her. 'Pinks and blues are all very well when you are a girl, but the darker greens are much more distinguished. More suitable. Unless you would prefer a dark blue, such as my mother favours?'

'No, thank you.'

Master Nicholas, who knew his taste to be impeccable, considered this exchange unworthy of his notice. 'And I believe I have a length of Kendal green wool which would do very well for an informal house gown.'

'But my eyes are blue, not green.'

'I do hope, dear lady,' chirruped Master Nicholas, 'that you do not insist on a match between garment colour and eye colour?'

He was wearing a rather dashing scarlet pourpoint that day and Susanna realised, after a moment, that he had been trying to be humorous. She smiled weakly.

Suddenly, she felt lonely, and to her own and Isabelle's considerable surprise, found herself wailing, 'Oh, how I wish Gervase were here! What if he has gone off to the wars without telling me?'

Did the silly girl know nothing about how the world worked? Isabelle wondered absently.

'Unlikely,' she replied. 'Now, Master Nicholas, about this house gown . . .'

CHAPTER EIGHT

1

Gervase, in fact, was still in London trying and failing to discover whether the mother—and, indeed, the future wife—of such a junior baron as he would be allocated seats in the Abbey for the coronation ceremony.

Although he would have liked to believe otherwise, he knew that his womenfolk would not be satisfied to be summoned to London simply for the pleasure of admiring him, on the day preceding the event, riding in the young king's procession from the Tower to Westminster, his best crimson doublet and cloak newly embroidered with golden vines at shocking expense. He winced at the thought of what his mother would have to say not only about the cost but about the quality of the workmanship.

As it happened, by the time he had extracted a grudging allocation of seats for them halfway down the nave, it was too late for them to make the journey from Vine Regis. Susanna would have enjoyed it, he thought, and he might even have enjoyed showing her off, pretty little thing that she was, but he consoled himself with the reflection that he had honestly tried, and gave himself up to enjoyment of the spectacle. It was ironic that the arrogant John of Gaunt, Duke of Lancaster, took a leading part in the ceremonial as Steward of the Realm but was not to be one of the council of administrators chosen to guide the boy in the early days of his rule.

It was fifty years since the last coronation, and it seemed that there was no one still alive who remembered the correct ceremonial. So there had been much unproductive rummaging through ancient, crackling parchment rolls and, in the end, it had been settled that an extravagant splendour was what was required. It was necessary, the Duke of Lancaster had decreed, that the sweet little prince, with his curling yellow hair and pink-and-white complexion, should be endowed with all the trappings of majesty.

It seemed to Gervase, watching Richard enter the abbey, a golden canopy borne over his head and the greatest nobles of the realm no more than shadows in the glory of his radiance, that the boy believed in his own transformation. Gervase tried and failed to imagine what it must be like to know yourself to be king by the grace of God. Did it make the burden greater or less? Or was it not a burden at all?

The Abbey had been designed for the worship of God, not for an audience of thousands. There was so much noise, bustle and glitter that, for the mass of those present, what was actually happening was a matter of muttered reports passed back from those in front to those behind. There were only occasional moments of silence—when the childish voice repeated the coronation oath; when the boy was anointed with the holy oil; and then when he was invested with the crown.

It had all been too much for him, it seemed. After the High Mass and the homages, as he left the Abbey rumour flew back that the king had swooned and had to be carried across to Westminster Hall, where the coronation banquet was to be held. Fortunately, he was able to retire and rest for two hours while the guests left the Abbey and made their way, chattering noisily, to their seats in the great Hall, and seemed revived when he appeared again to preside over the event. But the crown weighed too heavy for him, and he complained of a headache, so that during the last three interminable hours of the banquet his cousin, the Earl of March, had to stand behind him, holding the crown above the royal head.

Gervase's neighbour, a pleasant young knight who, like Gervase, was hoping to join Thomas of Woodstock's expedition to France, murmured, 'Not a good augury, I feel. I hope you are staying in London rather than rushing away? It will be interesting to see how things develop. And I hear there's a splendid new whorehouse over on the south bank of the river . . .'

2

Back at Vine Regis, it had taken the better part of a day before the scaffolding fire abandoned its sporadic attempts to break out again and made it possible to investigate the origins.

Master Emile had no desire to know the origins. As far as he was concerned, it was an act of God. The weather had been relentlessly hot, the sun bright, and no doubt some stupid skivvy had thrown out a shard of broken bowl or goblet which had acted as a burning glass.

Master Hal was not so sure. As dusk began to

fall and the lodge bell rang for the end of the working day, he sat with Hamish MacLeod perched on the well-head in the main courtyard. 'The fire began in the heart of the pile,' he said thoughtfully, 'and burned up and out.'

'Queer.'

'Very queer.'

'Ye're saying it wasn't an accident, in fact?'

The younger man ran smoke-blackened fingers through his hair, but made no reply.

Hamish MacLeod's pale eyes were friendly and amused. 'Ye're wondering about me, are you? Ye see me as a wild Hielandman, one of the auld enemy. Can ye trust me?'

'That thought did cross my mind.'

'Well, I came here twenty years since, and if the Lady can trust me, then I think you can. She even trusts me enough to let me go home to Skye now and again to see my folk, though it takes weeks for me to get there and back, specially when the war's on.' He paused. 'Mind ye, I don't see where trust comes into it. If ye think the fire was not an accident, what hinders ye from saying so?'

Their conversation had been low-voiced, for there was much coming and going in the courtyard, but now Master Hal's voice dropped even further.

'What hinders me? Master Emile hinders me,' he replied. He had a pleasant smile, even through the coating of black ash that shrouded his features, and his eyes and teeth flashed in the light of the flaring torches being brought out by a procession of servants and fitted into the sconces round the courtyard walls.

Hamish had a shrewd idea of his meaning. 'Aye,' he agreed. 'It's not good policy to criticise your

179

employer in public.'

'It's not good policy to criticise him at all. I'd never work again if the masons' guild heard about it. I'd be banned for breaking my oath of engagement. I shouldn't even be talking to you.'

'That seems a bit extreme.' Hamish was intrigued. 'Are there a lot of rules you have to abide by?'

'Pages and pages of them! We masons are required to be good little boys at all times, at home as at work. No consorting with women. No living with any woman other than a legally wedded wife. No gambling. Going to confession every year.'

'My, my. There goes my hope of being accepted into the profession. But I take it ye're not thinking Master Emile was the one guilty of setting the fire?'

'No, of course not. It's just . . .'

With perfect timing, one of the kitchen boys emerged from the Buttery Tower bearing an ale jug and two wooden drinking cups. Master Hal no doubt regarded it as a happy coincidence, but that was because he was not well acquainted with Hamish MacLeod who, being a man of foresight, had anticipated that their conversation might be the better for lubrication.

Rumour had it that the weather in the Channel was stormy, but here inland it was developing into a long, hot summer and, although the stone walls of the castle, twelve feet thick, had so far kept it tolerably cool indoors, the still air of the central courtyard trapped the day's heat and held it until well into the night.

'It's just—what?' Hamish repeated when they were settled again with cups in hand.

180

Master Hal swallowed gratefully. 'That's good! Master Emile? He's set in his ways. He's a Frenchie. He blows hot and cold. His reputation matters more to him than life itself, and he won't brook even a hint of criticism or disagreement. It throws him right off balance. If anything goes wrong, you can be sure the blame will not be his.'

'And it falls on you?'

'Unless I am very, very careful.'

'Which you are?' After a moment, Hamish went on, 'There's been a good deal going wrong on this project. Is it always like this?'

'No. Everything usually runs smoothly.'

'So why not this time?'

'I don't know. Evil spirits, perhaps.'

'Do you believe that?'

Master Hal's mutter was barely audible, 'Not otherworldly ones.'

Hamish chuckled. 'Don't dismiss them. Skye, where I come from, is as full as it can hold of ill-doing faeries and kelpies. Then there's the ghosties and ghoulies and long-leggity beasties, and things that go bump in the night.'

'Indeed?'

Clearly, Master Hal wasn't convinced, so Hamish reverted to more immediate matters. 'If ye have no great opinion of Master Emile, why do ye stay? There must be plenty of openings for a bright lad like you.' Hamish was curious about Master Hal's background; clearly, he was no mere peasant. But to ask outright would, he suspected, be regarded as intrusive.

'Thank you, but I'm not a lad any more and I have to think of my future. I have served seven years' apprenticeship and am now a head journeyman. I hope soon to become a master mason myself, and undertake commissions on my own account. But to achieve that, I need four master masons to speak for me before the masons' guild. So I cannot afford to make an enemy of Master Emile.'

'Ah, I see. That's how things work, is it? And there's no other way?' It seemed to Hamish that, if there were, bright young Master Hal would be aware of it.

'None so reliable,' Master Hal replied absently. Staring down into his cup, he failed to observe the sparkle of interest in Hamish MacLeod's eyes.

There was a sudden whickering from the stables as someone rode in through the great gate and clopped across the courtyard in a stately manner that would have sufficed to identify Sir Walter Woolston without further evidence.

Hamish said, 'Ah yes. And what about the fire?'

Master Hal was quick to make the association. 'Not the steward. Not this time.'

'No?'

'The fire must have been burning unnoticed since about last Friday. The innermost poles were almost like charcoal when we raked them out. I believe he has been away from Vine Regis for longer than that, so unless he sneaked back unseen . . .'

'You know what started it?'

'I think—I *think*—some smouldering oily rags, pushed deep down in the pile. We found a second bundle that hadn't caught.'

'Uh-huh.' Hamish cocked his red head. 'So it was deliberate, then? But failing Sir Walter, who? And why?'

'The two sawyers seem to me the likeliest culprits, assuming they had a few minutes alone after they were released from the pillory and before they were marched away into the countryside.'

Hamish could not recall the sawyers being granted a single unguarded moment before being marched away. But he said merely, 'And if they were the who, then we don't need to wonder about the why.'

'Spite,' said Master Hal.

'That's a relief.' Hamish stood up and flexed his shoulders. 'Och, well. No great harm done.'

'You think not?' said Master Hal. Hamish looked down at him and he went on after a moment, 'It could set the building work back for weeks. Depends how long it takes to get replacement poles. The ones Master Emile favours have to come all the way from the Baltic.'

Hamish surveyed him meditatively. 'Well, well. How interesting. Who would have thought it?'

3

The master carpenter, whose name was Joseph, was an unpleasant man who considered himself just as fine a craftsman as the master mason and went through life resenting the implication that he wasn't. More than anything, he disliked having Master Emile tell him what to do.

'No,' he said, turning away. 'You're in charge of the site. If you can't manage things, you'd better hand over to someone who can.'

Master Emile was shaking with fury. 'You will

do what I tell you!'

'Save your breath, little man. Or I will walk out and take all my carpenters with me.'

It silenced the master mason only for a moment. 'Go, then! I need you not!' He looked as if he were about to burst into tears.

Master Hal sighed, casting a resigned glance at Sir Walter, who had made his stately way on to the scene, looking quite unconcerned. Even his 'Tut, tut' of disapproval was far from convincing. Everyone knew by now that he disliked Master Emile intensely and rejoiced in his troubles.

'You need me not?' jeered Master Joseph. 'Ha! My men are craftsmen. Who else can make the window and door support arches, and shape the roof timbers as they must be shaped? But you want us to waste our time and skills on searching out fir trees and splitting them into struts and braces, a task any ham-fisted clod could carry out? No, no. If you have allowed your scaffolding to be destroyed, then it is for you to replace it or find some other solution.'

Master Emile was several inches shorter than Master Joseph, but he launched himself at the carpenter with his arms flailing. Master Hal's move to hold him back came too late and Joseph simply met the assault by placing the flat of his hand on Master Emile's chest. The master mason went down with a crash on the ground, a crash accompanied by sarcastic cheers from the audience which had assembled. Scaffolders, most of them.

Some time later, Hamish, who had witnessed all this from the gatehouse, remarked to Master Hal, 'The wee man's nerves are getting bad.'

'And his English to match.'

'But,' Hamish went on, '"replace the scaffolding, or find some other solution"? Such as what?'

Master Hal waved an irritable hand. 'If you look, you can see that we have been raising the scaffolding as a kind of tower, standing on the ground, which means two ranks of poles, front and back, joined by struts across and with diagonal braces to hold them stable. The alternative is to use only one rank of poles and anchor the cross-struts into the wall itself as we build it. That way, we'd probably have enough poles to see us through.'

Hamish thought for a moment. 'But then the courses would look uneven, would they not? Or when ye remove the scaffolding, ye'd leave dozens of holes in the wall where the cross-struts were?'

'Yes, of course, but we'd fill them in with mortar. There were always going to be a few holes, anyway, particularly near the base, to stabilise the whole thing.'

'The Lady is not going to like it.'

The Lady did not, indeed, like the idea of mortar-filled holes disturbing the gracious symmetry of her new walls, and said so in no uncertain terms. And when long delays were put to her as the only option, she replied crisply that this was not necessarily so. 'We might well be able to borrow the scaffolding we need from Stanwelle. They should have a plentiful supply at present, with the building there only just begun.'

William, who had developed a close interest in the building works and was showing a tendency to tread almost in Master Hal's footprints, to that gentleman's increasing annoyance, chirped up,

185

'That's a good notion!'

'Thank you.' Dame Constance's half-smile was mechanical. 'John, ride over and ask Abbot Ralph if he would do us this favour.'

'Yes, mother.'

'I'll come, too.' It was William again.

'And so shall I, if you do not object,' said Susanna. 'I would like to see more of the countryside. And the abbey also, of course.'

4

It was a sedate little procession consisting of John and his groom, Susanna and hers, with Margot as chaperone, that set out later in the day, William trailing along behind. John, who had initially envisaged his mission to Stanwelle as a brisk canter there and back, dutifully—if unnecessarily—held everyone to the ladylike pace favoured by Isabelle on the rare occasions when he went riding with her.

Susanna, who would have enjoyed a gallop, accepted this without complaint because it gave her an opportunity to fish innocently in waters that interested her. As they passed the pleasant manor of Amerscote, she was able to say brightly, 'What a number of delightful manors there are on the estate. I should be happy to live in any of them. I wonder, does the Lady not wish sometimes that she could be rid of all the responsibilities of the castle and move to somewhere smaller and more home-like?'

John, aware that she had already asked Isabelle much the same question, merely laughed. 'I cannot

186

imagine what she would find to do with her time.'

After a moment, as if the thought had just occurred to her, Susanna went on, 'I am surprised that she has not married again. Any gentleman would be fortunate to have her as his lady.'

'Any gentleman would be fortunate indeed, but the lady might have her own opinions.'

'I suppose so.'

Mentally raising his eyebrows, John wondered where all this was leading. What was Susanna up to? Because she was clearly up to something.

Not until they were making polite conversation with Abbot Ralph in his richly decorated lodging, with its Great Hall and mosaic tiled floors, did light begin to dawn.

They had been able to see the massive walls of Stanwelle for several miles, but the sheer sprawl of it always surprised even John, who was familiar with the place. Approaching from the north, as they did, it was the abbey church that first met the eye, the long line of its nave and choir with the heavy ribs and traceried windows hiding many of the lesser buildings that lay beyond.

They skirted the site to the east, John waving an informative hand as they went. 'Chapter house with the cloister beyond, the monks' parlour with dormitories over—the lay brothers have their equivalent on the west side—then the infirmary, and here we are! The abbot's lodging, complete with its own kitchen and a good many other rooms as well. Ralph likes his comforts. All the butter and cream from the dairy are reserved for him, with all the choicest birds and fish. When he goes on bread-and-water as a penance for something, everybody knows about it because they're able to guzzle his butter and cream and other luxuries to their hearts' content. Vows of silence or no vows of silence, you can't keep anything quiet in a monastery.'

'I wonder where they are building the new chapel? I don't see any signs of activity.'

'Over on the west side near the Guest Hall, probably. Far enough away for it not to disturb Ralph. We can ask.'

The abbot greeted his unexpected visitors with his usual stateliness, though without warmth. He had known John since infancy, and supposed that fact might account for the young man's lack of proper respect towards him, but to be called upon to welcome a very young and flighty-looking lady— whom he vaguely remembered from the foundation-laying ceremony at Vine Regis—went beyond what he saw as fitting. So he bade her be seated and then ignored her.

Susanna sat virtuously silent while John explained the predicament that had arisen at Vine Regis and waited hopefully for Abbot Ralph to volunteer his assistance. When he didn't, John said, 'My mother wondered whether you might find it possible to help her out—just until our new scaffolding arrives from the Baltic, you understand. She will come and explain everything to you in person, if you so wish.'

Abbot Ralph saw no need for that. Had his complexion not been naturally pallid, he might well have lost colour. 'Let me consult with Monsieur, my architect.'

M. Bernard duly presented himself and reluctantly conceded that it would be some weeks before all the chapel scaffolding would be needed.

How many lifts, he asked, did the gracious Lady require, and for how long?

Waving an eager William to silence, and reflecting that he should have brought Master Hal, John confessed his ignorance, whereupon, in response to a nod from the abbot, M. Bernard said, 'I will visit in a day or two. Or perhaps three. And we may then assess the gracious Lady's requirements.'

'Excellent,' said John. 'My lady mother will be most grateful.'

It seemed a trifle impolite to take leave there and then, so he made a few enquiries about the progress of the chapel and was showing signs of running out of inspiration when Susanna, tired of being ignored, raised her voice.

'It seems a shame,' she said, 'that Stanwelle does not have a nunnery. There must be many young ladies in the district who are desirous of taking the veil.'

'Possibly,' replied the abbot repressively, then, thinking to put an end to such foolishness, went on, 'but, aside from the obvious difficulties, much new building would be entailed, and an endowment would of course be essential.'

Gaily, she smiled. 'Surely there must be some local lady, some rich widow, who would be prepared to endow such an institution and even become its first abbess? I can think of one at least.'

William, whose idea it had been, looked as if he would like to applaud, but it was as much as John could do not to choke.

Abbot Ralph looked as if he were in much the same case. 'Indeed?' he rejoined icily.

Susanna bit her lip. Perhaps she shouldn't have

put it quite so obviously.

Fortunately, at that moment the bells began to ring out from the abbey church. It was time for the office of *hora nona* and Abbot Ralph rose to dismiss his guests.

As they set out homeward, John demanded of a subdued Susanna, '*What* were you thinking of?'

She could have said that she was being considerate of Dame Constance's wellbeing, that the Lady might not wish to share Vine Regis with her daughter-in-law when she and Gervase were married. 'It was only an idea that suddenly came to me,' she lied. 'It just popped out before I thought. Forget that I said it, please.' Then, observing the frown on John's normally good-humoured face, she did her best to change the subject. 'Abbot Ralph *is* very large, isn't he?'

'Yes,' replied John, breathing heavily through his nose.

5

And so, for Susanna, temporarily abandoning the problem of Dame Constance and the future, it was back to the demands of her wardrobe, to days of intermittent cutting and stitching and fitting, discussions about gores and gussets and seams, embroideries and trimmings.

It was all going beautifully when Susanna, hurrying round the corner of the building site, fell over a pile of ashlar blocks which had not been there the day before—and broke her ankle. The ache was unbearable, but the physician at first said it was only a sprain, and he would bind it up. As the hours passed, the ankle swelled and swelled until a sobbing Susanna had to tell her women to take the binding off and summon the physician again. He was displeased, having little time for tearful young ladies whose sprains turned out to be fractures. The swelling would have to go down before he could do anything about setting the bone, he said, so her ladyship would have to resign herself to lying in bed for a day or two. He would give her a soothing draught to ease the pain.

Dame Constance did her best to ensure that Master Emile also suffered pain, giving him the tongue-lashing of his life and dismissing, with contempt, his defence that building sites were necessarily hazardous to people who did not look where they were going. It was—of course—Master Hal who offered to make himself responsible for tidying up the site.

'Thank you,' said Dame Constance, and stalked off to discover how Susanna was feeling.

She found Susanna still in bed, palely holding court and continuing the discussion of her fashion transformation with Isabelle. They had reached the stage of hairstyles and headdresses, and Dame Constance stood listening while Isabelle conceded virginally loose hair until Susanna was married, but insisted on its being covered by a small goffered veil held in place by a gold fillet.

Dame Constance nodded approvingly, handed over the small bunch of roses she had brought from her private garden in the courtyard, and departed feeling moderately reassured.

It was several days before Susanna decided that she must, she *must*, get up and face the world again. The invaluable Hamish carved sticks for her to lean on, made to just the right height, and she began to feel more friendly towards him. She even smiled at him when she said, 'Thank you, MacLeod.'

Hovered over by her gentlewomen, and with William at her side uttering yelps of advice and encouragement, she succeeded in mastering the problem of walking with sticks, and even discovered that it was possible to negotiate the stairs on them.

In the meantime, much cutting and stitching had been going on, and her new wardrobe was finished, save for a few minor fitting adjustments. Everyone was exhausted, but delighted with the result.

Except Susanna. 'If only,' she wailed, as one of Isabelle's gentlewomen held up the hand mirror before her, 'if only someone would make a really big mirror in which I could see *all* of myself, instead of just bits.'

Isabelle said thoughtfully, 'I couldn't possibly wear that green, with my colouring, but it is excellent with your complexion.'

'Yes, I can see that.'

'And the darker colours flatter your waist and make it look tiny.'

'Really?'

'Yes, really.'

Master Nicholas danced around her tugging here and tweaking there, and pronounced himself satisfied. 'All that now remains,' he declared, 'is for you to present yourself in public in your new guise, and wait for the compliments!'

'From whom?' Susanna's voice held a touch of acidity.

And it was true enough. Dame Constance

192

congratulated Isabelle and Master Nicholas on the excellence of their choices while favouring Susanna with no more than an approving, 'Yes, that is much better.' Gervase—still no word from him other than that he had attended the coronation!—was not there to say what he thought. And what the lesser male inhabitants of Vine Regis thought was not permitted to be spoken and could not, in any case, be of interest to the future young Lady of the Castle.

6

The Lord Gervase, not a natural communicator, was in any case too absorbed by events in Westminster and the City to concern himself with what might be going on at Vine Regis. His mother, he knew, would have everything under control there—including, he supposed, his frivolous little wife-to-be.

Waiting around in his lodgings in the City, preparatory to joining the expedition under the king's youngest uncle, Thomas of Woodstock, Duke of Buckingham, whose object was to destroy the Franco-Castilian fleet moored at Sluys, Gervase found himself witnessing the continuing clash between the court and the Commons more closely than ever before.

John of Gaunt had withdrawn from court a few days after the coronation, ostensibly to spend more time with his family but leaving trouble behind, as always, so that Gervase found himself caught up in an attempt to recapture two offending squires who had escaped from the Tower of London.

Responding to a call from the Constable of the Tower and a court knight by name of Sir Ralph Ferrers, Gervase discovered too late that the two squires had taken sanctuary in Westminster Abbey. Breaking into a holy place and shedding blood therein was not at all what Gervase could approve of, but neither was he confident enough to refuse, which would have entailed royal displeasure and endangered not only himself but everyone at Vine Regis and the estate itself.

The Bishop of London promptly excommunicated both the Constable and Sir Ralph. John of Gaunt denounced the Bishop of London. The City showed a strong inclination to riot. Gervase went to confession.

Confessors in the City of London had their own realistic priorities—nothing too harsh for young men attached to the court, and great care when dealing with City merchants and their associates, who had developed an acute distaste for the Church and its money-grubbing ways. Gervase's penances were therefore light—bread and water for a week and no sexual intercourse for three months, which, since the new whorehouse on the south bank of the river had not lived up to expectations, was no great hardship.

He went back to fretting about when Thomas of Woodstock's expedition would finally sail. It was not at all clear whether the new Poll Tax would be sufficient to subsidise it.

And then, one day, he was summoned to the Queen Mother's residence in Kennington, to meet two nobles of the Continual Council and several senior members of the young king's household. Thereafter, he found himself before the blond and

beautiful young king himself, who said,
'Tell me, my lord . . .'

7

Susanna, searching for Sir Guy, whom, in the absence of his son, she worshipped by default, caught him one day, collapsed on the grass on the west side of the castle, by no means his usual impeccable self but grey with exhaustion and stone dust. She hesitated and began to turn away but, aware of someone standing over him, he opened his eyes and, blinking against the light, said, 'What a refreshing change from seeing nothing but mules and carts and barges!'

She had watched him often, from a distance, urging on the endless lines of drivers with their loads of dressed stone. 'Must you be responsible? Is there no one else?'

'Yes, but no one with my genius for getting things done.' He grinned. 'Without a steady supply of materials, the work will never be finished and we will never be rid of these builders, whose natural instinct is to be lazy and unreliable and slow. The longer they take, the longer they are assured of their wages.'

'I suppose so.'

She went on staring at him and, after a moment, he asked, 'Did you want to say something to me, or are we just passing the time of day?'

'May I ask you something?'

'What?'

'Do you have a mother?'

He gave a small splutter of laughter. 'Most

people do.'

'I didn't mean that.'

'No, I don't imagine you did. My mother died some years ago.' He gave her a moment to digest that, then added, 'So did my wife.'

'Oh, I'm sorry,' she said lamely. But she was committed, so she went on, 'Did you always think your mother was right? Did you always say, "Yes, mother"?'

The dents at the corners of his mobile mouth deepened. 'I don't recall.'

'Oh, don't you?' and then in a different tone, 'I'm sorry, I didn't mean to disturb you. It was just that I have never thanked you for dealing with those wicked sawyers, or making clear that their tale of M. Alain was quite untrue. So, please, accept my gratitude.'

'Well,' he said, 'at least you know now that you should not allow yourself to be alone with any gentleman who is not your betrothed or your husband.'

She glanced around nervously, and he laughed. 'No, you are quite safe with me, especially in full view of the castle and with a hundred workmen just round the corner. I like your new style, by the way. It's elegant and it suits you. Even the crutches add a certain panache.'

As soon as he said it, intending only to ease an awkward moment, he knew it to have been a mistake. Experienced as he was, he had no difficulty in recognising the signs of girlish infatuation—the blush, the averting of the eyes, the slight intake of breath. He swore to himself.

And then it was as if he had ceased to exist.

A young man strode round the corner. 'Oh,

196

there you are, father!' he began, and stopped as if he had walked into a sheet of glass. 'I'm—ah—sorry. Did I—ah—interrupt . . . ?'

His eyes were on Susanna.

'Not at all,' she gasped.

It was the thrilling young man she had seen on the first day of her arrival at Vine Regis, and never since. She had dreamed of him many times, knowing who he was but wondering where he had gone, her dreams warmed by the remembered pleasure of that illicit kiss from Robert Salvin—the kiss that had been so wrong, and yet so right. She had wanted to be kissed again, but not by Robert Salvin.

The young man smiled at her now, and she discovered, heart pounding, that close up, with his dark hair, handsome features, flashing smile and brilliant eyes, he did indeed powerfully resemble his father.

That gentleman said, 'Piers, welcome back. You have made good time, and we need the timbers you have brought.' Then, to Susanna, he went on, 'Piers has been bringing the great timbers for the roof beams and rafters from Shrewsbury. Six wains, each drawn by twelve oxen. Seven weeks coming and going. Two hundred miles at—what?—five miles a day?'

Piers said distractedly, 'Yes, about that. And I've lost count of how many other weeks I spent waiting for the timbers to be prepared.'

He had seen Susanna only once before, weeks ago, in a rush, and without any real interest. But now, as she stood there leaning on her sticks looking exquisitely pretty and fragile and helpless, he was entranced. And more than entranced.

They made conversation of a sort, about Piers' journey, and the heat and how the builders were getting on, and Sir Guy watched with intense interest as the breath fled from the young people's lungs, as their eyes clung and melted into each other's, as an overpowering warmth and excitement possessed them. It was so charming and so moving that, for a moment, he did not even think of the complications such an attraction must bring in its wake.

In the end, he had to clear his throat slightly and break the spell. 'Have you two met?' he asked amusedly.

There was no reply. They were lost in another, a blissful, world. So he rose to his feet. 'You will forgive us, Susanna, if we go in search of Master Emile? He will be restored to equanimity, I hope, by the knowledge that the first floor rafters have arrived.'

8

As if guided by some mutual instinct, Susanna and Piers made no effort to seek each other out, gave no hint to onlookers of what was between them. Their secret had nothing to do with any practical consequences; it was just something too important to share. Behaving like distant acquaintances, they resumed normal life in a daze, doing what was expected of them but detached from it.

Sir Guy watched the pair of them when they were in the Great Hall after meals, observing their careful reticence, but said nothing.

There were many problems the young couple

would have to confront if and when the first rapture began to fade. Piers was twenty-two years old, and mature enough to handle his own affairs without interference, but Sir Guy did not feel that he could place any reliance on Susanna's good sense. He could not tell whether her ingrained belief in propriety would hold her to the pre-contract with Gervase or whether romance would conquer. He couldn't be sure whether she was even giving any thought to it. Quizzically, he wondered which she would choose, to love and be loved, or to be Lady of the Castle. It might be wise to test them by sending Piers out of immediate reach—home to Lanson, perhaps, which Sir Guy had been neglecting in the interests of Vine Regis. He would wait and see.

9

Voluntary the public distance between them might be, but the strain on the young lovers—the desperation for a word, a touch—grew as the days passed. It was a starvation of the senses, and each was subtly aware of it in the other. To meet in private was impossible, could not be planned for in the bustling context of Vine Regis, especially with Susanna unable to go out riding or even walking any distance.

And then, one day, from the other side of the courtyard, he saw her limping into the north-west tower and, hurriedly confecting an errand for himself, ran lightly up the stairs after her. Laying his hand on her arm, he said, 'May I help you, my lady? Those sticks must be very inconvenient.'

199

His subterfuge was unnecessary. There was no one else there to hear.

She turned towards him, her heart beating lightly and rapidly somewhere around the base of her throat, and her eyes looked to him as blue as the summer sky as he moved his hands to rest on her shoulders. Her own lips trembling, she could feel the faint tremor running through his limbs, and even his voice vibrated a little as he said softly, 'I love you, Susanna. I love you so much.'

She stared back at him wordlessly. It wasn't possible. It couldn't be true. But she knew that it was.

He said again, 'I love you so much,' and shook her slightly. 'I love you, I love you, I love you beyond bearing.'

Where her words came from, she had no idea. Not from her conscious mind, to be sure. She whispered, 'But you don't know me. And I don't know *you*.'

'Does it matter?'

She answered with absolute certainty. 'No.'

He drew her into an alcove and, laying her sticks carefully aside, kissed her gently, and it was heavenly, so he kissed her again. As she stood within the circle of his arms, her mouth soft under his, she felt all the strength drain from her, felt her very bones melt. Nothing mattered in the world except the contact between their lips.

At length he drew his head back and, murmuring her name, buried his lips in the hollow at the base of her throat.

She realised that there was something she had left unsaid, an omission that ought to be rectified. 'I love you, too.'

He gave a choke of laughter. 'I should hope so. Otherwise, my lady, you have been behaving quite shockingly.'

She laughed back at him, and then they sat hand in hand, exchanging blissful nothings as lovers do, until she said dreamily, 'I thought your father was wonderful . . .'

'Well, he is!'

'Yes, I know. But I found him amazingly attractive. He is so like you!'

He raised her hand to his lips. 'My darling! How could you tell, when you had barely seen me except as I went rushing past you that day on the hill?'

'It was enough.' She blushed. 'I knew! And then you vanished, and I didn't know where you had gone, and I couldn't very well ask . . .'

'My darling!'

They might have gone on like this for hours, except that they heard someone coming, and had to part, Piers into the treasurer's office and Susanna continuing to the physician's eyrie in search of something to ease the cough little Blanche had developed from breathing in so much dust.

CHAPTER NINE

1

While Piers was explaining to Master Emile what the suppliers had told him about the relative strengths and weaknesses of the Shrewsbury timbers—explanations heavily punctuated with apologies for his occasional lapses in concentration—Susanna wafted dreamily through her days, her earthly attention prosaically occupied with spinning and weaving.

The Vine Regis sheep had been manhandled into the village ponds to clean their fleeces, and had then been sheared, this time legitimately. Diverting her mind from the building works, Dame Constance had decreed that, since August had arrived and the long hot summer must come to an end some time—and the sooner the better, in her opinion—it was necessary for everyone to get on with the spinning. It needed a dozen spinners to keep each weaver supplied and, with winter approaching, however slowly, everyone would soon feel the need of good warm clothing. The village women had been occupied in the unenviable task of using teasel heads to card the fleeces, and there should by now be a sufficiency of fluffed-up wool for the spinners to work on.

'Ugh!' said Blanche. 'I don't like it when everyone's walking around with distaffs and spindles all the time. They're too busy wondering when the spindle will hit the floor to listen prop'ly to what other people are saying to them, and they don't have a hand free to throw a ball or anything like that.'

Susanna thought for a moment. 'Perhaps we could ask MacLeod to make special small distaffs and spindles for you and Eleanor. He's good at carving, I know. And then you could annoy everyone else by walking around not paying attention to what *they* are saying.'

Predictably, Blanche said, 'Ugh!' again, but Susanna was beginning to get the measure of the child. 'Your grandmother would be proud of you.'

Her proposal was not entirely disinterested. She herself had always been clumsy with the distaff and it occurred to her that teaching the children to use it might disguise, or even help to remedy her deficiencies. 'But for the moment, why don't we go down to the village and see how the women are getting on with the carding? If we take MacLeod with us, perhaps he could help us carry some wool back.'

Although she was now limping around the castle with only one of her sticks, there was no question as yet of walking as far as the village. So old Tom, her groom, heaved her up into her side saddle and she was delighted to find herself quite comfortable in it. Even a trip to the village, after the weeks of incarceration, was as splendid a prospect to her as it always was to Blanche.

After dinner they set off with their bodyguard in attendance and a pack pony for company. Hamish MacLeod knew, if Susanna did not, just how much a few fleeces'-worth of wool could weigh.

They were lucky not to miss the fun, as Blanche was to tell her grandmother importantly when they reached home again. Because, arriving in the village, they discovered Father Hoby, his hair flying in greasy yellow strings around his tonsure, his skirts hitched up in one hand to reveal bare and bony knees, tearing along the street in pursuit of a terrified mendicant friar, brandishing a knife and cursing the man at the top of his voice.

'. . . dare you . . . preaching outside my church . . . taking money . . . no permission . . . speaking ill of the Lady . . . I'll cut your lips off when I catch you . . .'

'Och, dearie me!' said Hamish. 'We can't have that.'

He tossed the pony's reins to old Tom, took a few swift strides, and the priest found himself stopped dead by a large hand twisted in the neck of his cassock.

'Now, now, wee man,' said Hamish amiably. 'What happened to the peace of the Lord?'

Father Hoby gobbled, 'They come here and preach without permission in front of my church, and take contributions from everyone . . .'

There wasn't, of course, a contributor in sight—although there were faces enough peering inquisitively through windows and doorways—and Hamish would have been very surprised to hear of any of the villagers prepared to part with good money to an itinerant preacher.

'Aye?' he said.

'And he was preaching that women's love of fine clothing is a mortal sin—and he meant the Lady, and'—he cast a meaning glance at an astounded Susanna—'the younger Lady. And he deserves to have his lips cut off for it.'

'Oh, aye? Well, not by you.' Hamish removed
204

the knife from the little priest's grasp and tucked it into his own belt. 'Just be grateful that I've saved you from appearing before the justice of the peace.'

'There's no law against cutting a blasphemer's lips off!'

'Is there not? We'd better ask Sir Guy about that.'

The erring friar had vanished into the distance, so Hamish used his grip on the cassock to lift the priest right off his feet before setting him down again, not gently, and releasing him. Then he retrieved the pony's reins from Tom and said, 'Right, then. The fleeces, my lady?'

'We can't just walk away,' said Susanna.

'Why not? Father Hoby isn't going anywhere.'

'I suppose not.' But Susanna felt she had not pulled her weight. She should have done, or said, something befitting her station, though she had no idea what.

Regaled with this saga when they returned to the castle, Dame Constance was not pleased. Summoning her younger son, she told him, 'John, ride over to Stanwelle and tell Abbot Ralph that I am in urgent need of a new castle chaplain. I am at fault for not having looked for one sooner. But we cannot possibly continue to rely on such an unlettered oaf as Father Hoby for our spiritual guidance. Where did he come from in the first place?'

It was a very strange question. John raised one eyebrow, and reflected that Dame Constance's mind must be wandering. It happened, he knew, as people got old. 'I have no idea, mother.'

'I don't suppose you have. As it happens, I was

205

thinking aloud. It was Abbot Ralph's predecessor who wished him on the village. Unforgivable! Jesu! What was that?'

A strange, creaking noise outdoors had been followed by a loud, dull thud and the inevitable outburst of shouting and swearing. John went to the window but the walls were too thick to allow him to see what was happening directly below. 'I'll go and find out,' he said, and ran from the room.

He returned a few minutes later, breathless and trying not to laugh. 'One of the hoist ropes broke,' he reported, 'and a huge chunk of stone hit the ground about six inches behind Sir Walter. It would have pulverised him if it had landed on him. The poor old boy's still shaking, and threatening Master Emile with every penalty you can think of. "Criminal incompetence", he says. The master mason is useless, he says. He should be instantly dismissed, he says, and that's just the polite bits!'

'And what does Master Emile say?'

'He says it's a conspiracy to ruin his reputation.'

'Indeed? And who is doing the conspiring?'

'That,' her son told her, 'is the question. Even he now recognises that it can hardly be Sir Walter, though he has suspected him of everything that has gone wrong since the episode of the flooded foundation trench.'

'John, this is not funny!'

'No, I know. But that perpetual calm of old Walter's has taken a nasty dent. I wouldn't have believed it, but he's human underneath.'

'I will have to speak to Master Emile, I suppose,' his mother sighed. 'Accidents will happen, but I would not have anticipated quite so many as in these last few weeks.'

Susanna, who had taken considerably more interest in the building work since her own accident, remembered William's speculations about the episode of the hod carriers, when Sir Walter had sustained a nasty blow from flying rubble. She said, 'Sir Walter seems to be more the victim than the villain. But it can't be deliberate, can it?'

'I can certainly see no way of ensuring coordination between victim and weapon,' said Dame Constance. 'It must have been pure chance that Walter was in the wrong place at the wrong time. Conspiracy, indeed!'

Susanna thought, pure chance that Sir Walter had been the one to suffer? Perhaps, but it was odd, just the same.

'Anyway,' said the Lady, 'let us return to business. Ralph will know what kind of man we need as chaplain here at the castle. And, John, do tidy yourself up before you go! Don't forget to ask him how his building work on the chapel is progressing, but don't give him the opportunity to ask for his scaffolding back!'

John ran his fingers through his hair. 'Yes, mother. No, mother.' He knew better than to say, 'What, again?' or to complain that he would not be back in time for supper.

On the other hand, the Feast of St Peter's Chains had just gone and the Vigil of St Lawrence still lay ahead. And it wasn't a Friday. So Abbot Ralph might not be fasting but supping in style. It was a cheering thought and the full moon promised a pleasant ride home through the soft summer air. He could ride along quietly and dream of the Lady Emilia, on whom his romantic heart was currently set.

2

In this he was frustrated. He had ridden no more than a couple of miles in the direction of Stanwelle when he met a majestic procession coming the other way—Abbot Ralph with his customary train of attendants, and M. Bernard of Dol, the architect, desirous of inspecting the scaffolding situation at Vine Regis.

Abbot Ralph said, 'I myself have come only out of vulgar curiosity,' which successfully deprived John of speech, so that the miles back to Vine Regis were accomplished in silence.

They arrived to find the workmen swaying one of the first floor beams into position. Two labourers plodding away in a treadmill had hauled it up, roped in a cradle arrangement attached to a sturdy central hook. The trick now was to guide one end of the beam into the hole excavated for it in the existing castle wall and to drop the other end into the gap left for it at the top of the new wall. This required some precision, much pushing and shoving on the part of the workmen perched on top of the new wall, and much shouting by Master Hal of, 'No, back a bit . . . no, forward again . . . and to the left . . . no! I said left, *gauche*, you bloody fools . . . and up a bit . . . and lower it now, slowly, I said *slowly* . . . oh, God's bones!!!'

The free end of the beam dropped with a crash into its appointed place, but the vibration caused the other end, embedded in the masonry of the castle, to give a jerk and loosen a segment of ancient stone which went catapulting through the air and missed Abbot Ralph by the merest whisker. The abbot flinched slightly and ducked his head aside, but took only a moment to recapture his usual Olympian calm.

The Stanwelle architect pursed his lips and remarked, 'It is a surprise to me that no one has yet been killed. The treadmill is balanced on planks and therefore unstable, and the workmen cannot be expected to perform such manoeuvres satisfactorily when they only have makeshift scaffolding to do it from. It is, of course, up to the Father Abbot to decree whether we are prepared to lend any more of our scaffolding until your own supplies arrive—not too long now, I trust?—but I myself would advise it.'

Abbot Ralph inclined his head graciously in return. 'I could not have men's deaths on my conscience.'

Then they all dismounted and went indoors, where Dame Constance welcomed them and asked for Abbot Ralph's help in finding a new chaplain.

He thought for a moment, in his hand the glass of spring water which was the only refreshment he would deign to accept. He was not usually so abstemious, and Dame Constance wondered if he were deliberately trying to lose weight or if she was imagining things. He said, 'I believe I have someone who would suit you. Father Sebastian. He has every quality save for the ability to fit in with monastic life. I will speak to him about it.'

'Thank you. I hope he will not be deterred by the danger of flying masonry?'

'Unlikely. I should have thought you yourself would have had enough of building works by now?'

209

'Don't speak of it. Never again. Never, ever, again.'

'Not even for the nunnery?' he asked whimsically.

She stared at him. 'The nunnery? Which nunnery?'

'I—ah—understood from a remark made by the Lady—ah—Susanna, is it?—that endowing a nunnery at Stanwelle and becoming its abbess might be a project that would appeal to you.' His voice tailed away as her expression moved from mystification to disbelief and then to something that was half amusement, half anger.

After a moment, she said with a metallic laugh, 'You understood wrongly. I cannot imagine what gave the Lady Susanna such an idea.'

Then she saw the relief on his face, and the laugh became more genuine. 'No, Ralph. Have no fear that I will inflict myself on Stanwelle.'

Chivalrously, he assured her that fear was not his predominant emotion, adding mendaciously that disappointment was more what he felt.

They parted on the best of terms, and Dame Constance promptly summoned John to her side, demanding to be told precisely what Susanna had said to Abbot Ralph to put such a notion into his head.

John floundered. He had put two and two together and come to the conclusion that Susanna was looking for ways to ensure that she, as the future Lady of the Castle, would have sole possession. He could not imagine why she should feel that way. Most new brides, according to his observation, managed to come to terms with their mothers-in-law and were grateful for their guidance. Susanna was an attractive but sometimes silly girl, and more transparent than she knew, but no good purpose could be served by setting her at odds with Dame Constance.

'It's just,' he essayed, 'that after her own two years in a convent, she feels it is a subject she knows something about. She was only looking for something intelligent to say. Your name wasn't mentioned. Truly. She was suggesting that some local lady might endow a nunnery at Stanwelle—that there was certainly a need for it—and Abbot Ralph jumped to conclusions. I did myself, but I think now she was just trying to make the general argument sound more practicable.'

His mother surveyed him suspiciously. 'Hmmm. I'll believe you. But it seems very strange to me.' Then, without a pause, 'And look at your hose, all wrinkled round the ankles. Oblige me by endeavouring, at least occasionally—I try not to ask the impossible—to look moderately tidy!'

'Yes, mother.'

Casting a rather chill glance at Susanna that evening, Dame Constance wondered what was the matter with her. From being determinedly vivacious, the girl had suddenly become calm, almost vague. Isabelle, absorbed in designing the wardrobe for her own forthcoming marriage, was no less vague when Dame Constance asked her what she thought. 'I hadn't noticed any change,' she replied absently.

Dame Constance simmered. What had she done to be surrounded by such a limp-minded family? Why did she have to do the thinking for everyone?

Sir Guy could have told her but, observing the tension in her, thought it wiser to hold his peace.

'Susanna, a word, please,' said Dame Constance after supper and stalked off towards her chamber.

Nervously scanning her conscience, Susanna, unaware of what had passed earlier in the day, could think of no way in which she had recently erred—until Dame Constance turned to face her and, without preliminary, said frostily, 'Perhaps you would be so good as to explain to me why Abbot Ralph received the impression from you that I might wish to endow, and preside over, a nunnery at Stanwelle?'

Susanna gulped. 'I—er . . .'

'I also understand that you have been wondering whether there is any manor of which I am fond, and where I might choose to live if not at Vine Regis?'

Susanna drew in a nervous breath, expecting the next accusation to relate to her interest in whether the Lady might marry again. It didn't come, but it could scarcely have made things worse.

'Well?' said Dame Constance.

Susanna stared at her blankly.

'Well?' Dame Constance repeated. 'I am waiting.'

'There was nothing as—as—direct as that,' Susanna stammered.

'Indeed? Then let us consider the indirect.'

'It was just that . . .'

Dame Constance was standing facing her, upright as always, hands clasped at her waist. There was a cold tension about her that suggested no explanation would be acceptable.

Susanna had never been spoken to like this,

couldn't believe that Dame Constance was actually in a rage—and with her, Susanna. What to say? How to put an end to it? She was tempted to run away, but self-respect forbade it.

Trembling, unable to meet the Lady's eyes, she said, 'When I marry Gervase . . .'

'Yes. You will become Lady of the Castle.'

Her words came out frantically then, in a rush. 'And it seemed to me you might not wish to stay at Vine Regis and watch me—making mistakes. As I am bound to do.'

'Certainly that cannot be denied, and I am relieved that you are conscious of it.' Dame Constance turned away, while Susanna stood twisting her fingers, and praying that it would soon be over.

But the Lady resumed, 'However, making mistakes is one thing, recognising them is another. And learning from them is what is important. Do you have any idea, for example, how often you have exasperated me over what you no doubt regard as minor matters?'

Susanna tried to think. 'Employing Alice?' she faltered.

'And?'

'Er . . .'

'And?'

Susanna couldn't think of anything else, other than the nunnery idea. She pouted and shrugged.

'Precisely! Your lack of simple common sense astounds me. It was necessary for me to lecture you on the very obvious need to learn about the people of Vine Regis. I had to drag the tale of the sawyers out of you, and I am not convinced that we know the full truth about that episode even yet.

You resent criticism—of your gowns, for example. You cannot face even the minor unpleasantness of sending an impertinent troubadour about his business. I have watched you flutter your eyelashes shamelessly at Master Robert Salvin . . .'

Just in time, Susanna bit back a 'Not any more!'

'And you are not even sufficiently interested to ask to see the model of the castle extension which is being built largely for your convenience!'

'No! That is not fair. I would have expected to be shown it, without having to ask.'

But Dame Constance was not to be stopped. 'And now we have you speculating on *my* future. Which is intolerable.'

Susanna, suffering a strong sense of injustice, contrived to murmur shakily, 'I'm sorry. I didn't know I was annoying you so much. You didn't let it show.'

In truth, it was not so much the episodes Dame Constance had quoted at Susanna that had caused her patience to snap. It was her own constant, nagging sensitivity to the girl's immature cast of mind, the predictability of her responses, the increasingly unbearable succession of small irritants that, singly specified, would have seemed too minor to be worth mentioning.

Dame Constance said, 'It would help if you could cure yourself of some of your unfortunate mannerisms.'

'My mannerisms? I don't understand.'

'Talk to Isabelle about them. And then perhaps we might find it possible to start again.'

When the tearful resentment and foot-stamping fury had begun to wear off, Susanna braced herself to go and talk to Isabelle.

'The Lady was horribly unkind to me! She just looked through me. She didn't shout or anything . . .'

'Would you rather she had shouted?'

'Yes. No. I don't know. But I've never been spoken to like that before. I'm sorry, what did you say?'

Isabelle shook her head. 'Nothing.' Better not to repeat that Susanna would have benefited from being 'spoken to like that' years ago.

'And it all came right out of the blue! When I had thought we were beginning to get on quite well. She never even gave a hint that she didn't like me.'

'It's not a question of not liking. It's a question of you getting on her nerves. My mother can put up with an amazing amount of vexation, far more than most people, before her patience runs out. But when it does, it happens suddenly and unexpectedly, which makes it quite startling. I *know*. She puts up with my lethargy for ages and ages without a murmur, and then, without warning—bang! She's back to normal next day, and at least she rarely says anything personally hurtful.'

'Well, if you think it's not hurtful to be told to cure myself of my mannerisms . . .'

'Did she specify them?'

'No, that's why I'm asking you.'

Isabelle murmured, 'Thank you, mother!'

'I should have stood up for myself, but I didn't.'

'It would have been a waste of time. When her patience snaps, there's nothing you can say.'

'Do I get on your nerves, too?'

'Sometimes. Do you really want to know what you should try to overcome?'

'I suppose so.'

'Can I be sure you'll pay attention, and really make an effort?'

'Yes. I wouldn't like you to—to waste your energy.'

Isabelle was perfectly accustomed to criticism, real or implied, of her natural languor, so she merely smiled at this.

Then, 'Let us consider only the most obvious of your mannerisms. You do pout a lot, when someone says something you don't like. Rather as if you're thinking, "You're wrong, but I'm not going to argue." It's very annoying.'

'Oh.' Susanna, who had been reviewing her supposed bad habits and was expecting something on the lines of intruding into other people's conversations, was taken aback.

'And you toss your head, and shrug, too, as if you are dismissing what is being said to you as quite unimportant.'

Gathering herself together, Susanna said, 'No, it's *not* that. It usually means I'm not—not at ease, that I can't think of anything to say.'

Isabelle took a delicate stitch in the girdle she was embroidering. 'Well, it makes people think you feel yourself superior.'

Susanna's voice was hollow. 'Anything else?'

'Those are the worst. But why do you keep your eyes lowered for so much of the time, at dinner

216

particularly? We all know you have beautiful eyelashes—indeed, Mr Salvin made a remark one day about using them to sweep up the crumbs—but you do display them in a way that suggests flirtatiousness or vanity.'

The juxtaposition of flirtatiousness and Mr Salvin was something Susanna preferred to pass over. Sweeping up the crumbs, indeed!

'Vanity? No, it's *modesty*! The nuns taught me all about correct behaviour. A lady should always smile faintly without showing her teeth, look down most of the time with her eyelids half closed, and toy with her food.'

She spoke almost mechanically. She had been half-heartedly trying to decide how, or even whether, to warn Isabelle that her husband-to-be was not to be trusted and here was an opening.

And then it was gone. Isabelle said, 'If that is correct behaviour, I would advise against it. And as for modesty—well, you do have a habit of, I was going to say "intruding" but it's not that. It's more a matter of drawing attention to yourself . . .'

'I don't like being ignored!'

'No one does. But when you are young and inexperienced, you cannot expect other people to value your opinions as highly as you do yourself.'

'Are you saying I have no judgement?'

Wrinkling her nose, Isabelle murmured, 'Not quite that. Just that *true* modesty means staying quiet unless you are absolutely sure that what you have to say will make a worthwhile contribution. You have to think things through before you speak. You have to be quite sure that you know what you are talking about.'

Susanna sighed heavily. 'Is that all? Have you

217

finished?'

Isabelle, quite worn out by the mental exercise so unexpectedly imposed on her, said, 'Yes, I think so.'

'Well, if you see me pouting or shrugging or putting myself forward in the future, please just say, "Susanna!" and glare at me.'

Isabelle laughed. 'I don't think I know how to glare.'

'No, I'm sure your mother will do that.'

5

No more than anyone else did Susanna like being criticised and her resentment grumbled on, deep down, even while she made a genuine attempt to mend her ways. It helped, she found, to look at other people's flaws—flaws which, if she had been so minded, would have irritated her intensely. For a start, there was Dame Constance's air of unassailable competence! And Isabelle's limp lack of interest in anything other than clothes. And John's incorrigible untidiness and unrelenting cheerfulness. And Master Emile rubbing bits of this or that between his fingers. And Sir Walter smoothing a hand over his perfectly smooth hair in moments of uncertainty. Looked at in this way, even Sir Guy's habit of seeming to regard everything that happened at Vine Regis as a source of private amusement could be seen as a flaw. Only Piers was exempt. It did not occur to Susanna that Gervase figured nowhere on her list.

She was just beginning to feel better when, as once before, Piers met her on the stairs and offered her his arm. She smiled at him gratefully. Stairs were still a problem, but it was a problem far less demanding than the need to see him and speak to him. Her love for him welled up inside her, and all the nightmarish memories of the encounter with Dame Constance—who had been unnervingly pleasant and normal ever since—were wiped out. It was like being filled with sunlight.

After a flashing glance up at him, she lowered her eyes to the stairs leading to the courtyard and the refuge she sought in the Lady's little garden. They moved together, unspeaking at first, her hand on his arm and the sides of their bodies touching, then, 'My darling,' he murmured. 'My love.' She felt herself in heaven.

And then he went on, low-voiced, 'What are we to do?' and the radiance was dimmed.

'Do?' she repeated blankly, as if it were a word she had never heard before, a concept that had no meaning.

She was so innocent, so adorable, so blissfully happy in the here-and-now of their love, but Piers had been torturing himself with thoughts of the morrow. It was not in his nature to sit back and let things take their course. If they were to carry their present delight in each other forward into the future, planning was essential—and an appreciation of the difficulties.

He phrased these as simply as he could, smiling down at her. 'My dearest, you are contracted to marry Gervase, who also happens to be one of my oldest friends. If I were to steal his betrothed, it would present not only legal difficulties but appalling personal complications in more relationships than ours. I love you enough to face

219

all that, but do you love *me* enough?'

'Of course.'

'Have you thought about it?'

She hadn't. She had been lost in her private wonderland, into which harsh realities did not—could not—intrude. 'Why do we have to do *anything*?'

If they had not reached the courtyard by then, so that they were in full public view, he might have taken her in his arms and kissed her brimming blue eyes and said, 'Leave everything to me,' but it would not have been a solution. 'What do *you* want to do?'

'I don't know.' All she knew was that she was not prepared to be tipped off her idyllic rose-tinted cloud. Everything had suddenly become too much for her. She didn't want to do anything. She didn't want to think. She only wanted to *feel*. 'I just want to see you.'

'That will not be easy.' He had been wondering how to break it to her. 'My father is sending me back to Lanson. He has been neglecting the stables and the stud in the interests of Vine Regis. And I'm afraid I have to go, my darling.'

'Oh, no. No! No! I can't bear it.'

'I'll come to Vine Regis often, I promise.'

In the end, he left her in the scented garden, wide-eyed and shocked, surrounded by thyme and rosemary, mignonette and pinks.

After a while, the tears drying on her cheeks, she began to find the sweetness oppressive. And when she tried to resurrect her lovely dreams, they came with horrid realities attached. What could she do? What should she do? Her betrothal to Gervase was as binding as marriage; her love for

Piers something apart. She must think. She must think!

Before Piers, she would have said that she was resigned to the belief in which she had been reared, that life was simple as long as one submitted to the laws of God and the Church.

The laws of God didn't have much to say about domineering mothers-in-law or future husbands who, when complained to, replied, 'I know she always behaves as if she is right, but the truth is that she *is* always right. If you ever question what she says, you discover that, unlike most of us, she has thought everything through before she speaks.' But even as she had tried to think of some way of easing Dame Constance out of Vine Regis, Susanna had come to realise that there was truth in what Gervase said.

Resigned though she had been to marrying to suit her father and the Church, she had been disappointed by the Church's definition of the meaning of perfect love between husband and wife. A wife's love was said to be perfect when she was blinded by her feelings, so that she sincerely believed that nobody was wiser, stronger, or handsomer than her husband; when she was pleased by everything about him; when she found everything he did or said to be right and just.

If the husband had been Piers, she would have had no difficulty with any of that, however much she might regret that the Church required no more of a husband than that he reciprocate his wife's 'perfect' love with merely 'moderate' love, which was never to be too ardent but just well-tempered and measured.

At first, the longer Gervase had stayed away, the

more Susanna had found herself hoping that he was not being ardent with some other woman in London, though now she knew that, if it had been Piers, she would have had no doubts on that score, because she believed his love to be as 'perfect' as her own.

But it was marriage, not love, that was the issue. She was legally committed to Gervase. If only—*if only*—he did not go to war! If only he had made some personal impact at Court, or even only in the discussions of the barons! That would be good for him, she thought. An awareness of success there might give him the strength to look for success closer to home. And although, now that the air had been cleared, Susanna was beginning to feel better about her own relations with Dame Constance, it did not for a moment diminish her desire for Gervase to take up his proper role at Vine Regis as Lord of the Castle, with herself, of course, as his Lady of the Castle, as was her destiny.

Gervase! Piers!

Suddenly, everything came together in a cold, clear light. Not a solution, but the knowledge that she had lost touch with herself. She had been behaving unnaturally ever since she had arrived at Vine Regis—showing off, at first, in an attempt to impress. Then, overawed by Dame Constance, desperately self-conscious and adopting her much-criticised mannerisms as a kind of defence. And now possessed by the madness that was her love for Piers, with all sanity, all sense of balance, flung to the winds.

What to do?

She had relied on instinct to guide her during these last months, and instinct had failed her badly. She must mend her ways. She wasn't clever, but when she set her mind to some ordinary problem she was perfectly competent to deal with it. It was just that—she heard herself give a little wail—*this* problem wasn't ordinary. She knew she needed advice and there was no one at Vine Regis she could talk to, certainly not Isabelle or Dame Constance. Never Dame Constance! She would have to write to her mother.

6

Just before Compline, she sat down with quill and parchment to compose a letter that would reassure her mother as to her general contentment at Vine Regis, while asking for the guidance she needed.

> *Most well-beloved mother,*
> *I have not written before because of the difficulty of having my letter delivered to you, but you will wish to know that I am well. Everyone at Vine Regis is very kind to me. It is a huge castle with great estates, and I have learned a great deal. The Lord Gervase is a pleasant gentleman, who earlier in the summer was called away to Court, which was very exciting for us all. He even attended the royal coronation. He might have to go away to war soon, though we hope not.*

She stopped suddenly, preparing to write about something that was intensely private and aware of a difficulty she had not foreseen—the trustworthiness of her messenger.

She had meant to ask William ro ride to Cernwell with her letter and bring back her mother's response, but William could read perfectly fluently and would have no hesitation in scanning what she had written. Susanna could not bear the thought of him knowing her feelings. She could put the important part in cypher, she supposed, but all that would do would be to tease him into decoding it and any cypher that her mother would understand would, in any case, have to be of the simplest. No, she would have to send old Tom, who had never learned to read. But he was the slowest thing in Creation, and would probably get lost on the way. Perhaps she could send both of them, entrusting the letter itself to her groom, who had always disliked William and would never let him see the letter except on pain of death. With a sigh, she resumed her writing.

But I am now in something of a dilemma, because in Lord Gervase's absence I have fallen very much in love with a local gentleman whose name is Piers Whiteford, and he is in love with me too. I cannot live without him. I do not know what to do and I am writing to you, my dearest mother, for guidance. Please let me have your advice as soon as you can.
Your most dutiful and loving daughter, Susanna

7

'Why should I take old Tom?' William demanded. 'I'd get there and back a whole lot faster alone.'
'Even if you have to take time to read my letter

on the way?' said Susanna tartly.

'Would I do that?'

'Of course you would.'

He pursed his lips and sniffed loudly. 'What's so private about it, anyway?'

She had an inspiration. Dropping her eyes modestly, she said, 'There are certain things—feminine things—which one does not usually talk about, but on which a young woman may wish to ask for advice from her mother.'

'Oh.' He stared at her for a moment, his colour slowly rising. 'Oh,' he muttered again. '*Women's things.*'

'Yes, William. *Embarrassing* women's things, which you wouldn't understand!'

'Oh, all right. I won't read your letter, then.'

But she still made him take old Tom with him.

8

Matilda of the Eyebrows was in charge of the raw wool, but when Susanna went to collect a supply for spinning she found her in a state of mild distraction.

'The Lady's best girdle, the silver-gilt one set with pearls—it's lost. She only wears it on special occasions, and I can't think where it has got to. It should be in its box inside her painted clothes chest, but the box is empty.'

'Have you looked all through the chest?'

'Of course I have! I have had everything out on the floor, searching, but there's no sign. I don't understand it.'

'She couldn't have put it somewhere else?'

225

'No, or not without telling me.'

'Is it valuable?'

'Yes. And it has a sentimental value for her, too. It was a wedding gift.'

Susanna said, 'I . . .' and then shook her head. 'No, never mind. It's nothing.' Which wasn't true, but she needed time to think.

Gratefully, she accepted Matilda's offer of help in tying the clump of raw wool to her distaff, a knack she had never mastered. 'I always make it too tight or too loose,' she said, 'and then either the spindle refuses to turn or the whole thing collapses.'

'And you don't want the children teasing you about it, do you?'

Startled, Susanna looked up and observed an understanding gleam in Matilda's eye. It made her feel much better. So she smiled and said, 'No, I don't!' and limped off in the direction of the schoolroom.

Reaching it, she found the girls sitting there under Anna's eye, looking seraphic while doing their best to irritate the patient gentlewoman by misusing the miniature distaffs that Hamish MacLeod had whittled for them.

Anna said, 'Blanche! You must not hit the spindle like that! You are not playing with your spinning top now.'

'It makes it go round quicker.'

'But it is jerky, which means the spun wool will not be as smooth and even as it should be.'

'Oh, pooh!' said Blanche. 'Who cares about that?'

Susanna knew that their mother had been fair-complexioned and that both children resembled

226

her in looks. In temperament, however, Eleanor was very much a smaller version of her Aunt Isabelle, whereas Blanche . . .

For the last day or two Blanche had clearly been looking for mischief and Susanna was preparing to speak to her sternly but, before she could say anything, the child danced across to her, exclaiming, 'What a lovely big fluffy ball of wool you've got! I want to pat it and cuddle it!'

Reaching up, she began stroking it and sinking her fingers into it.

There was a slight clatter as something fell to the floor, and she jumped back with an unconvincing giggle. 'Oooh! What's that?'

It was one of Susanna's rings. 'It must have slipped off your finger into the ball of wool,' Blanche exclaimed. 'Didn't you notice you'd lost it?'

Susanna knew very well that she had lost it, and that it had not slipped off her finger into the wool. She held out a hand. 'I will have the other two back, as well, please.'

The child's surprise seemed genuine. 'The other two?'

'Three of my rings were missing. You remember, I was looking for them the other day.'

'Oh, *those* rings!'

'Yes, those rings! Now I want the other two—my favourite with the balas rubies, and the one with the sky-blue sapphire.'

'*I* haven't got them!'

'Come along, Blanche. You can't play that trick more than once. The others, please.'

'I haven't *got* them.' The child stamped her foot. 'I haven't, I haven't!'

227

Eleanor put a sisterly arm round Blanche's waist and, in her usual small voice, confirmed, 'She hasn't. Truly.'

Susanna thought, but did not say, 'Then who has?' One ring she might have lost, but not three. It would have been more comfortable to disbelieve the children's protestations of innocence, because the alternative to childish mischief was grown-up theft. And not only of Susanna's rings but of the Lady's valuable girdle—which Blanche would admittedly never have dared to touch.

She smiled at the flushed and tearfully furious child and said, 'I'm not going to eat you, my pet. We must try and think where the other rings can have got to.'

Blanche sniffed noisily. 'Just because I'm little, I always get the blame.'

'No, of course you don't. Come here and give me a hug, and let's be friends again.'

After a moment, Blanche obeyed, though with no great show of enthusiasm.

9

Susanna worried away at the problem of who she could talk to about her suspicions, and eventually decided that there was no one but Isabelle. She should have gone straight to Dame Constance, but didn't dare.

'I don't want to annoy her again by seeming foolish,' she told Isabelle. 'It's easy enough for rings to get lost, even for your mother's girdle to be mislaid, but both at once?'

'At least we can't hold Gervase at fault this time,

228

after that stupid affair over the missing cups and platters when he went off to Westminster,' Isabelle murmured. She brushed a hand over her amber skirts. 'How I dislike spinning. These horrible little crimpy threads stick to everything, and make me cough, too.' Then with neither pause nor change of tone, 'Have you questioned your women?'

'Yes, of course. Well—indirectly. It's not something one can ask about outright.'

'Mmmm. I don't think I myself have mislaid anything of value, but John was complaining about a missing cloak brooch. The St George one, you must have noticed it. He thinks he may have lost it when he set out for Stanwelle the other day, but can't remember whether he was even wearing it to start with. *Just* like him!'

'Oh, dear.'

'The trouble with a place like this,' Isabelle said, 'is that there are too many people. Half the time, it's only by accident that you find out what is going on. You need to trip over a corpse before you discover that someone has died.'

'Isabelle! What a dreadful thought.'

'It was meant to make you smile, instead of sitting there looking so miserable.'

Susanna said disconsolately, 'Well, it didn't. But your mother probably knows, anyway? I'm sure she is aware of everything that goes on.'

'In general. But most of us mislay something now and again, and she doesn't necessarily know about it unless it is specifically mentioned to her.'

'You mean, she wouldn't know if there happened to be a spate of small losses.'

Isabelle smiled with relief. 'Well done, Susanna. That is exactly what I mean. So, if you want your

229

suspicions confirmed, what next?'

Susanna sat down with a thud on the window ledge and massaged her ankle with a soothing hand. It still ached at the slightest provocation. 'I suppose I will have to go round talking to people, finding out if there *is* a spate of small losses or whether it's just coincidence. Will you help me?'

True to form, Isabelle extricated herself gracefully from a project requiring the expenditure of effort. There was also enough of her mother in her to feel that Susanna should be encouraged to take responsibility. 'You should try John. He can talk to the men more innocently than you or I could.'

She was quite right, of course, when Susanna thought about it. 'Yes, I suppose so,' she said. 'It would look very suspicious if you or I started questioning the men, and I don't want to stir up a fuss unnecessarily. Thank you.'

10

For the next few days, Susanna found herself watching John like a mother hen with only one chick. When he wasn't gossiping with anyone, she willed him to start and, when he was, she was unable to tear her eyes away as she tried to guess what was being said. When she drifted unobtrusively closer, she usually found that they were talking about horses.

He knew what she was up to and, boyishly, was determined to keep her in suspense. Grinning mischievously at her, he was taken aback by the intensity of the look he received in return. Not for the first time, it struck her how unlike his brother and sister he was; he had none of Gervase's detachment or Isabelle's languor. With a small gust of irritation, she reflected that he had more in common with Blanche.

For the briefest of moments, she had a glimpse of why Dame Constance might be so tolerant of the pair of them, disarmed by the vitality that set them apart from the laconic Gervase and Isabelle. And then her perception was dimmed again by the problems she faced in having to deal with them.

'Well, why shouldn't we be talking about horses?' John demanded. 'Guy Whiteford is doing some very clever breeding. The late king had extensive stables and a good few running horses, and Guy believes that racing has a future. We're all interested in his results. You should ride out some morning and watch Piers exercising the barbs.'

He had no conception of how desperately she desired even a glimpse of Piers. 'That would be interesting,' she said carelessly.

She was rewarded. Halting her palfrey at an unobtrusive distance from the broad sweep of green turf on which half a dozen barbaries were quietly circling, waiting for a signal, she had no difficulty in recognising Piers mounted on one of the first pair to set off on a gallop up the gentle slope. Even had she not been blindingly in love with him, her feeling would have been a mixture of exhilaration and pure delight. He was clad in a plain brown tunic and leggings and his mount's trappings made no more concession than its rider to the showy fashions of the time. Fast and smooth, they moved together with sleek-muscled grace, the man bent low over the horse's neck, two perfectly balanced and coordinated figures covering the ground with dazzling speed and ease. When they reined in and began to walk back down the hill, the horse was scarcely blowing at all and the man, upright now, showed his satisfaction by his very posture. He looked businesslike and effective, a man to be taken account of, and not only by the girl who loved him.

11

Old Tom was waiting to help her dismount when she and John returned to Vine Regis.

'Already!' she exclaimed. 'It has been only ten days!'

He ducked his head, smiling bashfully. 'Didn' get lost once.' Then, from the wallet at his belt, he produced a slightly crumpled piece of parchment. 'Wouldn' let Maister William see it, though he wanted to. Your lady mother says to tell you she wishes you happy.'

'Thank you, Tom. Where is Master William?'

'Gone fer to have summat to eat.'

Upstairs there would be her gentlewomen and the children, so she turned away into Dame Constance's scented garden. Her mother's letter was short and unsurprising, and the words she dreaded leapt out at her from the page.

You must be strong. You must marry the Lord Gervase as you are committed to do and put this Master Whiteford out of your mind. You say you are 'in love' with him, which simply means that you are suffering from a youthful infatuation. Do as I say, and you will overcome it. Your elders know better than you what makes a successful marriage. Believe me, my dearest daughter, it may seem cruel now but you will thank me in the end. Your loving mother.

It wasn't an infatuation! It *wasn't*. She couldn't possibly put Piers out of her mind. But her mother had more experience of the world than she had. Perhaps her love for Piers would indeed fade and die? It was a truly terrible thought.

She sat in the garden for more than an hour, arguing back and forth with herself, emotion at war with reason, but when she finally rose to go indoors she had reached a wavering conclusion. If there was the remotest danger of her love for Piers fading and dying, she must test it now. Later would be too late.

12

Next morning, John gave in to her impatience about the suspected thefts and waylaid her in the Great Hall, saying, 'You'll be *amazed*!'

'Will I?'

'Thirty—*thirty!*—brooches and chains and rings have gone missing. And everyone thought, as we guessed, that they were simply mislaid!'

'You're sure they weren't?'

'As sure as it's possible to be. I even helped search for some of them.'

Anxiously, she demanded, 'You didn't mention the word "theft"!'

'No, of course not. I know better than that. Oh,

233

and you'll enjoy this!' His grin widened. 'Even Guy Whiteford had lost a cloak chain. I helped him hunt in the stables for it, but we didn't find it, of course.'

Susanna gasped. 'How embarrassing!'

'What's embarrassing about it?'

She flapped a hand. 'Oh, nothing. Just that he is supposed to catch criminals, not be a victim.'

'Well, anyway, Piers hasn't lost anything, though he's been away so much that he hasn't given our thief much opportunity.'

'Piers?' faltered Susanna.

'Guy's son. You know him! There he is, over there. He seems to have invited himself to dinner. He came to our rescue that first day you were here, and you saw him exercising the barbs yesterday morning.'

'Oh, yes. Of course.' How *could* she put him out of her mind? He turned, and caught her eye, and smiled politely at her, and somehow she contrived to smile distantly back at him. He frowned a little.

Pulling herself together, she said to John, 'Are you quite, quite sure about all this?'

'Yes. So what do we do now?'

'I don't know! I don't suppose anyone knows where or when they lost their things?'

'Not really. Mostly, it was a case of, "I think I last wore it on such-and-such a day." Why?'

'Indoors or outdoors?'

'Everyone's in and out all the time. What difference does it make?' Then, after a moment, 'Oh, I think I see. The builders aren't allowed indoors, so in that case they couldn't be the guilty parties.'

'No. It would have to be someone creeping

234

around inside the castle. Someone we're acquainted with.' She shuddered.

'Ugh. Not a pleasant thought. We'll have to report all this to my mother, you know.'

'Yes, I know. You're quite, quite sure?'

'I said so, didn't I?'

He had no idea how important it was. Dame Constance might be grateful, or she might think Susanna was being impertinent, putting herself forward. But it was too late to back down, now, and Susanna was convinced that her suspicions were correct. So she sent a brief prayer heavenward and went off with John in search of the Lady.

13

Dame Constance, who had in general reverted to her usual calm and controlled self, nevertheless appeared to be slightly on edge when they found her. Susanna pretended not to notice, but John said, 'Are you all right, mother?'

'Yes, of course I am all right. I am only suffering from lack of sleep. I have no idea whether it is deliberate, but the builders seem to make maximum noise when they begin work at dawn, and only stop to break their fast when they are quite, quite sure that every single soul in the castle is as wide awake as it is possible to be.'

'Do they? They don't wake *me*!' said John.

'No, it would take the crack of doom to wake you,' his mother told him straitly. 'This looks like a deputation. Did you want me?'

'Susanna does.'

'Yes?'

Susanna exclaimed reproachfully, 'John!'

'Well, you started it.'

Reluctantly, shaking within, she embarked on the tale of the missing jewels, and Dame Constance listened without interrupting. When Susanna reached the end, she said with a sigh, 'I cannot fault your reasoning. I wish I could. And you have behaved very sensibly.'

Susanna's relief was almost overpowering. 'Thank you,' she gasped.

'The question is, what do we do now?'

John said, 'Find the thief, of course!'

'My clever son,' remarked Dame Constance. 'How?'

'I don't know. Why don't we ask Guy to investigate? He'll know what to do.'

'He can hardly do it formally. It would make every man and boy in the castle feel under suspicion. Their loyalty to Gervase—and the family—matters greatly to us. They deserve that we should return that loyalty, don't you think?'

Susanna was taken aback. It was something she had not considered. After a moment, she essayed, 'What about the mummers? The troubadours? The strolling singers?'

'The outsiders, you mean? The natural suspects? Yes, but there is the question of access.'

'Access?'

'Most of the men in the castle sleep communally, which would make things easier for the thief. But my girdle and your rings, Susanna? Our women would chase away any intruder who even approached our private chambers.'

'I wondered about that. But your girdle might

236

have been valuable enough to persuade the thief to take a risk, to wait until he knew your room to be empty. In the case of my rings—well, rings are easy enough to slip off. When someone takes your hand . . .'

Dame Constance's eyebrows rose and, characteristically, John exclaimed, 'Oh ho!'

Susanna hurried on, 'And, of course, a good many people have taken my hand to help me when I have been limping around these last few weeks.'

Dame Constance seemed to have lost interest. 'I think we should have a full conference later on—you two, Sir Guy, Hamish MacLeod and perhaps Guy's son Piers. Or has he gone off to Lanson? In the meantime, I intend to retire to the orchard in search of peace and quiet.'

Susanna, slightly above herself at having done something of which Dame Constance approved, had to resist the temptation to advise her to take her bodyguard with her, because one never knew what dangers might be lurking beyond the moat.

CHAPTER TEN

1

In normal circumstances, Dame Constance would have retreated to her garden in the corner of the main courtyard, with its scented beds and the canopied bench that protected her from the sun. But although the garden was separated from the building site by the whole east wall of the castle quadrangle, there were days when the noise seemed to bounce over the roofs and echo back and forth across the courtyard, so that there was little peace and quiet there.

She was sitting under an apple tree in the orchard, inhaling the perfume of ripening peaches from the south-facing wall, when Sir Guy came to find her.

'My poor dear,' he said, joining her on the grass and putting an arm round her shoulders. 'You are having a bad time, are you not?'

She smiled back at him. 'You are going to say, "Let me take you away from all this".'

'I live in hope.'

'You would be almost as astonished as my children—and my household—if I said "Yes".'

'Why don't you?'

'Perhaps, some day. When Gervase is competent to look after Vine Regis.'

'Leave him to it, my dear! He's competent enough at fighting, when you are not there to tell him what to do! In the case of Vine Regis you have

238

overshadowed him for too long. He must learn to stand on his own feet, to use his judgement and reach the necessary decisions. He will never do that while you are here, taking responsibility for everything.'

'Are you criticising me?'

He reflected for a moment. 'I suppose I am.'

'Well, don't!'

'Someone must,' he said seriously. 'For his sake, for your sake, for everyone's sake. You are too successful, too good at everything you do. You make everyone else feel small.'

'No. That is not kind!'

'It was not intended to be. But, as for Gervase, it is time you allowed him to grow up.'

'I wish he would! He is still very young in some ways—only physical action seems to wake him out of his inertia. If he would just take a proper interest in his estates, but he won't even ride out to inspect them unless I tell him to do so.'

She stopped abruptly, conscious of his quizzically raised eyebrow. 'Oh, yes—telling him what to do! And you are telling me that it is *my* fault that he lacks vitality and decisiveness and all the other characteristics he needs to manage Vine Regis? But look at John. He has those traits in abundance, although they are not fully developed yet. He was born with them. Gervase was not.'

'Well, perhaps they have some innate differences of temperament, but you have seen no need to oppress John by making him feel inferior to you.'

'Guy!'

'You hate that, don't you? I'm sorry, my dear. I know it has not been deliberate, that you have

239

been quite unconscious of it, but I'm afraid it is something that has to be said. Give Gervase a chance to gain self-assurance and he might—he *will*—surprise you.'

She studied him thoughtfully for a moment. She had always put Gervase's weaknesses down to a fault of character, but perhaps she *had* been inclined to be impatient with him. It was always so much easier and more satisfactory to do things one's self in the knowledge that they would be done properly.

She said, 'I find myself wondering whether you have an ulterior motive in speaking up for Gervase.'

'If it makes you feel more comfortable!' he laughed. 'Of course I do. I want you away from Vine Regis. I want you at home with me, at Lanson. I know Lanson is smaller, but there is less to worry about. We could be peaceful and happy there.'

'Yes.'

'I take that to mean that you agree with what I have just said about peace, rather than consenting to marry me?'

She laughed back at him, disarmed as always. 'Bless you! You know too well how to get round me. Did the children tell you about the thefts?'

He had been wondering how—or indeed, whether—to warn her of the breakers ahead for Gervase's intended marriage, but realised that he had lost the initiative. So he said only, 'Of course.'

'And?'

'With well over a hundred possible suspects, it is not an easy situation. We will have to investigate the outsiders first, but they would hardly have secreted the spoils in the pouches at their belts. So the first question is, where would they be likely to have hidden them.'

'I hadn't thought of that.'

'I don't suppose you had.'

She had picked up a fallen leaf and was shredding it with her fingers. 'There must be any number of possible places in the castle. Far too many.'

'But there are disadvantages to hiding the loot indoors.'

'Disadvantages?'

'The possibility of accidental discovery.'

'Yes.'

'And more importantly, the guilty man would still have to carry everything on his person or in his baggage when he left Vine Regis on the next stage of his travels. He would go in constant fear of discovery, and be afraid of being searched when he leaves the castle for the last time.'

'I see. So—he would choose a hiding place outside the walls? To which he could safely return to collect his booty?'

He grinned at her lovingly. 'Clever girl.'

'Thank you. A hole in the ground, perhaps?'

'You're thinking of buried treasure, which is not the same thing. Just think! Digging a hole, and opening it up for every new trinket, then filling it in again, would greatly multiply the risks of discovery.'

She gave a small moan of frustration, and he laughed. 'You sound like young Susanna!'

Her reply was a mock glare. 'Who finds you scandalously attractive.'

'No. That has worn off. She has . . .'

241

'I hope so. I lost patience with her the other evening and gave her a most unkind talking-to about her general behaviour and all those irritating mannerisms of hers. And it seems to have had some effect. She has behaved quite sensibly, even intelligently, over these thefts.'

'How frustrating for you!'

Again he had lost the initiative. But his eyes were sparkling, and she had to look away. Their light-hearted banter had been her most reliable defence over the years, but it was not always impregnable.

She fanned herself with a vigorous hand. 'This heat is unbearable. We need a good storm. How do you suggest we proceed?'

He was sitting up straight now, and looking thoughtful. 'First, we must weed out the unlikely culprits, and then watch the more likely ones with care. Let us be grateful that Susanna and John had sufficient sense not to broadcast their suspicions, so there is no reason for the thief to feel uneasy. Who do you fancy as the villain or villains?'

'I have no idea!'

'The mummers, the strolling singers, the troubadour?'

'I know nothing about any of them personally, only whether they are good at what they do— which is to entertain us.'

'If you told them all to leave, it could force a revelation and we might learn something.'

'We would certainly learn that we were very dull company without them. Which reminds me. It is high time that Susanna told that objectionable troubadour that he is no longer welcome here. She has been putting it off, because she has still to learn that postponing disagreeable tasks makes them no more agreeable.'

'And what if he is the thief?'

'Then that,' Dame Constance told him sweetly, 'becomes *your* problem.'

2

As Susanna and John sat in the alcove of the Great Hall, waiting for Dame Constance's meeting to convene, John asked in an artificially casual voice, 'Have you—er—met the Bucktons?'

Susanna struggled to recall the stream of visiting knights and their ladies who had put in a passing appearance at dinner or supper in the last few months. 'I believe I have.'

'And what did you think of Buckton's sister? The Lady Emilia. Pretty, isn't she?'

Brown-haired, Susanna seemed to remember, and desperately shy. Beyond that, the girl was a blur. 'Very pretty,' she said.

'I'm so glad you think so. It's time I was wed, and . . .'

Susanna sat open-mouthed for a moment and then sighed heavily. 'John, prettiness has nothing to do with anything. If you have marriage in mind, you should be looking for property. If you don't have marriage in mind, you should not be swooning over a lady of gentle birth.'

John was offended. 'You'd rather I went to that girl in the village, would you?'

'Which girl in the village?'

'Oh, never mind. But I would have expected more understanding from you.'

She said, 'I *do* understand, John, but you know very well that marriage is a business arrangement, first and foremost. Love in marriage is something you can only hope to grow into. It's a question of affection rather than passion, I suppose. That's what I think, anyway.'

In a snatched few words with Piers earlier in the day, she had told him what her mother had said, and that perhaps it would be wise to test the depth and strength of their love by avoiding each other's company for a time.

'Help me!' she had begged him, and had been shocked when he laughed at her and called her his beloved innocent.

The only future she could see was her yearning for him settling into something treasured in her heart, not something that could have any influence on the everyday reality of her life.

'Poor Susanna! Girls do have a harder time than men, don't they,' John said, 'with everything arranged by their parents. You'd barely even seen Gervase before you were told you were to marry him.'

'Barely?' she repeated indignantly. 'Never!'

He teased her. 'But you are learning to love him, of course.'

'I don't know,' she said slowly. 'But I can probably learn to live with him.'

3

Dame Constance, with Isabelle, Sir Guy and Hamish MacLeod beside her and William, trying to be unobtrusive, trailing along behind, arrived in time to overhear Susanna's last words.

She raised her eyebrows slightly. 'If you are talking of Gervase, I can tell you that he is on his way. A messenger has just arrived to say so. You will be relieved to know that he does not mention rushing off to France with sword in hand, but has been appointed to some office at Court . . .'

'Oh, has he?'

'He does not, unfortunately, say what. We will find out in a few days, no doubt.'

When they were seated, Dame Constance summarised what she and Sir Guy had agreed about the thefts, concluding, 'We feel that John and Hamish might have views on the likeliest suspects. Both of you are better acquainted with the entertainers than we are.'

John and Hamish nodded at each other lugubriously. 'Aye,' said Hamish. 'That fairly puts us in our place, does it not? We're the ones who hobnob with the lower classes.'

'Not at all,' responded Dame Constance serenely. 'It merely occurred to me that Hamish might have some special insights. Some member of his extensive family must surely have experience as a singer or mummer?'

Appearing to give this some thought, Hamish finally said, 'No-o-o. Callum can just about keep a tune in his head, but no more than that. His voice isn't up to much.'

'Callum?'

'My third sister's fourth husband.'

'Ah.'

'This is no laughing matter,' John told them. 'After all the trouble Susanna and I went to, you might at least take it seriously.'

William exclaimed, 'Four husbands sounds pretty serious to me.'

'Och, they're aye fighting in the glens and getting killed off.'

Susanna's attention was caught. Her mind had been diverted from the thefts by the idea of Gervase finding favour at Court, and she now tried to imagine herself working her way through four husbands. It was impossible. Two, perhaps.

She said, 'The short, fat one of the mummers always looks to me as if he has a shifty eye.'

'Yes, but he has short fat hands, too,' interposed William. 'Not a thief's hands. Too noticeable.'

Sir Guy grinned. 'A good point, young man,' and William, unaccustomed to compliments from his elders, preened himself.

Hamish said, 'I wouldny trust that wee thin singer, the fair-haired laddie with the high voice.'

'No,' agreed John. 'But he smells. You couldn't not notice him if he came too close.'

And so it went on. Even the troubadour, M. Alain, was thought to be too lofty, too self-satisfied, to dabble in petty crime.

'Talking of M. Alain . . .' Dame Constance said, her eyes on Susanna.

Reluctantly, Susanna replied, 'I know. Tomorrow.'

'Good. It seems, then, as if the task of detection falls mainly to Hamish.'

Sir Guy said, 'Yes, he must get on gossiping terms with all our suspects.'

'I'll help,' chirruped William. 'I'm good at gossiping with people. They think I'm harmless.'

Sir Guy half-smiled at him. 'Fine. Now, Hamish, you know what to look for? Anything slightly out of the ordinary. Anyone who even hints at future plans requiring more money than you would expect a travelling player to be possessed of. That kind of thing.'

'Spying, in fact.'

'If you want to see it in that way. And you and John—and William—must be wide awake for any new thefts. I'll get Piers back from Lanson by way of reinforcement. The more investigators there are, the better, because the sooner we hear of a loss, the easier it will be to track everyone's recent movements.'

John, restored to humour, declared, 'I'm going to enjoy this!' and William clearly felt the same.

Susanna sat and felt sorry for herself, torn between her passionate desire to see Piers and her hopeless attempt to put him out of her mind. Everyone and everything seemed to be conspiring against her. She pouted miserably.

And then she heard a murmur of, 'Susanna!' and saw that Isabelle was trying to glare at her. She wasn't very good at it, and after a moment Susanna stopped pouting and began giggling instead. It was infectious, and all the younger members of the company found themselves joining in.

Susanna felt much better.

4

The following day began, as so often, with trouble among the builders. The additional scaffolding had arrived from Stanwelle and the new walls had begun to rise rapidly again, but the lime mortar holding the stones was setting too quickly. It should have started off as spreadable as butter but was more like moist crumbs.

'It won't hold,' declared Master Hal, and the mortar mixer brandished his trowel, yelping, 'What do you expect, in this weather! The lime has to mature in the damp for at least a month, and keeping it damp has been hard enough for me and my men. And then, when we mix it with water and sand, the water begins to evaporate almost at once.'

'Well, put in more water!'

'You're the boss, but the stones'll slither around all over the place when they're being laid. If your men would use it a bit faster, you wouldn't have this problem.'

'They can't lay any faster than they are doing!'

'Maybe we could,' muttered a surly man beside him, one of those whose job it was to mortar and lay the stones, 'if the stones were prepared right.'

Then Master Emile came hurtling down a long ladder and, reaching the ground, also showed a tendency to yelp and wave his arms about, though not about the texture of the mortar. 'The stones! I have observed some that do not lie in the same natural layers as in the quarry. This will not do! They will not settle as they should.'

'How can we tell?' demanded the surly man, who was known as Bald John. 'It's them at the quarry, the hard hewers. They must've dressed the wrong face of the blocks. The stones aren't rightly squared off, neither. Makes them hard to lay.'

Master Emile's voice rose an octave. 'How can you tell, you ask? Have you not looked for the positioning marks? And if you cannot see them, do you not know enough to look at the grain of the

248

stone? You must remove the blocks that are not right!'

Master Hal swore under his breath. To Hamish MacLeod, an interested passerby, he remarked, 'And now we'll have to find somewhere to stack all the rejects to be carted back to the quarry.'

Hamish said, 'I'm surprised you didn't notice the fault yourself.'

'God's bones! It's only the last two or three courses, and I've been doing everything else on the site. I don't have eyes in the back of my head.'

Young William, lurking as usual, offered helpfully, 'It's true. Hal has far too much to do.'

Master Hal ignored him, as did Hamish, who said pacifically, 'You'd need eyes in the *top* of your head to see the grain from here, would you not? Och, well, I have to ride over to Stanwelle and bring back the new chaplain. I'd better get on with it before yon thunderclouds break. We look as if we're due for a storm.'

'It'll be a while yet,' opined Master Hal, glancing at the heavy grey sky before turning his attention back to the mortar mixer.

5

Much later that afternoon, having been summoned to the presence of the Lady Susanna, M. Alain de Niort found her sitting bolt upright in an alcove in the Great Hall, looking as stern as she knew how, and with scarcely an inch of flesh on display. Hamish MacLeod, back from Stanwelle, was seated unobtrusively not too far away, whittling peacefully at a new knife handle he was making and appearing to have no interest in anything else.

Even after all these weeks, Susanna still felt guilty over having, if only by implication, exaggerated M. Alain's bad behaviour that day in the wood, the day when Isabelle's husband-to-be, Master Robert Salvin, had been the true wrongdoer.

Now, she shuddered at the memory of that day, and her voice quavered almost imperceptibly as she began, 'M. Alain, I believe you have been here at Vine Regis for several months now. I do not know how long troubadours are accustomed to accept the hospitality of each place they visit, but I am persuaded that it is—er—time for you to move on.'

That wasn't too bad, she thought.

M. Alain thought otherwise. 'Move on? Why should I move on? I pay for my lodging daily by entertaining your company. That they are coarse and noisy, unable to respond to the fine quality of my music and poetry, is their misfortune. Indeed, it would not surprise me to learn that their tastes lean more towards the inane warblings of the ballad singers and common minstrels.'

Only later did Susanna realise that her haughty response reflected how deeply she herself had been absorbed into the society of Vine Regis. 'You are impertinent, sir,' she said. 'I myself, as one who knows a good deal about music and poetry, can perfectly understand why others choose not to give yours their full attention.'

She had resisted the temptation to say outright that he was not very good, but she had come close enough.

He stiffened even more, his round cheeks

scarlet. 'You demean me!' he exclaimed.

'M. Alain, I merely suggested that you go. I had no particular wish to criticise. It is you who are making an issue of it.'

He was seething, and for an unpleasant moment she thought he was about to strike her and was grateful for the reassuring nearness of Hamish MacLeod, who was poised, she sensed, to leap to his feet.

M. Alain's rosebud lips were compressed and his eyes hot as he said contemptuously, 'You are not, I believe, the Lady of the Castle. It is not for you to tell me to go.'

She gasped. 'How dare you speak to me like that! Take care, or I will have you thrown out.'

He tossed his head. 'There is no need for that. I prefer not to stay in such a place. I shall leave now, this minute.'

Without thinking, she said, 'But there is no moon tonight and a storm is coming up.'

He shrugged his shoulders as if such considerations were beneath him, then turned and stalked out.

Hamish MacLeod, looking after him, sniffed and remarked, 'I wouldn't mind searching him as he leaves, him and his wee pageboy, but Sir Guy says we wouldn't find anything hidden about his person. Aye, well, ye could be doing with a cup of wine to make ye feel better after that, my lady?'

She knew, suddenly, that she could not go on calling him 'MacLeod'. He might be a servant, and an over-privileged one, but he was a good and kindly man. So she said, 'Yes—er—Hamish. Thank you. That would be very welcome.'

He noticed, and was invisibly amused.

An hour later, buoyed by the wine as well as by her sense of achievement, Susanna watched the troubadour ride away with his page mounted behind him and his small dog running at his heels. Seeing him off, she thought, was like seeing off the most unsettled weeks of her life, as if he had come to symbolise all that had gone wrong, all the mistakes she had made, her feeling of being an outsider in her new home.

The relief was immeasurable. She found that she was smiling foolishly to herself.

CHAPTER ELEVEN

1

The storm did not break, and did not break, but the sky became black as pitch and all the candles had to be lit at supper. The heat was unbearable.

Susanna felt her hair becoming soaked with perspiration. Every few moments, surreptitiously, she had to dab at her forehead with her scarf. Her kirtle was clinging to her like a second skin. Even the sight of food revolted her. She felt ill, and the prospect of thunder and lightning, of which she had always been terrified, made it impossible for her to concentrate on what the new chaplain was saying to a Dame Constance whose face was almost as white as the barbe she wore.

Glancing round, Susanna thought that the men did not seem nearly as badly afflicted as the women, although the sweat was pouring down their temples and seeping through their shirts and doublets. Was it cooling them? she wondered. And then she was diverted by the discovery that Sir Guy was watching Dame Constance with intensity, almost anxiety.

No. He couldn't be. She was imagining things.

Father Sebastian, the chaplain, was saying, 'As you are of course aware, Lady, the world is in terminal decline and rushing toward the Judgement Day, the final and inevitable day of doom. There have been many signs of God's anger—plague, pestilence, and tempest. We know not what disaster will ultimately bring about the end of the world.'

Dame Constance moistened her lips. 'Indeed, no. Although at this present, tempest might be considered a blessing rather than a curse.'

It was verging on blasphemy, but Susanna thought, 'Yes, yes.'

A new voice intervened. It was M. Bernard, Abbot Ralph's architect who, after a few private words from Hamish at Stanwelle, had chosen to ride back with him to observe the continuing progress of the work at Vine Regis, and to assess how soon he might reasonably ask for his scaffolding back. 'The Vox Domini bell will assuredly need to be rung tonight,' he observed, 'to frighten away the evil spirits of the air that drive the storm.'

Dame Constance inclined her head slightly. 'I do not doubt that Father Hoby will have his bellringers ready and prepared.' It was said in a tone that, to those who knew her, implied that she thought Father Hoby would be not only ready but revelling in it.

Just then, all the candle flames swerved madly as a hot wind swept in from the kitchen end of the Great Hall, a wind from outdoors that presaged wild weather to come. At almost the same moment, John exclaimed, 'Rain!' Although the windows were open, so that there was no rattle against the panes, the candlelight sufficed to define the first, scattered drops falling heavily outside.

Rising to her feet, Dame Constance collected Isabelle and Susanna with her eyes and began to make her way, followed by the chaplain and architect and a few others, out of the Hall, gesturing to other members of the household to keep their seats. Susanna, conscious of looking less than her best with damp, bedraggled hair and heated complexion, kept her eyes lowered as they passed the table where Piers was seated, and missed the look which would have told her that all he wanted to do was take her in his arms and protect her.

When they reached the courtyard and went out onto the island, they found the hot wind persisting, blowing in great sweeps from the south-west. The rain was not yet a downpour, but there was enough of it, warm though it was, to promise relief at last. They stood with their faces turned towards the heavens as it fell with increasing vigour and only withdrew into the protection of the Great Gate when they were in danger of being soaked.

Dame Constance had been leaning heavily on Hamish's arm, but now he handed her over to the support of Sir Guy and hurried in to the courtyard garden to bring out a small bench which he set up at a spot sheltered from the wind but on the fringes of the rain. She sank into it gratefully and, after a moment, signed to Susanna and Isabelle to join her.

They sat there for almost an hour as the Vox Domini bell clanged out, uneven and deafening, while the thunder and lightning came ever closer. At one stage there was a momentary silence and they heard, faint and far away, the bells of Stanwelle also ringing out and knew that every bell for miles around would be tolling to defeat the storm.

At last the point came when Susanna was no

255

longer able to control her nervous shudders, and Dame Constance said, 'There is no shame in fearing thunder. Would you prefer to go indoors?'

'Yes—oh!—I think so. If you wouldn't mind?'

When she reached her chamber, she found it in possession of the children, who were wide awake and perched on the window sill with hands stretched out to catch the raindrops. Fortunately, the sill was deep and Anna and Margot were there to make sure they did not fall.

'Ooh, you're all wet,' Blanche exclaimed. 'Anna wouldn't let us come down and get wet, too, though we wanted to.'

Just then there was a great peal of thunder almost overhead, and Susanna was unable to control her sharp intake of breath. Eleanor's small voice said, 'Don't you like thunder?'

'No, not very much.'

'I don't either, and Blanche just pretends she doesn't mind it. But she does, really.'

Susanna smiled weakly. 'Oh dear. Perhaps we should all sit down and hug one another, and play some game to occupy our minds. What do you think?'

'No,' Blanche said bravely. 'I'd better go and get *my* bell.' Reaching out for Margot's hand and clinging to it, she marched from the room.

Eleanor said, 'She has a little bell that's been blessed, just like the one St Salaberga had for her daughter Anstruda, who was frightened of storms—you remember? If we ring it in here, it might help to keep us safe and drive the storm away.'

'Yes,' Susanna replied. 'Perhaps it might.'

They took it in turns to ring the little handbell

and tried to persuade themselves that the storm was not moving back and forth above the castle as it seemed to be, but passing, however slowly. Susanna, exhausted, found herself wishing the children would fall asleep so that she herself might lie down and try to shut out the noise and the blinding flashes from the heavens.

But before that could happen, there was a flash of lightning directly overhead followed by a sound quite distinct from the sounds of the storm. The sound of falling stones.

The sound of a wall crashing down.

2

'Blood,' said Hamish.

He was on his knees under the pale morning sky beside a pile of fallen masonry and his eyes and his voice were grim.

The top few courses of the newly built outer skin of the wall—the courses whose mortar had been deemed unsatisfactory—had blown down at the height of the storm, taking with them a wedge-shaped section of the previous work where the rubble filling had not yet set. There was a stain at the foot which, partly washed-out though it was by the rain, could not be mistaken for anything other than what it was.

'Is anyone missing?' Dame Constance asked tightly, but no one was, though it took more than two hours to be sure of it.

In the meantime, someone—no one knew who—had muttered the words, 'building sacrifice', and they had taken possession of everyone's mind.

257

If there had been an ordinary accident, where was the body? There was too much blood to speak of anything but death. A body there must be.

Sir Walter said, 'I would have expected a traditional blood sacrifice to take place *before* building work began. Indeed, I was surprised that Master Emile did not insist on it.'

Dame Constance said, 'Yes.' She, too, had been surprised and also relieved, though she understood that, in these modern times, the blood for baptising new buildings in the name of the Lord was usually supplied by a pig or a lamb.

She glanced at Sir Guy, who was frowning thoughtfully. 'It is possible,' he offered, 'that someone may have taken the recent difficulties on the site to be a consequence of there having been no such sacrifice in the earlier stages. A case of better late than never.' But he was clearly unconvinced.

John, who had his own priorities, broke in with, 'Can't we discuss this over breakfast? I'm hungry.'

It was a welcome diversion, although Dame Constance did her best to look disapproving.

When they were settled at a table in the Great Hall, John demanded, 'Who cares whether the building goes up or not?'

'I beg your pardon?'

'Don't look at me like that, mother. It was a perfectly serious question.'

'And an intelligent one,' contributed Sir Guy.

'Indeed?'

'Well, who *does* care?' said John.

'I do, of course.'

'Obviously,' exclaimed her son. 'But who else? Who cares enough to shed blood for it?'

258

She was silent for a moment. 'Ah, I think I understand. Though I wish I did not. No, no. It was an accident. It must have been.'

'Then where is the body?'

She sighed heavily. 'I have no idea. Your reasoning, I take it, is that the only people who would need the—er—assistance of a blood sacrifice would be those who have responsibility for the works. Whose reputation depends on their success?'

'Yes.' John threw down his knife and sat back. 'I would have said Walter, except that everything that goes wrong is a source of pleasure for him. He loves to imply that he'd do a much better job than Master Emile.'

Dame Constance knew that Guy thought the same, and certainly Sir Walter had detested the master mason right from the beginning, even before he had been struck by falling rubble, and almost crushed by a block of masonry. Dame Constance found herself wondering for the first time whether those had been the accidents they seemed. 'And if not Sir Walter?'

'Then it must be Master Emile himself, mustn't it? Everything that's gone wrong has cast a slur on his reputation, which means the world to him. He probably feels he needs all the help he can get.'

'I cannot believe it,' said his mother. 'Such a flimsy little man. Surely he would not go to the length of murdering someone!'

'First,' said Sir Guy, 'we need to know who, *if anyone*, is dead!'

Dame Constance gazed back at him, meeting the challenge in his eyes even while conscious of a powerful desire to weep. 'Very well,' she said after

259

a moment. 'Let us go and investigate further.'

3

'*Non, non, non!*' Master Emile was declaring. '*C'est ridicule, monsieur! Ignorance crasse!*'

'No such thing,' replied Sir Walter with all the hauteur at his command. 'Quicklime destroys, slaked lime preserves. The lime kiln has been soaked by the rain, therefore the lime has been slaked. Therefore anything—any *body*—hidden therein will be preserved. The kiln must be dug out and searched.'

'*Non, non, non!*'

Dame Constance glanced round in search of Master Hal, who appeared to have detached himself from this particular confrontation and was supervising a preliminary sweeping up of the site. Like everyone else he looked weary and pallid after the sleepless night and she could understand his preferring not to be involved.

The Stanwelle architect, however, was there to put his inferiors right. 'One has no personal experience of destroying or preserving bodies, of course,' he stated magisterially, 'and lime is a dangerous substance when heated. But I believe that Sir—ah—Walter overstates the dangerous qualities of quicklime. Slaked lime, on the other hand, is undoubtedly harmless *except* when the act of slaking takes place. Water thrown on hot quicklime generates a brief but intense and highly destructive burst of heat.' He stopped, as if there were nothing more to be said.

'So are you telling us,' John asked, after a

260

moment, 'that for anything such as a body to be destroyed, it would have to be in position before the rain reached the lime?'

'One might so infer.'

'I do not,' said Dame Constance forcefully, 'believe any of this! It seems to me that you have all gone mad. Ah, there you are, Susanna. I hope the children are safely out of the way?'

'Yes, Lady. They are still fast asleep, as I was until an hour ago. What has happened? Was someone hurt when the wall collapsed? Who could have been out of doors in such terrible weather?'

She was startled to see Sir Guy and Dame Constance exchange glances. Had she said something clever?

It seemed that she had. 'That,' remarked Sir Guy, 'is a question no one has previously asked. Well done, Susanna. We believe someone may have been killed, but no one in the castle appears to be missing. The workmen also seem to be accounted for, though I have little faith in Master Emile's assurances in that direction. On the whole, the workmen sleeping in the mason's lodge seem likelier candidates than anyone in the castle. Any one of them might have ventured out to relieve himself.'

'Perhaps we should ask Master Hal,' Hamish suggested.

Waved over to join the little group, Master Hal said, 'If I may advise, I believe you should stand further back from the wall. There may still be some loose rubble liable to fall.'

They all moved back. Hamish, glancing up, asked, 'Should ye not go up on the scaffolding and find out?'

261

'Not until I have made sure the scaffolding itself is stable, though it probably is. But the planks have been blown off.'

Master Hal looked like a worried man, but that was understandable in the circumstances. Sir Guy said, 'Are we quite sure that all the workmen have been accounted for?'

'There were four missing this morning,' Master Hal replied, rubbing his eyes wearily, 'but it turned out they had all gone down to the village before the storm broke in search of more comfortable beds. Now, if you'll excuse me, I have a lot to do.'

'Yes, of course,' said Dame Constance, 'but I think we may need some of your men to move the fallen stone in search of . . .'

She was halted by an exclamation from Susanna. 'It's . . . that's . . . oh dear!'

'*What* is "it"?' enquired Dame Constance a little crisply.

Susanna pointed and they all turned. A small dog had come running round the corner from the gatehouse to sniff at the fallen masonry—a small tan-coloured dog with a sharp snout and an erect and feathery tail which Susanna had seen before. She said, 'It's the troubadour's dog. It went with him when he left. Yesterday.'

'The Lady Susanna is right,' Hamish said. 'And not just the dog.'

A few swift strides took him to the corner from which the dog had appeared. There were the sounds of a scuffle and an unmistakably human yowl and when Hamish returned he had a damp and unhappy pageboy by the ear.

The boy, having been fed on the instructions of Dame Constance and fitted out with some dry clothes, was perfectly prepared to talk. In fact, it was hard to stop him.

'Never spoke to me, he didn't, not properly. Never told me anything. But yesterday we hadn't ridden far before he said, "I've forgot summat. Have to go back." I said, "What about the storm?" but he paid me no heed. I was scared, all that noise and the flashing lights in the sky. I'd have run away if I'd had anywhere to run to, but it were safer staying with him.'

Susanna thought, poor boy! He couldn't be more than about ten years old and it must have been terrible for him to have to be dependent on someone like the self-centred and self-satisfied M. Alain. *Poor* boy!

'Well, I don't think he'd forgot anything really,' the poor boy went on. 'I think he was just coming back to collect something he shouldn't, and the storm meant he'd stand less chance of being caught. A thief, that's what he was. Didn't think I knew, but I did. Well, I ask you. All them rings and brooches! Anyway, we came back, and that's when the wall fell on him. Can I have some more of that cheese? I'm still famished.'

Mutely, Dame Constance signed to John who went off towards the kitchen archway shouting, 'Master Robert! More cheese, please.'

'You saw exactly what happened, did you?' asked Sir Guy, and the boy nodded, his mouth once more full of bread and cheese.

'Tell us.'

'Well, drawbridge were up so he left me and the horse on the other side of the moat, and found himself a plank and poled himself across. And then he went to the new wall, and there was a flash and I *think* he shifted one of the stones and stuck his hand into the gap. And then there was this huge crash and the wall fell on him.'

'And what did you do?'

'Ran away, o' course. I reckoned he were sure to be dead.'

John said, 'And you've been hiding in the woods ever since, have you?'

'Aye. But then the dog got away and I was trying to catch it.'

'What about the horse?'

'Still in the woods. I'm not big enough to ride him.'

Sir Guy said, 'Did you see anyone else?'

'No, my lord. 'Twere only him and me. Didn't see no one else at all.'

5

Dame Constance said, 'An accident, then. Not a blood sacrifice. Well, that is a relief.'

William couldn't hold his tongue. 'Not a murder, either,' he said. 'I mean, you couldn't rely on lightning striking at exactly the right moment.'

Susanna, remembering his doubts about the two previous accidents involving Sir Walter, looked at him, frowning thoughtfully, but everyone else ignored him.

Dame Constance resumed, 'Sir Guy, perhaps you would explain everything to Sir Walter, and then I think we must take Master Hal into our confidence.'

'Not Master Emile?'

She grimaced. 'Yes, I suppose so, although I have very little faith in him. It is the excellent Master Hal who will finish up doing the work, as always.'

Master Emile, rubbing a fragment of the fallen masonry between his fingers, did indeed conclude that the labour of clearing up should be left to Master Hal, while he himself devoted his mind to the best way of repairing the damage so that the main structure remained sound. It was a challenge, he declared, which only a fully fledged master mason was competent to meet.

M. Bernard, not quite repressing a snort, indicated to Master Emile precisely how much of the surrounding wall would have to be removed and rebuilt, and Master Emile, failing to repress an answering snort, thanked him for his advice and declared his intention of marking out a very much wider and shallower area for demolition. M. Bernard rode off back to Stanwelle in a supercilious rage.

Dame Constance summoned her treasurer, who had agreed the original contract with Master Emile, and demanded to know whether she would be within her legal rights in dismissing him. She was told no. The thunder had been an act of God and not the master mason's responsibility, and there was no compulsion on him to agree with the opinion—which was only an opinion—of an outside expert, even if he did bear the title of *magister cementarius*.

'You dare laugh!' she challenged Sir Guy, who

was fighting a strong desire to do just that.

'It is not your troubles that delight me. It is the expression on your face. I don't think I have ever before seen an expression of such concentrated exasperation.'

'Well, you may stop being delighted and offer me some solution!'

He could not resist. 'As I recall, Susanna has always wanted to take over as Lady of the Castle . . .'

She stared at him for a moment and then, suddenly cordial, said, 'What an excellent idea. I must think about it.'

They were standing on the grass on the relatively quiet west side of the castle, across from the orchard which had also suffered in the storm. Much of the fruit, already ripe, had fallen to the ground and Dame Constance hoped that Master Robert would soon set someone to collect it for present sauces and future preserves. Dried apples and peaches and plums were invaluable in the kitchen.

She said, 'Do you have an orchard at Lanson? I don't recall.'

The logic of her thoughts escaped him, and he frowned and was just saying, 'Yes, of course, on the south-facing side of the hill behind the manor,' when Master Hal appeared before them. He was bearing a small leather bag, dusty and damp, its neck drawn tight with cord.

'We've cleared all the fallen masonry and found no trace of a body,' he said, 'but we discovered this in a gap in the stonework in the third course up from the ground.'

'A gap?'

'Scaffolding hole.'

Sir Guy was more interested in the absence of a body than in the presence of a bag, but he stopped Dame Constance before she could loosen the cord at the neck and peer inside at its contents. After a moment of careful study, he handed it back to her and she opened it and found that it was weighted at the bottom with her pearl-studded girdle but did not contain nearly as many rings and brooches as she would have expected. She frowned.

'More mysteries,' Sir Guy was saying to the journeyman.

'Yes. The troubadour must have had an arrangement with one of our builders to leave extra space behind that particular hole. Clever of him.'

'But you or Master Emile might surely have been expected to notice?'

The younger man shrugged. 'There is inevitably some unevenness in the laying of the first few courses, and we cannot inspect every single stone. Otherwise the work would never be done.'

It sounded reasonable.

'It would, however, be useful to know which of the men laid that course of stones.'

'I suppose so. It might have been Bald John,' Master Hal murmured reflectively, 'but I can't be sure. I'll try and find out, though I can promise nothing.'

Sir Guy thought, but did not say, 'We still lack a body. Where is it? And, above all, why is it not where one would expect it to be?'

And then a trumpet sounded in the distance.

'Can it be?' Dame Constance wondered.

It could.

By the time Gervase and his retinue reached the drawbridge, Susanna had descended to the courtyard again and emerged from the gatehouse in a rush, somewhat out of breath but remembering her dignity just in time. She sailed across to greet her betrothed with nervous politeness.

'Well, what a night *that* was!' said Gervase, tossing his reins to his groom. 'I was pleased I had decided to stop at Wellcombe instead of riding on. I'm glad to find Vine Regis still standing. You are looking charming, my dear Susanna. I hope you are well? And my lady mother?'

But his mind was obviously elsewhere, and as the tail of his retinue wound into sight Sir Guy gave a sharp exclamation. Draped over the saddle bow of one of the grooms' mounts was what looked like a drowned body.

Gervase glanced at him and then told Susanna. 'I believe you should go indoors. You too, mother.'

Neither of them showed any inclination to obey but preferred to continue standing, gazing in horror and distaste at the remains of the young man whom they had not liked, but who had not deserved to die.

After waiting hopefully for a moment or two, Gervase resigned himself. To Sir Guy, he said, 'I think it's that troubadour fellow, isn't it? The one who couldn't sing? We found him in the river a mile or two back. Looks as if he took a battering on the rocks.'

'Not on the rocks. The wall fell on him and almost certainly killed him. How, I wonder, did he get into the river?'

'No idea,' said Gervase. 'You're the expert on that kind of thing. Maybe the wall didn't kill him but just set him staggering around, so that he fell in and drowned. Wouldn't surprise me. That's the kind of thing that happens.'

Whistling absently under his breath, Sir Guy replied, 'Maybe.'

Dame Constance turned gratefully as Hamish's voice from behind said, 'Ye'll be wanting Father Sebastian to take charge of the poor man, will ye not?'

'Yes,' she said. 'He will have to make the necessary arrangements, otherwise we will be standing here all day, uselessly speculating. Please be so good as to fetch him. Now, come indoors, Gervase, and tell us what has been happening and all about your new Court appointment.'

'If you're sure,' he said doubtfully.

'Go ahead,' Sir Guy told him. 'I'd like to have a closer look at the body. I'll follow you later.'

'All right. Fine.'

But Gervase seemed less relieved to have matters taken out of his hands than he would formerly have been. His mother found it interesting.

7

'I have been appointed as a Chamber knight to the king,' Gervase said airily.

269

'How wonderful,' exclaimed Susanna, and then, 'What's that?'

'It means I have to keep him company, and act as his equerry, and generally run around after him.'

'Why you?' enquired his mother, and was much entertained to receive a reproving glance from Susanna, who was determined to behave as she ought.

Gervase, characteristically, had given that question no thought. He had simply been pleased to be asked—although the asking had been more like ordering. Now, he said, 'I would have preferred to join the expedition against France that Thomas of Woodstock is recruiting for, but the council was setting up the king's household and I suppose they thought it would be good for him, since he's just a boy, to have young Chamber knights around him rather than older ones. They did interrogate me, though, to make sure I was responsible and reliable. And it did no harm'—he grinned unexpectedly at John—'that I happened to have a younger brother whom I was accustomed to keeping in order.'

This struck his nearest and dearest as exquisitely funny, and Sir Guy, rejoining them, found them all laughing as if they had not a care in the world.

'Just the man I need,' said Gervase. 'The young king is very interested in horseflesh and discovered, when he was giving me my first audience, that I am, too. So I am to have a special role, acting as his intermediary with the royal Master of the Horse.'

'Is it still Bernard Brocas?'

'No. He's going off to be Captain of Calais.

There's a new man, Thomas de Murrieux. All I know about him is that he's from Suffolk. As far as I can tell he'll hold the title while I do the work.'

'Interesting work, though. I know one or two small studs you could go to for special mounts for the Court, but the royal studs should supply you with all the coursers and amblers you need. Otherwise, there's the horse market at Smithfield, and I'd advise you to take a trip to Prague. But you'll have to go to Spain for North African barbs. The king will want some of those. Lovely animals. And no, you can't have mine!'

Susanna said, 'It sounds as if you'll be spending all your time at Court, or travelling around buying horses. We'll never see you here at Vine Regis.'

He had forgotten how pretty she was, and she was more refined looking than he remembered. Was it something to do with her clothes, perhaps? He didn't know. He wasn't an expert. He put a reassuring arm round her shoulders. 'It's all right, my dear. In general, I will only have to be at Court for three months, then I will have three months off to attend to my own affairs at home. And you'll like coming to stay with me at Court, won't you? You'll enjoy all the entertainments. When I left, the City was making plans for the king's first Christmas. Minstrels and torches and knights and squires. Someone dressed up like an emperor, and someone like the Pope with more than a score of cardinals in attendance. And other men with black visors looking like emissaries from foreign princes. It should be well worth seeing.'

She brightened up at once, though a little artificially. 'Oh, can I come? Will I really meet the king? How exciting! How clever you are!'

He smiled down at her and then, from the corner of his eye, caught sight of an old friend. He raised his voice. 'Piers! Haven't seen you for a while. What have you been up to?'

Piers waved back at him, but turned away, signing that he had things to do and would see Gervase later.

Susanna found herself shaking. But she didn't pout and she didn't shrug. She just felt sick with nerves.

8

The horses had to be rubbed down and turned out in the fields, and Gervase's retinue had to settle itself back into the castle, and the children had to be brought to welcome their father home, and then it was time for supper. Only afterwards did Dame Constance have an opportunity to consult with Sir Guy, Hamish, John, Isabelle and Susanna about the contents of the leather bag that the late M. Alain had returned to collect. Gervase had to be brought in and have everything explained to him.

In her private chamber, she tipped the bag's contents out on the bed and spread them over the coverlet. 'What is missing?' she asked.

Susanna said disappointedly, 'My balas ruby ring isn't there.'

Sir Guy's cloak chain was also missing, and John's St George brooch.

'What else, John? You have a better idea than anyone of the trinkets reported lost.'

He frowned heavily, trying to remember, and they gradually put together a list of what should

272

have been in the bag, but wasn't.

'It's the most valuable, or least identifiable, pieces that aren't here,' Hamish said eventually. 'The saleable ones, or the ones that could be broken up—the ones with a fair weight of gold or set with good-quality gems. So where are they? Who's got *them*?'

'Someone,' said Sir Guy, 'who had them *before* the wall fell. They weren't removed in the interval between the bag being found and Master Hal handing it over to us.'

'How do you know that?' demanded Dame Constance.

'I looked at the bag before you opened it, remember? And the dust and the damp had not been disturbed. In other words, if the bag had been opened after the storm but before you opened it yourself, it would have been apparent from the distribution of the dust and damp in the creases round the neck.'

The admiring silence following this revelation was interrupted by Gervase, who succeeded in irritating everyone, notably his betrothed and his brother, by exclaiming, 'I don't know how you can have let this happen!'

'Ho, ho!' John erupted. 'You should have been here, shouldn't you, and none of it would have happened!'

'Well, I . . .'

'And if it hadn't been for Susanna and me, no one would ever have known!'

'Yes, well . . .'

Dame Constance said, 'Susanna will tell you all about it in due course, Gervase. In the meantime, you ought not to criticise.'

But Gervase did not respond with the expected, 'Yes, mother.' Instead, he declared, 'We should set up a system. For notifying losses. Then we would know at once when something like this happens.'

Everyone stared at him.

Sir Guy gave a chuckle. 'Is that what they do at Court?'

'I don't know. But they should.' He corrected himself. 'I mean, *we* should.'

'Thank you, Gervase,' said his mother in a tone of such extravagant amiability that Sir Guy nearly suffered a relapse. 'I am sure you are right.' Then, remembering what Guy had said about her habit of overriding her son, she softened her tone and went on, with no trace of sarcasm, 'Perhaps you and Susanna could give some thought to how we might design such a system for Vine Regis?'

'Certainly, mother.' Gervase answered with aplomb, but Susanna's eyes were wide with astonishment as she murmured, 'Yes, Lady.'

'In the meantime, however, we have to decide how to resolve the present difficulty.'

Isabelle raised her voice for the first time. 'We can't just return all these trinkets to their owners, can we?'

'Why not?' Dame Constance knew perfectly well why not, but could never resist the temptation of jolting her daughter into either mental or physical effort. Not for the first time, she reflected that the sooner the marriage with Robert Salvin was finalised, the better.

'If we do return them, all at once, they'll guess about the thefts. And those whose jewels are still missing will be annoyed and—and suspicious. We don't want that to happen, do we?'

'No, we don't. So what should we do?'

'I have no idea. Find the thief, I suppose.'

'The *other* thief? The second one.'

'Yes. Oh dear, it is complicated, isn't it!'

Her mother smiled. 'Let us all go away and think about it. We can talk again tomorrow.' She began gathering up the scattered rings and brooches. 'Sir Guy, perhaps you would wait for a moment and then you can take charge of all these?'

'Certainly, Lady.'

CHAPTER TWELVE

1

Except at dead of night, there was no real privacy in a castle, not even in the Lady's private chamber, so he had to content himself with kissing her very thoroughly. Fortunately, she had removed the formal linen barbe before the family conference, which made kissing her much easier and more pleasurable.

Smiling down at her and sliding his hand inside the neck of her gown, he said, 'Some day . . .'

She shuddered lightly, deliciously, and smiled back at him with a softness that would have astonished most of those who thought they knew her.

It took longer than he would have expected for her expression to begin to lose its vulnerability, which was satisfying. 'Yes, my love?'

'Tell me.'

'What? That I love you beyond belief?'

She sat up sharply. 'Of course not. You know perfectly well what I mean.'

He gave a mock sigh. 'What *will* we find to talk about in all those trouble-free years ahead?'

'Guy!'

'Oh, very well. As I see it, the unfortunate troubadour was in league with someone else, perhaps one of the builders, perhaps not. Between them, they stole anything that was there for the stealing. M. Alain made the mistake of coming back for the bag containing his share of the spoils at the height of the storm. The second thief had already appropriated what was due to him. For some reason, someone—presumably the second thief—decided to throw the troubadour's body in the river. He was almost certainly dead beforehand, because I could find none of the outward signs of drowning. There's a kind of froth that comes from . . . No, you don't want to know the gruesome details. The question is, why try to dispose of the body? Was it too close to the jewels' hiding place, which might have exposed the thefts—which we were thought to know nothing about? Was it because the fact of the troubadour's death might have led us to investigations that could have become awkward for his associate? Or was there something more? I feel there must have been, but I have no idea what.'

'No?'

'No.'

'What do we do, then?'

'Nothing. We wait and see.'

2

Susanna had no idea what to expect when Gervase sent to say he would come and visit her just before Compline. Suddenly confronted by the physical reality of a future husband rather than the blissful dream in which she had been living, she took several deep breaths and reminded herself that her fate was sealed and there was nothing she could do about it. Then she waited.

There was no fond embrace when he arrived—though she knew that would have been too much to hope for—merely a peck on the cheek and a demand to know where she kept her writing blocks.

'We need to note down how losses and possible thefts should be reported and recorded while the subject is still fresh in our minds,' he told her. 'Sit down and concentrate, like a good girl.'

'I don't want to,' she said rebelliously. 'I want to hear all about the coronation, and what you have been doing at Court, and all about everything!'

'I sent you messages.'

'Yes. "Witnessed the coronation", "attended the king's robing", "crossed the river to Battersea". *Very* informative!'

'I'll tell you about it all in good time, and you can tell me what has been happening here. Now, to work.'

It took more than an hour before Gervase was satisfied. There would be a lost-and-found register—no mention of thefts—and the castle steward would have charge of all unidentified finds. All losses were to be reported to him, in case the items in question were already lodged with him. The junior members of the household, who could not be expected to report to someone as elevated as Sir Walter, were to report to their immediate superiors, who would in turn report to Sir Walter.

Susanna said, 'I can't imagine anyone as junior as the pageboys having anything worth stealing. Must it all be so complicated?'

'You never know. Some of the boys may have valuable trinkets from their families. No, if we are having a system, it must cover everybody at all levels of the household. And a spate of losses must be identifiable.'

'I suppose so.' She raised a hand to hide a yawn. 'Oh dear, I am so tired. The storm kept me awake all last night.'

'Mmmm?' He was busy rereading his notes.

'Gervase!'

'Yes, my dear?'

'I—er . . .'

They stared at each other blankly for a moment, neither of them with any sense of what the other was thinking, two people with no feeling for each other beyond the knowledge of a shared future. They had barely been acquainted before the months of separation, and knew each other less now.

So much had happened to Gervase since he had been away that he could scarcely remember what kind of person Susanna was. Pretty, fluffy, flirtatious, with an occasionally shrewish tongue. Although he would have preferred a quiet domestic life, it did not matter too much what kind of person she was. There was no need for him to have very much to do with her, except in bed, and then only until she produced the sons he wanted and needed.

That their relationship had greatly changed was something that, even if it had been explained to him, he would not have understood, for Susanna scarcely understood it herself. Where separation had made her more of a stranger to him, it had made him less of a stranger to her. During the early part of his absence, when she had been feeling alone and lonely, there had been reassurance in thinking about him, in magnifying his good points and minimising his failings—while

279

reflecting on how she might correct these in a suitably wifely way when the time came—and in persuading herself that his return would make everything right. He was hers, and she needed him. Or so she had thought, until she had met Piers.

And now it was too late.

Gervase said, 'We are both tired. I shall bid you goodnight and perhaps we may talk again in the morning.'

3

Wait and see, had said Sir Guy. So they waited, but did not see. Nothing happened except that for a whole week the builders became unnaturally well-behaved.

The only other factor of note was that not once did Gervase say, 'Yes, mother.'

The Gervase who had returned from Court, they soon discovered, was not the same man who had left Vine Regis in June. His mother could not tell whether those months had changed him or whether, as Sir Guy believed, they had simply brought the real Gervase—the son of Lord Nicholas—to the surface. Either way, his new personality came as something of a shock to those who had thought they knew him well.

Especially when he chose to be disparaging about the whole building project and its management. 'I am not impressed,' he began. 'Whoever designed the gunloops obviously knows nothing about warfare. Look at those on the first floor! The splays are such that using light cannon would make shooting hazardous even dead ahead.

And there's no traverse. Couldn't even use a crossbow with any comfort. And—*and!*—they're so positioned that the only thing you'd hit would be the wall of the castle itself. Shocking, that's what it is.'

Weakly, his mother said, 'But, Gervase, you saw the model before we even embarked on the works, and you didn't mention these problems then.'

'A model a few inches high!' Gervase shrugged. 'Who can tell from that? The man in charge of things ought to know better. Gunloops aren't meant to be just decorative, you know.'

Susanna murmured, 'But surely we're far enough from the coast . . .'

Gervase ignored her. 'And I'll tell you something else. I don't like all these Frenchies all over the place. Can't tell where they come from, can we? Could be from our own territories across the Channel; could be full-blooded Frenchmen; could be Burgundians. Wouldn't surprise me if they're in the pay of Charles of France and deliberately undermining things. Think how useful it would be to Charles if his troops made a *chevauchée*, a foray, towards Vine Regis, knowing in advance that it was indefensible!'

His mother said, 'Really, Gervase!'

'Besides, I would have expected the work to be almost finished by now. I know people who've built whole castles in half the time. After all, it's only a matter of piling blocks of stone on top of one another. Nothing complicated.'

His family, getting its breath back, looked at him pityingly.

'You'll learn!' John told him.

'Perhaps,' suggested his mother, 'you yourself

281

would like to have a word with Master Emile about it?'

'Yes. Why not?' And off he went.

Obedient to the Lady's expressive eye, Hamish found that he had something urgent to attend to by the Great Gate. It was not therefore entirely by chance that he happened to overhear what ensued.

'Now, see here, Master Emile, this will not do.'

If Master Emile had not been standing on the first lift of the scaffolding, Gervase would have overtopped the little man by head and shoulders. But the mason, for once at no physical disadvantage, had the courage to say, '*What* will not do, my lord?'

'You are working far too slowly. You should be finished by now. I know men who have had whole castles built in the time you have taken to raise barely half an extension.'

Master Hal, who had materialised at Hamish's shoulder, muttered, 'They must have been very small castles,' and Hamish grinned.

'I require an explanation,' Gervase continued, 'not only of your slowness, but of all these accidents which you are no doubt using as an excuse for taking so long.'

Abruptly, Master Emile's bravado deserted him. 'This has never happened to me before. I am renowned, as far away as Bohemia, for the smoothness and excellence of my work. On my sites, there are *never* accidents! I do not understand it.'

Oblivious to the little man's unhappiness, Gervase drew his own conclusion. 'You are saying that the fault is not yours? That it is Vine Regis where the fault lies?'

'What other reason can there be?'

'Nonsense. I have never heard anything so ridiculous. But if you feel like that, why do you not take yourself off elsewhere? I am sure we can manage perfectly well without you.'

'Oh, oh,' murmured Hamish. 'The poor wee man. Look at him shaking.'

Master Hal said, 'He won't go. Not voluntarily.'

Hamish, who had had a highly instructive private conversation with M. Bernard from Stanwelle two days previously, took a silent breath. 'Not involuntarily, either. The Lady would like to dismiss him, I believe, but his contract is watertight.'

'Oh. Is it?'

'Aye. But ye'll not tell anyone I said that, though, will you?'

'Of course not.'

The mason drew himself up. 'I will not go. It is my bounden duty to stay and finish the building.'

'Well,' Gervase said, 'I recommend that you finish it fast, otherwise I will have to report you to the masons' guild for failing in your duty to your clients.' He had no idea what the masons' guild did but, if there was one thing he had learned at Court, it was to sound as if he knew what he was talking about even when he didn't.

On the way back up to the Great Hall, he said to Hamish, 'What *is* the masons' guild, anyway?'

4

With an expression on his face that a disbelieving Sir Guy identified as mild embarrassment, Hamish

283

told him later in the day, 'I've stirred things up a bit. We might see some action soon.'

'Hamish, do you *know* something?'

'No, no. But there are a few wee indicators. We'll have to keep our eyes open, though. I mind when Rob—that's my second brother—tried stirring something up in the glen and made too good a job of it. Someone got murdered and Rob found himself an outlaw, though he hadn't laid a hand on anyone.'

Sir Guy breathed deeply through his nose. 'Have you ever thought of writing your family history?'

'Me? No. Dull stuff. Who'd be interested?'

5

The weather having cooled down, the mortar mixer was a happy man, or as happy as it was in his nature to be.

Not so the other workmen on the site. Master Emile began pushing them for all he was worth. Speed was what he wanted and speed he would have. But no one took him seriously, so they paid very little attention to his increasingly shrill demands. The hod carriers plodded a little less slowly up the ladders with their loads of stone or mortar; the masons scanned every block less arbitrarily for the positioning marks; the men turning the windlass that operated the hoist turned it faster but had to take more rests to compensate for the strain on their muscles; and the scaffolders, waiting to be told when to raise the next lift, amused themselves by kicking a ball around and getting in everyone's way.

Only Gervase was impressed. It was the first time he had seen action on the building site and he flattered himself that his rebuke had had the desired effect on Master Emile. No one was so unkind as to disabuse him.

Everyone else waited for the next crisis, except John, Hamish and an eager William, who were too busy keeping their ears open for any further thefts. There were none.

Piers was nowhere to be seen, and Susanna thought miserably that he must be helping her obey her mother. She wished he wouldn't.

6

Riding out with Sir Guy to his manor at Lanson, with Gervase and Susanna for company, Dame Constance sighed pleasurably at the clean, dust-free air and the silence, and said, 'I cannot believe it. Two whole weeks and no more accidents. No more thefts. Was it all that wretched troubadour's fault?'

'Wishful thinking, my love,' Sir Guy murmured.

'I know. He can hardly have arranged the accidents, and we still have the mystery of the missing jewels.'

'Arranged the accidents?' Sir Guy repeated after a reflective moment. 'I wonder. I can't see any obvious link.'

'There isn't one. I was just thinking of all the things that have gone wrong since the builders arrived. How delightful to be away from them, and how rich the countryside looks after the rain. And those fluffy little white clouds. I don't think I shall take pleasure in a cloudless blue sky ever again.'

Just then, they breasted the hill and Lanson lay before them, not a castle, but a large and friendly grey stone house, low-built, with many outbuildings and fat cattle in the fields around.

Behind them, they heard Susanna exclaim, 'Oh, how lovely. How comfortable and *human* it looks.'

'It's hardly Vine Regis, though,' responded Gervase repressively.

'No, no, of course not.'

Gervase called forward, 'Guy! Have you ever thought of building on an extension? Or adding another floor, perhaps?'

He was perfectly serious. It had always surprised his mother that he had almost no sense of the ridiculous. On the evidence to date, neither had Susanna, so they should get on well, she thought.

Guy's strangled, 'On the whole, no, Gervase,' was enough to send Dame Constance off in a peal of laughter, which astonished Susanna, who had never heard her do anything as undisciplined as laugh aloud.

Piers was there to welcome them, which Susanna had not expected. She succeeded in suppressing her small gasp of shock—delight—desperation—but the expression in her eyes gave her away to anyone who happened to be looking. Fortunately, Gervase wasn't, but Dame Constance was. Her own eyes narrowed slightly, and she cast a glance at Sir Guy who responded with raised brows and a shrug of mock ignorance, which she recognised as such. Nor had he any difficulty in interpreting the answer on her face—'I will speak to you later.'

His steward supplied them with an excellent

wine and some spice cakes, after which they were shown round the house—Dame Constance remarking that some fresh furnishings would not come amiss—and inspected the in-fields and the orchard.

Susanna, at the tail of the little procession, found her arm caught in a vibrant grip. It was Piers, passion, anxiety and frustration warring on his handsome face. 'We must arrange to meet, somehow. We must talk again.'

'How? When? What about?' she gasped nervously. She shouldn't, she shouldn't. She reminded herself that she was trying to put him out of her mind.

'Can you set out for a ride one day? With your women, of course. If you go in the direction of Amerscote, I could meet you by accident. Please, my darling.'

'Yes. All right. I will send a message to you.'

Just then, they reached the stud farm, where Susanna was able to recover her composure by declaring herself captivated by two little barbary foals.

'Gervase, could we not have a stud farm, too? Oh, *please* say yes.'

'I don't know. You can't just rear horses in your spare time, you know, and we already have plenty to do at home.'

No implied reference to whether mother might or might not approve! Sir Guy overcame the temptation to flash a delighted grin at his beloved, who was herself smothering a smile while sighing internally over what she had earlier seen in Susanna's eyes.

'Oh, but, *please*, Gervase.'

'Well, I'll think about it.'

When they set off again for Vine Regis, they were all—with the exception of Dame Constance—feeling relaxed and cheerful.

7

It did not last. It was a Saturday, and pay day for the builders. Or should have been.

But when they arrived back they found Master Emile perched on the second lift of the scaffolding with all his workers clustered on the ground below, shouting and waving their fists at him. Master Hal was standing on the first lift, holding on to the scaffolding with one hand and gesticulating for quiet with the other.

Dismounting in the courtyard, Gervase demanded of Hamish, who was lying in wait for them, 'What is all this? What is going on? Why are they all standing around instead of working?'

'They always stop at three on a Saturday.'

'Oh, do they?'

'That's when they get paid and go off to the town to spend their wages.'

'And?'

'And Master Emile says he can't pay them today.'

'Oh, can't he?' Gervase looked thunderous. 'We'll soon see about that!'

As he went marching off, Dame Constance murmured, 'I wonder why not? I clearly remember that we gave him a sum to cover the wages when we agreed the contract.'

To Sir Guy's questioning eyebrow, Hamish

responded with a look of translucent innocence which said as clearly as words, 'Nothing to do with me.' Sir Guy didn't believe him.

The arrival of Lord Gervase on the building site quietened the irate mob, partly because of his lordliness, the distinction of his tall and splendidly dressed figure—hooded green shoulder cloak over green-and-white patterned surcoat elaborately belted with gold, one leg of his hose white and the other green, and his spurs brightly gilt—and partly because they wanted to hear what he said.

What he said was, 'What's all this? What is going on?'

Master Emile shouted down at him, 'The men are angry because I cannot pay them.'

'And why can you not pay them?'

'I have not the money.'

There was a renewed howl from his workmen.

Gervase said, 'Why not? You should have.'

'There is not enough.'

Gervase looked down his nose at him, something of an achievement when the little man was standing several feet above him. 'Don't look at me as if you expect me to bail you out.'

Fortunately, Sir Guy had appeared beside him and had little difficulty in silencing the renewed uproar. The men knew him and trusted him. He said, 'Master Hal, I think we need an explanation and perhaps you might be better equipped to give it to us than Master Emile. Let us go indoors where we can talk sensibly and without interruption.' He raised his voice. 'No doubt the men will forgive us for leaving them, in the hope that we succeed in resolving the problem?'

The response was a grumble rather than a howl,

after which Bald John the stone-layer and Master Joseph the head carpenter announced that they wanted to come too.

It was agreed.

8

They trooped indoors and up the stairs, collecting John, Sir Walter and Hamish on the way and with Master Emile, whom Sir Guy had half expected to be required to leave as a hostage, trailing behind.

Arriving in the Great Hall, they found Dame Constance pretending to pore over some papers, and it seemed natural that, having been apprised of the situation, she should preside over the conference that followed.

To the disconsolate little master mason, she said, 'I believe that our advance payment to you, when we agreed the contract, included a sum sufficient to pay your workers throughout. There was even an additional sum for what were referred to as contingencies, and beyond that you declared yourself able to meet any deficit. Why, then, are you in difficulties?'

'There have been delays,' he muttered.

'We are all aware of that. But you cannot have run out of money to pay the men, surely?'

'No.'

There was a gasp of fury from Bald John and Master Joseph.

'No?' repeated Dame Constance. 'Then where is the problem? I think an explanation is required.'

'I have not run out *yet*. But I will.'

It was like drawing teeth. Turning to Master

290

Hal, she said, 'I believe we might proceed more rapidly if you explained things.'

'Yes, Lady.' He hesitated, a good-looking, fair young man placed in a situation which he did not relish. But when he spoke again, it was decisively. 'Because of all the accidents and delays, the work has proceeded more slowly than Master Emile originally estimated. It will be several weeks yet before the work is nearing completion. But there is only enough in the money-coffer for another two or three weeks' wages. Master Emile's choice, therefore, is between not paying the men at all for two weeks out of every three, or for paying them a much smaller sum than they are due for every remaining week.'

Bald John and Master Joseph both began talking at once, but Dame Constance waved them to silence. 'Was this explained to the men?'

'I—er—I don't know, Lady. Not by me, is all I can say.'

She turned to look at Master Emile, who seemed to have retreated from the discussion. 'Master Emile?' she said, and for the first time felt sorry for him. He looked like a lost child.

'This has never happened to me before,' he declared in a shaking voice. 'I am renowned, as far away as Bohemia, for the smoothness and excellence of my work. Nothing like this has ever happened in all my experience. I do not understand it.'

Gervase intervened. 'Yes, we know that. You've said it before.'

Dame Constance dropped her eyes to her hands, spreading them out on the table before her. Were the forefinger and thumb of her right hand

291

slightly more crooked than they should be? The distaff and spindle sometimes had that effect. It was a pity, because she had always been proud of her elegant hands. She sighed.

What to do?

Bald John said, 'Well, we're not working if we don't get paid.'

And Master Joseph echoed, 'No pay, no work. You'll have to find someone else to finish your extension, my lord, 'cos we're leaving. Every last man of us.'

Gervase went scarlet. Just like his father, Dame Constance reflected. She could tell that he was about to start sounding off about principles and not submitting to blackmail. Her own inclination was to submit; additional cost was the lesser evil, and there was allowance for it in her budget.

Sir Guy's cool voice dropped into the silence. 'There must be some solution.'

He was looking at Master Hal. So was Hamish.

But the answer came from Bald John.

Nodding his head towards Master Emile, he said, 'It's like this. 'E's broke all the rules of the masons' guild, and that means we're not *allowed* to go on working for 'im.'

Master Emile said faintly, 'The rules forbid you to criticise me!'

'Not if everyone knows about your faults and can testify to them. That's what the rules say— their very words.'

Curiously, Dame Constance asked, 'Do you keep all the rules in your head?'

'Well, we 'ave to, don't we? Only way we can tell if we're getting our rights. If 'e can't pay us, and my lord won't, we 'ave to leave and look for other work or find someone else to take over 'ere who *can* pay us.'

All eyes now were on Master Hal.

He flushed. 'If you are suggesting I might be the "someone else", I'm not a master mason, only a head journeyman. I can't step in just like that. The Lady would have to ask me first, and I'd have to consult the corporation master in Salisbury about whether it would be permissible.'

Dame Constance said, 'Consider yourself asked.'

Once more Sir Guy raised his voice. 'Your ability to take over is not, of course, the only issue. The question is whether you have the money that will enable you to pay the men.'

There was a protracted silence. Then, 'Yes, I do.'

Master Joseph grunted, 'We'd like to see the colour of it.'

'Well, you can't at this moment,' Master Hal replied sharply. 'I don't keep my personal funds about me at all times. I have them safe in Salisbury.'

'With the Tolomei?' John enquired cheerfully, but Master Hal failed to see the joke even when John went on helpfully, 'You know, the great international bankers.'

'No,' said Master Hal, 'with a merchant friend who happens to have a strongroom.'

Gervase, looking pleased, said, 'Well, you and your two witnesses here had better all go off to Salisbury on Monday or Tuesday and settle the matter with the—what did you call him?—the corporation master.'

'I'll come, too,' said Hamish. 'Ye'll need

someone to help you guard your money on the way back.'

'And perhaps I might join you,' said Sir Guy, who was beginning to see daylight. 'I have some business there and would welcome the company.'

His guileless look almost matched Hamish's, but only Dame Constance was suspicious.

9

'No, I don't know what Hamish is up to,' he said. 'That's to say, I don't *know*.'

'But you can guess?'

'I have an inkling.'

'Which you don't intend to reveal to me?'

'I might be wrong.' His smile, as always, was disarming.

She fought it. 'Let us then talk about another matter. And don't put me off again. You don't just have an inkling about Susanna and Piers, you *know* something. Is there some feeling between them? Because I am going to be very angry if there is.'

Serious now, he said, 'I couldn't decide whether to warn you. But she was talking to me on the day he arrived back from Shrewsbury, and the pair of them—well, it was magical to see. Think of every cliché you have ever heard. Love at first sight, made for each other, the meeting of two souls. I just sat and watched, and envied them their youth and enchantment.'

'Yes, that's all very well, but . . .'

'Indeed. "But" is the operative word.'

'The girl is contracted to marry my son. Have you spoken to Piers about the affair?'

'No. Or only in passing.'

'*No?*'

'He is concerned by the fact that he and Gervase have been friends for most of their lives. And the possibility of endangering your and my relationship—yes, he knows about it—is also an issue with him. But he is an adult and must make up his own mind. I can't interfere or advise.'

'Oh, can you not? Well, *I* can!'

The smile crept back into his eyes. 'And what will you say? That love doesn't matter? That marriage is a business arrangement? That he and Susanna must simply stop being in love? Come on, my dear, you're wiser than that.'

Decisively, she said, 'It will wear off. Infatuation always does. And Susanna is not old enough to know her own mind or to value romance at its true worth.'

'Perhaps, perhaps not. But if she is old enough to marry, she is old enough to choose. It concerns me that she may not know that she *can* choose.'

'You may be right,' Dame Constance admitted reluctantly. 'Since Gervase came home she has behaved towards him just as she did before he went away, as a dutiful, if not fond, future wife. And in his absence she was clearly giving some thought to the future.' She frowned. '*When* did she and Piers meet? Was it before or after she tried to set me up in a nunnery?'

He gave a shout of laughter. 'Before or after she did what?'

Her frown lifting, she said, 'Didn't I tell you? I discovered that she would prefer not to share Vine Regis with her mother-in-law, and was trying to think of ways to ease me out. She wondered to

295

Isabelle whether there was some manor I particularly liked and might choose to go and live in. And the nunnery was hinted at when John and Abbot Ralph were present. It sent Ralph into a state of purest terror, I may tell you.'

'I can well believe it!'

Dame Constance's frown returned. 'That must have been at least a week or two before she met Piers. Oh dear! The silly girl cannot now believe that she can marry Gervase while being head over heels in love with someone else. She cannot *possibly* be as innocent as that!'

He said carefully, 'When you were little more than a child and betrothed to Nicholas, did anyone ever tell you that it was possible for you to break the pre-marriage contract? If you wanted to.'

'I don't remember. I don't think so.'

'No. It wouldn't have suited your family for you to be made aware that you could break a contract they had gone to a good deal of trouble to arrange.'

She gave a little grimace. 'Just as it wouldn't suit *me* for Susanna to be made aware that she could break a contract *I* have gone to a good deal of trouble to arrange?'

'Precisely.'

'Hmmm. Does Piers want to marry her?'

He shrugged. 'I imagine so.'

'Guy, you are not being helpful!'

'Let me put it like this. Susanna probably thinks she is irrevocably committed to the marriage contract. You—we—may leave her in ignorance of the possibility of breaking it, but she will find out some time. And when that happens, everyone will be hurt, not least Susanna herself.'

'It doesn't worry you,' she asked tartly, 'that, if she breaks off the contract now, it is Gervase who will be hurt?'

He turned from the window to look at her, and even in the waning light she could see the humorous quirk of his eyebrow. 'Do you really think so?'

As she stared back at him, the tension drained out of her. 'No, of course not. Or only in his vanity. Hard though Susanna has tried—yes, I'll admit that—she has made no impression on him at all. He knows he must marry again and is prepared to bed her in the hope of sons. But, beyond that, nothing. I find it very odd because, although she has irritated me constantly since she arrived, she is quite a taking little thing when she wants to be. Most men would . . .'

More than once in the past, Guy had found himself wondering about Gervase's sexual inclinations but had come to the conclusion that, however common pederasty—or, as it was coming to be called, buggery—might be amongst fighting men, Gervase's problem was simple lack of interest. He was an unemotional young man, except when moved by some unpredictable force.

Dame Constance's voice had trailed away as she observed the small furrowing of Sir Guy's brow.

Now, he grinned at his beloved and said, 'Most men would respond, yes, but Gervase is not most men.'

She sighed. 'I suppose I must speak to him.'

'No, you must speak to Susanna.'

He did not immediately identify the expression on her face, which was, in fact, one of guilt. There was a reprehensible charm, she was thinking, in the

297

idea of freeing herself from Susanna's still irritating presence while simultaneously helping the girl towards her heart's desire.

'Yes,' she said. 'You are right. I must.'

CHAPTER THIRTEEN

1

It was a long day's ride to Salisbury, and Master Hal's little party was slowed down by the poor horsemanship of Bald John and Master Joseph, more accustomed to moving on foot or in a waggon. But they arrived at last and parted for the night, Sir Guy to stay with one of his fellow magistrates, Master Hal with the merchant friend who was no Tolomei, Bald John and Master Joseph in a tavern, and Hamish in a refuge unspecified. They arranged to meet in the morning at the residence of the corporation master.

Hamish did not manage a wink of sleep, since his refuge was in a doorway opposite the house where Master Hal was staying, and from which that young man obligingly emerged soon after first light, wearing a smart, clean surcoat, presumably borrowed, and making for the town's only goldsmith. Hamish gave him fifteen minutes' grace and then followed him in to the workshop, an enticing and colourful place whose walls were hung with necklaces, girdles, brooches and rings; with badges, pendants and chains; with nuggets of gold and branches of coral waiting to be mounted and made into babies' teething sticks. There were jewelled purses on the shelves, and ring blanks, and gemstones to be set in them according to the customer's choice.

As Hamish entered, the goldsmith was sitting at his table holding something up to the light.

A ring. A balas ruby ring. On the table beside him were his hand-scales and a pile of trinkets on top of which, instantly recognisable, was John's St George cloak brooch.

'Aye, aye,' said Hamish blithely to the young man standing at the goldsmith's side. 'So here you are, Master Hal. I see I've timed my visit well. I hope he's giving you a good price for all these? Ye'll never be able to pay Master Emile's workmen otherwise, will you?'

Master Hal stared at him tightly, began to stammer something about finding the jewels, then made a dive for the door. But Hamish was in his way and Sir Guy was waiting just inside, and the goldsmith's bodyguard had been alerted and was standing half-crouched like a wrestler ready for a bout. There was a violent struggle, during which the goldsmith pranced around trying to protect his valuable stock and moaning, 'Take care! Take care!' while Master Hal fought with all the trained power of his muscles to escape the trap.

In the end, when the young man was on the floor with Hamish sitting astride his chest, Sir Guy looked down upon him and said in his official voice, 'Master Hal Southern, in the belief that you may be guilty of theft, and by virtue of my position as magistrate and justice of the peace, I hereby arrest you in the king's name.'

2

Dame Constance had spent the better part of the day trying to decide how best to deal with Susanna, but had reached no conclusion by the time the sun

300

was beginning to go down. Susanna had been showing every sign of trying to behave well since Dame Constance's eruption, but Dame Constance suspected that her criticisms still rankled. However, no amount of postponement, she thought, was going to make things any easier.

One difficulty was that, coolly studied, Susanna's predicament was perfectly understandable. Gervase had many good qualities, though none of them—even his mother was forced to admit—instantly attractive to a young girl, whereas Piers was an unequivocally delightful young man, full of character as well as of charm. Dame Constance, had she been twenty years younger, could easily have fallen in love with him. Guy, twenty years before, must have been very like his son. If she had known then that she could break off her pre-contract with Nicholas, what would she have done? But she hadn't become acquainted with Guy until several years later, so the question had not arisen.

If it had, how very different her life would have been.

And now Susanna was at the same crossroads.

Looking back, Dame Constance knew very well that she should have tried harder to warm to a girl who was supposedly mature in age but was not so in temperament. The pangs of growing up, the uncertainty about who she was or wanted to be, the resistance to guidance, all were typical of adolescence and Dame Constance knew it. But only in theory because, Isabelle having been too lazy to be a troublesome daughter, she had not had to deal with it in practice. She had begun to despair of Susanna until, firstly, her own slow-burning anger had flared up and led to a scene she would have preferred not to have taken place—although the effect on the girl had been salutary—and secondly the discovery of the thefts, in which Susanna had shown both good judgement and sense.

Now, having suggested a stroll in the orchard, she said, 'I am aware of having lectured you in the past, but we have never really talked properly, have we? Not in a calm and adult way, I mean. And I think it is time we did.'

Not so long ago, Susanna would have thought, 'Oh, dear!' Instead, she raised a more mature mental eyebrow and thought, 'That will make a change!'

Dame Constance, eyes fixed on the path ahead and skirts slightly lifted to avoid sweeping up the fallen leaves, went on, 'I think perhaps I have been a little unfair to you, offering you too little encouragement to fit in at Vine Regis and expecting you to do it of your own accord.'

An apology? It couldn't be! Susanna murmured, 'I did try, but Vine Regis is so big, so grand, so—so stony!—compared with my own home at Cernwell.'

'Is Cernwell so very congenial and—er—snug? I know nothing of it.'

Susanna gave a small choke of laughter. 'Only because it is home. It's stony, too, and harsh in many ways. But it isn't full of strangers.'

Strangers.

Dame Constance, at Susanna's age, had been so self-contained that the very concept of strangers had been meaningless to her.

'Yet you must have known what to expect when you came here.'

'Knowing what to expect isn't the same as experiencing it.'

'No.' Dame Constance sat down gracefully on a convenient bench and gestured to Susanna to join her. 'But to you, strangers have remained strangers. Even the guests who so frequently come and go from Vine Regis rarely stay long enough to become friends. And most of them are, in any case, men. But some bring wives and daughters. With a little effort you could become better acquainted and perhaps be invited to visit them in turn.'

'I suppose so,' Susanna said listlessly.

'But you haven't liked them enough to make the effort?'

'Well, there have been too many other things to occupy me. I thought later, perhaps, when I am more settled.'

Dame Constance raised her eyes to meet Susanna's. 'You are not happy here, and I think you are the kind of person who needs to be happy. That is a state which it is not always possible to achieve.' Her eyes, darker than Susanna's, were intensely blue. 'What would make you happy?'

Susanna could not say, 'To be in Piers' arms forever and not have to think about anything or anyone else.' Disconsolately, she stared back at Dame Constance. 'I don't know. I thought I did. I thought it would be enough if Gervase could be persuaded to love me.'

Drily, 'And being Lady of the Castle would have helped?'

'Yes,' she admitted.

'But now?'

Weakly, Susanna repeated, 'Now?'

'Now that you believe yourself to be in love with

303

Piers.'

It was startling to hear it spoken. 'I—I . . .'

'You *can* choose, you know. You don't have to marry Gervase.'

There was a long, long moment of silence while Susanna tried to absorb what had been said—at once wonderful and so unexpected as to be almost unbearable.

Her eyes flew at last to the Lady's. 'That's what my guardian says, but I didn't believe him because he wants me to marry William.'

It was such a ridiculous idea that Dame Constance laughed. 'Which you never would.'

'Never in all eternity. Can I *really* break the pre-contract?' Her brain was beginning to function. 'My guardian probably thinks we could just ignore it—but then, if I were to marry someone else, the marriage would never be legal, would it?'

'No. And it is not so simple, I'm afraid. You would have to appear before an ecclesiastical court and state your reasons for wishing to cancel the contract.'

'I couldn't! I should be terrified!'

Dame Constance regarded her quizzically. 'Take care. Where is that new sense of responsibility I thought you were developing?'

And then she went on, 'Well, it is up to you, of course. Either you marry Gervase and become Lady of Vine Regis, hoping that love will follow, or you suffer an hour in the bishop's court and then marry Piers. In effect, you choose between making the best of what others have decreed for you, or you take your destiny into your own hands.'

Shaken and confused, Susanna jumped to her feet and stood staring blindly into the sun, a paling

304

disc against the twilight sky. 'Can I really take my destiny into my own hands?' She couldn't grasp it at first. 'I must think! I must think! Is love everything? Yes, no, I don't know.'

Dame Constance wondered whether she had heard aright. If she had, then Susanna really was growing up, and not just on the surface. Gently, she said, 'I can't answer that. Love alone is not always enough. When the first passion becomes less fervent, you discover that liking and friendship matter, too.'

'I must talk to Piers,' Susanna said breathlessly. 'I have arranged to meet him tomorrow, out towards Amerscote.'

Just then, they heard the familiar sound of a small body of horsemen plodding over the drawbridge. 'Ah,' said Dame Constance, rising to her feet. 'That sounds like the mission to Salisbury returning. Let us go and find out what has been happening.'

3

It was with his feet tied under his horse's belly and a rope binding his upper arms to his body but leaving his hands free for the reins, that Master Hal returned to Vine Regis.

No one could believe it at first. No one wanted to believe it. But Hamish had packed all the stolen trinkets into a bag under the watchful eye of Sir Guy, and the goldsmith had fixed a lead seal on the bag's tie, so that there could be no subsequent debate about its contents.

Next morning, Dame Constance summoned all

the members of the household who were known to have 'lost' brooches or jewels, and tipped the bag out on a table in the Great Hall. The cries of 'That's mine!' 'Oh, that's mine!' were proof enough of Master Hal's delinquency.

'What first made you suspicious, Hamish?' Dame Constance asked later, at a family conference in her chamber.

Hamish's two days on horseback and the sleepless night between had not dimmed his bright eyes, but his weariness was apparent as he gathered his thoughts together.

'I wouldn't say I was suspicious at first, just interested. I was having a wee gossip with him in the courtyard one night—when we'd had the scaffolding fire, remember? And he said he hoped to become a master mason himself some day soon, and needed four others to speak for him before the masons' guild. I asked was there no other way of making himself acceptable to the guild and he said none so reliable. His manner was a wee bit odd, and he implied that the sawyers must have set the scaffolding fire when I knew they couldn't have. So I wondered, that's all. I'm pretty sure he must have set it himself—all to land Master Emile in difficulties. And then, when I had the chance to speak to M. Bernard a while after, I asked him and he said that if someone like Master Hal—we named no names—was for some reason given independent responsibility for completing a project and carried it through well, it would put him in credit with the masons' guild and they might relax their rules in that case. All of which started me putting two and two together.'

He paused, and Gervase said, 'Yes, and?'

Hamish grinned. 'And it seemed to me that the young man had been going out of his way to worm himself into the Lady's good graces, and that he believed she would be happy for him to replace Master Emile.'

Dame Constance smiled wrily. 'Yes, whenever I insisted that something be done, he did it, not Master Emile. And he saved Blanche's life. And he is an attractive young man, and an intelligent one, and I found him very likeable. Oh, dear.'

'Well, when I thought carefully about it, I recognised that Master Emile had been exasperating you right from the start and now he was having a hard time with all these hold-ups. I found myself wondering about the other so-called accidents. Like the hod-men who slipped on the ramp and showered Sir Walter with rubble. Why did they slip? Mud or mortar on the treads? And when the hoist rope broke, why should it have done? Was it old, or badly maintained, or had someone deliberately frayed it with a knife? And how many men knew that replacement scaffolding would have to come all the way from the Baltic? And as for the mortar that wouldn't set on the day before the storm, because it was too dry, Master Hal told the mixer to make it much wetter, even though the mixer warned him it would make the stones slip around and hard to lay. If the mortar had been of the right texture, the wall might not have fallen down.'

Meditatively, Sir Guy said, 'I wonder if it was the foundation trench that first gave him the idea of making Master Emile's life a misery?'

Susanna, whose attention had been wandering, exclaimed, 'You don't mean he intended the wall to fall down? He can't have been trying to kill M. Alain, can he?'

'Don't be a silly little puss,' Gervase told her. 'He couldn't be sure the wall would fall down at the right moment.'

Had William been present, he would have chipped in with, 'That's what *I* said, ages ago.'

But he wasn't, so it was left to Sir Guy to remark, 'I think we will find that the two men were already acquainted when the troubadour arrived . . .'

'Coincidence!' exclaimed John dismissively. 'I don't believe it.'

'Perhaps not. But coincidence figures more often in everyday life than you might think. Troubadours move around a good deal, and they could easily have met when Master Hal was working on some other building site. Hal may well have known something to the troubadour's disadvantage. If Hamish's suspicions are correct— and I believe they are—Master Hal knew that if his plan to discredit Master Emile succeeded, he was going to be in urgent need of funds to see him through until he received the lump sum due on completion of the contract. So he reached an agreement with M. Alain for that young man to steal whatever he could lay his hands on.'

Gervase said, 'Yes, it's all quite obvious, really, isn't it?' causing his mother to reflect that if he had not been her son she would have felt sorely tempted to stick a very large pin in him.

Neither Sir Guy nor Hamish so much as blinked, but Susanna, chin on fist, told them, 'Well, I think you have been very clever, working it all out. I'm sure Gervase will see that, when he takes time to think about it, won't you, Gervase?'

'Will I? Yes, my dear. I am sure you are right.'

Although Dame Constance succeeded in suppressing her choke of laughter, her voice quavered slightly as she offered, 'I suppose that Master Hal must have been first on the scene on the morning after the storm and, finding the troubadour's body, dragged it to the river to be rid of it. He knew it would raise questions if it were left there. And of course he didn't know at that stage that we were already aware of the thefts, because we did not tell him until later in the day.'

Sir Guy nodded, but Gervase clearly thought that such minor details were of no interest. 'Let us get down to business. What happens next?' he demanded, but the question proved to be rhetorical. 'Guy will have to keep the fellow in the dungeon until he can be sentenced, but in the meantime we have to get on with the work. Either Master Emile will have to be reinstated, or we must find a new master mason, and I don't know how we do that. And we'll have to pay the workmen to stay until we find someone, I suppose. I can see that it's going to cost money, whatever happens. Why are you all staring at me?'

John said, 'We haven't quite got used to . . .'

But his mother, recovering her breath, told him, 'We have reserves,' and then, serious now, 'But before we go into that, perhaps Guy will tell us what the sentence on Master Hal is likely to be?'

'For theft, for killing a man even by accident and trying to dispose of the body, it should be death.'

309

With reluctance, Susanna rose to her feet. 'If you will excuse me, I have to see someone.'

Piers, Dame Constance remembered. She nodded a smiling dismissal.

Outside the door, which stood ajar, Susanna discovered William, all too clearly eavesdropping.

'What are you doing here?' she demanded in a sizzling whisper. 'What a dreadful boy you are! Go away and occupy yourself with something useful.' She waited until he had taken himself off, resentfully, down the stairs, and then went to her own chamber to collect Margot and on to the stables.

Telling William to go away had become such a habit that she never wondered what he did with his time other than hang about on the building site making a nuisance of himself. It did not for a moment occur to her that his hero-worship of Master Hal might have inconvenient consequences for everybody, including herself.

Now, reaching the courtyard, a worried William slipped unobtrusively along to the Mill Tower and down the steep flight of steps below it to the latticed iron gate of the castle dungeon. He found Master Hal in sole possession, sitting on the stone floor with his arms clasped round his knees and an air of absorption about him that was very unlike his usual cheerful vitality. The only furniture was a bucket and the only light came from the stairs and the tiny squint or peephole high in one wall through which the gaoler could inspect his prisoners without troubling to go all the way downstairs.

Desperate not to attract attention from anyone else who might be within earshot, William rattled the gate lightly and muttered, 'Hal! I say, Hal!'

Master Hal raised his head and William was shocked to see his bruises. His clothes, too, were badly torn after the fight in the goldsmith's shop.

William said, 'Tch, tch!' which was less than helpful, as Master Hal did not forbear to mention.

'Well, you look terrible. And your jaw's all swollen, too.'

'I am aware of that. What do you want?'

Remembering his mission, William said, 'They're having a conference up in the Lady's chamber and Sir Guy says the penalty for theft, and for killing a man even by accident, is death. I came to warn you.'

'Thank you for the warning. But it would be more useful if you did something to get me out of here.'

William was taken aback, but a moment's reflection told him it was the best answer. He didn't want to see Master Hal hanged. The only problem was, 'How?'

'There must be a key somewhere. It'll be hung on a wall in the gaoler's room.'

His mouth turning down meditatively at the corners, William said, 'There *is* a gaoler's room, I know, but the castle doesn't have a gaoler.' He had asked once, and been told that Vine Regis didn't need one. The gatekeeper did any necessary prisoner-minding in his spare moments. 'Who brought you breakfast?'

'The gatekeeper, I think.'

William nodded wisely. 'I'll go and investigate.'

Pattering along to the gaoler's room, he found it

locked, but peering through the iron lattice saw there was a single great key hanging on the wall. Would the gatekeeper go to the trouble of unlocking the gaoler's room and fetching the dungeon key every time he wanted to visit his prisoner? It seemed unlikely, gatekeepers being a notoriously idle breed. He would have a duplicate somewhere. William stared intently at the key and tried to memorise the wards. A wide one, then one that was short and thin, then a middling-sized one, and another short, fat one . . .

Down the stairs again and back to the damp and smelly dungeon. Master Hal was on his feet now. 'Well?'

'We need to divert the gatekeeper so that I can try and steal his key. He *must* have a duplicate, and it's too big to carry around. I'll go and have a gossip with him and, if you start shouting and making a fuss after a few minutes—the length of a couple of paternosters, say—he might come and investigate. I'll convince him that I'm harmless and he might leave me alone in the room.'

Grimly, Master Hal said, 'I'll have to take care not to make the kind of fuss that will persuade him to bring the key with him.'

'God's bones, I hadn't thought of that! Don't make it sound as if you're having an apoplexy, or anything of that sort. You could hint at wanting to bribe him, perhaps?'

'I've tried that already.'

'Well, try it again. I can't be expected to think of everything!'

On which slightly sour note, William took himself off to the gatekeeper's room to ask about the mechanism of the gate system and the portcullis.

'My father is thinking of installing new machinery at home,' he explained, and the gatekeeper, who knew Master William's inquisitive mind, sighed faintly and embarked on a less than lucid explanation.

'Yes, but . . .' said William, surreptitiously assessing the three great keys hung from rings on the wall.

He was studying the brake on the winch when Master Hal began shouting and the gatekeeper, with a shrug, went off to see what the fuss was about. The four guards asleep on the floor were undisturbed as William crossed hurriedly over to the keys and tucked the one he wanted into the waist of his hose, the key inside and the ring folded to the outside, hidden by his jerkin, to hold it in place. He was a picture of innocence, still engrossed in the winch brake, when the gatekeeper returned.

Sliding in and out of doorways, slithering down steps and along passages, William returned in triumph to the dungeon. There was an unnerving moment when the key stuck, but it was the right key and the iron lattice creaked open without too much noise.

'Thank you,' said Master Hal and, yanking William into the dungeon, slipped out himself, and relocked the door.

To William's indignant, 'Hey!' he responded with a laugh and the remark that the boy would only hinder his escape. And then he was gone.

In the meantime, the discussion in the Lady's chamber had been continuing.

Dame Constance had said meditatively, 'The death penalty. Yes, I thought so. But I cannot forget him saving Blanche's life the day she fell into the river. It doesn't matter what his motives were. We owe him something for that—a life for a life. I believe we should let him go free. If the masons' guild bans him from any further employment in his chosen trade, that should be punishment enough.'

Gervase was shocked, but everyone else had rather liked Master Hal. Sir Guy said, 'Well, it's one way of looking at things. And if he had been a different kind of young man, he could have saved himself a good deal of trouble by simply arranging a fatal accident for Master Emile. Murder is easy on a building site. Very well. I will be defaulting on my legal oaths, but we will keep him in the dungeon for a few days in order to frighten him, and then release him. Does that satisfy you?'

It did, and the conversation had progressed to other matters when a breathless gatekeeper was admitted by Dame Constance's gentlewoman, Matilda. He was scarlet with shame and by no means coherent, so that it was some minutes before they discovered that Master Hal had been released through the agency of young Master William, who had himself been locked up in turn by the prisoner and had taken some little time to attract attention. The lad was not best pleased, he remarked.

Neither were Lord Gervase or Sir Guy. Gervase,

indeed, was furious. 'All of a piece,' he exclaimed. 'Just what I would have expected from this whole misbegotten business. We'd better get after him. Are you coming, Guy?'

'Yes, indeed,' said Sir Guy, smothering a grin. He was finding it increasingly difficult to take Gervase's newly authoritative manner seriously, but suspected the entertainment value would soon pall. 'Let's not rush things, however,' he went on and turned to the gatekeeper. 'Arthur, how long since he got away? And how far do you reckon he can have gone?'

Arthur let his breath out in a puff. 'Depends. I arst a couple of the workmen but they swear they didn' see him. I don't believe them. If he took a 'orse, he'd be well over the hill by now. If he didn', he wouldn' be much further than the village. Unless he made fer the woods, o' course.'

Fortunately, when they reached the courtyard, one of the stable boys was able to report that Master Hal had led out one of the coursers and ridden off Stanwelle way. Bareback, he added, with reluctant admiration.

'Right,' said Gervase. 'We'd better saddle up. And where's my page? I'll want my longsword and my crossbow.'

6

Susanna, accompanied by her small party of Margot, old Tom the groom, and a young page, was so absorbed in the prospect of meeting Piers that she scarcely noticed how the season had changed. It was more than six months since she had arrived at Vine Regis, and they had been eventful months by any standards, though the summer had been so long and so hot that it had seemed to last forever, the days and the weeks floating by in a timeless haze. But now, suddenly, the landscape was brilliant with early autumn colours, the bronze and gold of the beech leaves, the amber bracken, the purple smoke of the dogwood leaves in the hedges, the hawthorns with their burden of redwings and fieldfares gorging themselves on the berries. A high wind and all would go flying and flirting over the low hills, but that time was not yet.

All Susanna could think of was what Dame Constance had said about her having a choice between making the best of what others had decreed for her, or taking her destiny into her own hands. She had suddenly realised that, put like that, it was no choice at all. Her whole future depended on what *she* decided, and if her decision proved to be a mistake, at least it would be her own mistake, not someone else's. All she needed was the ultimate reassurance of a few words from Piers, the proof that she had not misjudged his love.

Her little party was approaching the hill where they had agreed to meet, a hill identified by the great flat rock that formed its face. She was probably early, but had been too eager to risk being late.

She was lost in her dreams when, 'My lady,' said Margot uneasily, drawing her attention to another, solitary rider who was coming up fast behind them. It wasn't Piers. Beyond the rider was a small group of other horsemen, galloping hard.

Even as Susanna hesitated and drew rein, the solitary rider was closing up. Then he raised his head and she recognised him. 'Master Hal!' It was clear from the pursuit that he must have escaped, and his pursuers were easy enough to identify—Gervase, Sir Guy, John, and an assortment of pages and grooms.

They were still two or three hundred yards away when Master Hal reached her. She tried to draw to one side, thinking to let him pass, but he had no such intention. Shouldering his courser into the midst of her small party, he flung old Tom and her page aside with well-aimed blows to their heads, and then made a grab for Susanna's reins and began hauling the palfrey towards the hill with the rock face.

'No, no! Leave me alone,' Susanna gasped, wrestling for control of the reins. 'Ride on. I won't try and stop you.'

He gave a snort of laughter. 'You wouldn't succeed. But what a fortunate encounter this is, my lady! I rely on you to discourage his lordship from using that crossbow of his.'

Then he slid to the ground and reached up to drag her from her saddle. Too concerned about the risk of damaging her ankle again, she could not resist, even when he forced her over to the rock face. There, setting his back against it, he clutched her tightly in front of him like a shield, his arms around her waist and hers locked to her sides.

Feeling safer on her feet, but much too late, she began to struggle. She could see old Tom and the page sitting up, shaking their heads to clear them of the blows Master Hal had struck, but neither of them looked in a fit state to come to her rescue.

Hoarsely, he said, 'Enough!' and she felt one of his arms loosen and drop, and she thought, 'Mary Mother of God be praised. There are too many people for him to deal with. He knows he cannot win.'

She was quite wrong. His hand rose again, and in it was his big, triangular-bladed mason's knife. He placed one edge just below her chin.

She gulped in horror, and the tiny movement in her throat was enough to bring her skin into contact with the knife. The slight scraping sensation was unutterably frightening.

But, she told herself, it couldn't be! This was cheerful, helpful Master Hal! He couldn't—he *could not*—really mean to hurt her. Yet he was desperate. She might be terrified, but so, she realised after a moment, was he. He was sweating profusely and his hand was shaking. If it were to slip . . . She stood as still as a statue, only her eyelids fluttering with fear.

Then the shouting began. Gervase demonstrated that they were within range of his crossbow by firing a bolt over and to the left of them. But it was more an expression of fury than anything else, and Susanna saw Sir Guy lay a hand on his arm and say, 'No.'

Master Hal shouted, 'You can kill her if you want to. And I will kill her if I must. Otherwise I want two fresh, saddled horses and to be allowed to ride off with her until I am well away from this benighted place. I'll free her, then.'

'Don't you dare touch her. Free her now, this instant!'

'And let myself be caught and hanged? Why should I?'

Gervase made a move forward, and Master Hal yelled, 'Stand back!' His hand twitched and again Susanna felt the scrape of the knife against her skin. Every other part of her was shaking with terror, and she scarcely dared breathe.

And then Sir Guy raised his cooler voice. 'Hal, listen to me. We had decided to let you go, because you saved little Lady Blanche's life all those months ago and we were grateful and appreciative. But you are making it impossible. Let the Lady Susanna go and something might be arranged.'

' "Might be"? Why should I trust your "might be" when it's my life that's at stake?'

It couldn't go on like this, Susanna thought, her brain at last beginning to function. What if she fainted? What if she *pretended* to faint? Did she dare?

Master Hal shouted, 'If you want her back alive, you know what to do!'

All his attention was concentrated on his pursuers, who were milling about restlessly, pointing and arguing. Her stillness made him sure of her, and she was conscious of the knife at her throat being loosely held. It was now or never.

Did she, *did* she dare?

If only Piers would come!

Shuddering inside, she moaned and let all her muscles go limp, so that she slumped down on Master Hal's left arm and threw him off balance. He hesitated for the briefest of moments and then began to haul her upright again, her arms flopping at her sides.

But that moment was enough. Piers descended from the heavens.

Coming to meet her, he had heard the shouting and had dismounted to investigate. Rather than charging in to what sounded like a thoroughly tense situation, he had crawled into position above the rock face—only to discover his beloved in danger of her life. After the first shock, his mind racing, he had lain working through all the possibilities, such as they were.

His only advantage was that Master Hal did not know he was there, an advantage he could not afford to lose. With the other man backed right up against the rock face, bow and arrow were ruled out, and although a thrown knife would not advertise Piers' position so obviously, there seemed no risk-proof target point for the knife. Whatever the means of attack, it had to incapacitate Master Hal *instantly* if Susanna were to be kept safe.

A knockout blow to the head? There were rocks enough strewn around, and Piers hefted one of about the right weight and size. But he didn't dare miss. Master Hal still needed to be distracted, however briefly.

With all his being so closely focused on Susanna, willing her to be brave, Piers saw her mouth tighten, sensed the beginnings of her collapse even before Master Hal did. Rising to his knees, he aimed and dropped the rock on the other man's head and then, even as Master Hal groaned and shook himself, leapt down after it.

The fight that followed was short and violent, Master Hal fighting for his life, and Piers for his love.

Susanna, trying to scramble out of the way of the flailing arms and legs and fists, felt one of the fists connect with her temple and, this time genuinely, lost consciousness.

When she came to, seconds later, she found herself cradled in Piers' arms. He was bruised and bloodied, and his eyes were briefly anxious, but when she opened hers they changed instantly to brilliant, smiling and loving.

It was the end of any doubts she might have had. She loved him without reservation.

'I knew you would come,' she breathed. 'I knew you would save me.'

'You saved yourself.' Then, gently brushing her tangled curls back from her forehead, he murmured, 'My poor, dear love, you are going to have a beautiful black eye.'

She gave a hiccup of overwrought laughter. 'You, too!'

Gervase was offended to discover that Master Hal was dead, accidental victim of his own mason's knife, but Sir Guy said, 'It is for the best. And that was well done, Piers. We were at a loss.'

'Yes,' Gervase agreed belatedly. 'Thank you. I'll take her,' and leaning over to Susanna, lifted her clumsily from Piers' embrace. 'She can ride back with me.'

Struggling free, Susanna responded tartly, 'If by "she" you mean me, I detest riding pillion. If someone will just fetch Angel back from that lovely patch of grazing she has found, I can manage perfectly well by myself, thank you.'

It was partly bravado that spoke, but more a dislike of the close physical contact entailed in sharing Gervase's mount. Riding pillion would force her to grasp him round the waist; if he took her up in front, she would be held enclosed in the circle of his arms. She was repelled by the thought.

By the time they reached Vine Regis again, a noisy, talkative little procession with Master Hal's body bringing up the rear, draped over the courser he had stolen from the stables, Susanna had such a blinding headache that she had to retire to her chamber. The apothecary, forbidden by Dame Constance to bleed his patient, fussed around with cold compresses until Susanna was ready to scream. But he went at last, and a bowl of capon broth did much to soothe her, so that she was able to sleep more peacefully than she had expected, in view of the throbbing in her temple and her overactive brain.

In the morning, a sympathetic Isabelle constructed an embroidered cover for the apothecary's plain bandage, so that she was able to face the world looking perhaps a little raffish but with her swollen eye hidden from view.

Piers swore she looked charming when they met by arrangement in the courtyard garden, quiet and peaceful in the suspension of the building works.

She no longer had any doubt about what she wanted, so she came straight to the point. 'I had thought,' she said, 'that I was committed to marrying Gervase, but now it seems that I can escape that. If I want to. If *you* want me to?'

For a moment, he didn't answer, or not in

words. Then he said, his eyes alight, 'I will speak to Gervase. He and I have been friends for many years, and I would hope to make him understand.'

She was sorely tempted, but, 'No,' she said. 'It is only right that I should tell him myself.' If Dame Constance had been present, she would have applauded.

Not so Gervase, when Susanna gathered all her courage together and requested him to visit her in her chamber.

He asked politely whether she had fully recovered from the excitements of the previous day, and she said yes, thank you, she had.

He said it was a pity that Master Hal had turned out to be a bad penny, since he had seemed quite an efficient fellow, and she said yes, that was true.

He remarked on the probable difficulty of finding new builders to continue the work on the extension, and she said, indeed, it would not be easy.

He asked whether she had something particular she wished to say to him, and she said yes, she did.

'I wished to say that you have been very kind to me. Everyone at Vine Regis has been very kind to me. But I do not believe that I can ever feel at home here. Despite our pre-contract, I find that—I find that I would prefer not to be married to you. If you don't mind?'

'Oh.'

'I—er—understand it would be possible to have the pre-contract overset.'

'Yes.'

'And I would like that to be done,' she went on a little desperately.

'Why?'

'I don't think I will ever feel at home here.'

'Yes, you said that before.'

'It may sound a weak-minded reason . . .'

'It does.' He was beginning to absorb what she had been saying. 'And I *do* mind.'

She said in a small voice, 'But you don't love me. You don't even like me.'

'That has nothing to do with it. You are my betrothed wife.'

'You mean I am one of your possessions?' Her headache was building up again. 'Well, I would prefer not to be. I don't want to be owned. I want to be loved!'

Even Gervase, far from perceptive, was capable of putting two and two together. 'I see. Do I deduce that you are proposing to marry some other man? Someone who *does* love you?'

She gulped. 'Yes.'

'Who?'

She had been praying that he would not ask. But he did, and she had no choice but to answer.

'Piers Whiteford.'

Gervase's colour had been slowly rising. Now, his hollow cheeks were scarlet and his mouth clamped shut, like a trap, the indentations running from its corners to the base of his nose showing up deeply incised. But he said nothing, or not to her.

Instead, he drew in a sharp breath, then turned and rushed out, and she could hear him marching along the corridor and down the stairs, shouting, 'Piers, Piers! Where are you? Show yourself!'

Horrified, she picked up her skirts and hurried after him, down the stairs and into the Great Hall.

'Piers, Piers! Where are you?'

His smallsword was in his hand.

Piers, who had been sitting talking intently to his father and Dame Constance, rose to his feet. 'I'm here, Gervase.'

'Right. On guard!'

Piers' own sword hissed out of its scabbard, while Dame Constance's voice approached more nearly to a shriek than anyone had ever heard from her before. 'Not in here, Gervase. Not here. Don't you dare! I won't have it.'

Susanna clutched him by the arm, and was roughly shaken off, while Sir Guy exclaimed, 'Don't be a fool, Gervase!' and John demanded, 'What's going on? What's this all about?'

Then Gervase and Piers were dashing off out of the Great Hall, stripping off their tunics as they went, followed at speed by a small horde of open-mouthed spectators.

There was a patch of relatively uncluttered grass on the other side of the moat and Gervase, kicking a few abandoned tools out of the way, announced, 'This will suffice. Right. On guard!' And lunged at Piers with no more ado.

Piers skipped back to escape the attack, and stood holding himself ready for the next. This time it was a cut from above and Piers was prepared, forcing the blade aside by sliding it along his own and then grappling and locking Gervase's sword arm in the crook of his elbow. But Gervase broke free and tried a thrust which Piers smacked aside with his own blade, and then there was a succession of upward thrusts, downward thrusts and crosswise thrusts, with an occasional straightforward lunge.

There was nothing graceful about the fight, no ballet of thrust and parry, but Susanna discovered, when she dared to look, that no blood was being shed and that Piers seemed competent to hold his own. An occasional cheer rose from the audience at what she took to be some masterly stroke, though they all looked the same to her—horribly dangerous.

'Stop,' she murmured. 'Oh, stop!'

But it went on and on. Dame Constance was standing close by Susanna, seething with irritation. 'Men! *Really*. They have no sense.'

Sir Guy laughed—Susanna couldn't believe it; did he have *no* feeling for his son?—and remarked, 'They will feel better afterwards. Or would you rather they scratched each other's eyes out?' earning himself a glare from Dame Constance.

And then there was blood on Piers' sleeve and Susanna moaned 'No!' although it did not seem to trouble him. Indeed, when Gervase tried another downward thrust he pushed Gervase's arm aside and down, while at the same time dropping the hilt of his own sword behind Gervase's bent knee and using it as a lever to throw his opponent to the ground.

After that both men abandoned their swords—Gervase breathlessly demanding, 'Where did you learn that trick?'—and it all degenerated into a vulgar wrestling match. In the end, they both gave up from exhaustion and lay back on the turf breathing heavily.

'Whoooar,' puffed Gervase at last. 'That's better.'

Dame Constance went and stood over them. 'May I ask,' she enquired politely, 'who won?'

Sir Guy joined her. 'Both and neither, I should say. Gervase is used to laying about himself in battle with his longsword, whereas Piers is not a battle-scarred veteran but a man who has been well trained in the art of swordsmanship. Gervase has the brute force while Piers has the technique.'

Gervase sat up. 'That's true enough. Well, I don't know about you, Piers, but I could do with a drink.'

And off the pair of them went, battered but companionable, in search of ale.

Her legs feeling as limp as the stalks in a daisy chain, Susanna followed them, remembering 'cannonball day', the day when Gervase had lost his temper with the builders over the demolition of the window sill in the Great Hall. He had been much more human and cheerful afterwards, then, too. It was very odd.

CHAPTER FOURTEEN

1

'We need Ralph,' said Dame Constance decisively.

'You'll not get him to come here when it's pouring like this,' offered John helpfully. 'Anyway, why do we need him?'

'We need to ask M. Bernard if he can recommend a new master mason,' his mother sighed, 'and it would be impolite, at the very least, to go straight to the architect rather than to his employer.'

'Oh, is that all?'

'No, that is not all! There is also the little matter of freeing Susanna and Gervase from their pre-contract, and to do that requires an appearance at the consistory court of the bishopric, with legal representation.'

'Surely Guy can deal with that? He's a lawyer and it's his son who's the cause of the trouble,' John chuckled. 'Which being so, I should hope he wouldn't charge you for his services.'

'Very droll,' said Sir Guy. 'But I am qualified in civil law, not canon law.'

'Is there a difference?'

His mother sighed again. 'You are being provocative. Of course there is a difference. The point at issue is that Ralph holds not only an abbacy but an archdeaconry, and in that capacity he presides over the consistory court. I believe that it would ease Susanna's path considerably if he could be persuaded, before the case comes before him, to view her application favourably.'

'Oh, ho!'

Dame Constance, pained, closed her eyes. 'I do wish that you would break yourself of the habit of saying "Oh, ho!" in that suggestive fashion.'

But John was not to be silenced. 'Suggestive? Well, what do you expect? You're going to get your way by flirting your eyelashes at Ralph and turning him to a jelly, aren't you? You should be ashamed of yourself.'

'That is no way to speak to your mother!'

But, '*Touché*, I think?' remarked Sir Guy.

2

The rain stopped, the temperature dropped, and Dame Constance—with a train including Sir Guy, Gervase, and a full complement of richly dressed attendants—rode over to Stanwelle on a fresh, frost-sparkling morning that virtually guaranteed they would find Abbot Ralph indoors, comfortably ensconsed before a roaring fire. They did him a slight injustice. The fire was roaring so effectively that he had risked moving away from it to sit at a table covered with parchments, books and document rolls, every inch of him speaking of authority and distinction. If his air of imperturbability slipped a little at sight of his visitors, they could not tell that he was adjusting to the prospect of yet another fifty days on bread and water and wondering whether he might justifiably argue that his penances should run concurrently rather than consecutively. It was up to him to decide, since the penitentials didn't cover a problem such as his. Perhaps he had been over-conscientious in the past.

He welcomed them graciously, summoned wine and spices for their refreshment, and waited to be told the reason for their visit.

'The building works at Vine Regis,' said Dame Constance. 'We have had certain problems.'

Abbot Ralph had heard rumours and was dying to know more, but nothing would have induced him to show it. 'Oh, dear,' he said, absently straightening one of the document rolls which had strayed out of alignment.

'Sir Guy will tell you.'

To the inhabitants of Vine Regis the previous few days had felt like an eternity, but Sir Guy crisply reduced the saga to its proper proportions, without a word wasted. When he had reached the conclusion, Abbot Ralph nodded and said, 'Problems, indeed. How may I help?'

'We need advice about finding a new master mason.'

M. Bernard was duly summoned and the question put to him. 'A master mason,' he meditated, 'with a full team of craftsmen and workmen. Hmmm.'

Sir Guy said, 'Master Emile himself has gone but most of his team are still at Vine Regis, arguing their future. I believe they would accept employment under a new master, if it were offered and if they trusted him.'

'Hmmm. There is Master Raymond, perhaps, but he would wish to bring his own team. Or possibly Master Beke who, I am told, is close to completing the work he is at present engaged on down Shaftesbury way.'

Gervase exclaimed, 'But we'd have to wait on his convenience, wouldn't we? And we want to get on with the work.'

M. Bernard said politely, 'It is usual for good master masons to be fully employed, so it is in general necessary to await their convenience. If you prefer to take on someone who *is* immediately available, you may find that there is good reason for it. The builder who has to go looking for work is not always to be relied upon.'

In truth, M. Bernard would have been perfectly happy to take on the project himself, fitting it in with his work at Stanwelle, but he could hardly suggest it. The abbot would feel he was not giving his all to the new chapel and there was also the fact that, having now for the first time met the impatient Lord Gervase, M. Bernard did not fancy having any more to do with him. If someone from Vine Regis were to make the suggestion, of course . . .

Dame Constance had, as it happened, been thinking of doing just that, but Ralph's goodwill was too important for her to risk upsetting him at this point. Time enough, she thought, when the matter of the pre-contract had been settled.

'Perhaps,' she said, 'M. Bernard might give the matter some thought? As my son says, it would be convenient to have the work progress as soon as possible, though the urgency is less than it was.'

'Oh?'

'You may recall,' she took an invisible breath, 'that the original reason for the work was to make Vine Regis more convenient for Gervase's new bride?'

'The Lady—ah—Susanna? Yes.'

'Unfortunately . . .'

Gervase was marching restlessly around the room. 'The silly girl has decided she doesn't want to marry me, after all.'

Abbot Ralph raised his eyes from his steepled fingers and caught Dame Constance flicking an irritated glance at her son.

She said, 'Unfortunately, there is the difficulty of the pre-contract. May I ask when is the next meeting of the consistory court, at which she may put her case for it to be dissolved or set aside?'

He suspected that the Lady was up to something and was not prepared to let her get away with it—whatever it might be—as easily as that. 'Do I deduce that you favour her case?'

She very nearly blushed. 'I would not wish her to marry my son if she is destined to be unhappy.'

'Whether the court would consider the young lady's probable unhappiness as a valid reason for overturning a legal contract is doubtful. It seems to me, also, that it is rather late in the day for her to wish to withdraw from it.'

'What kind of reason would the court prefer?' Gervase demanded.

Coldly, the abbot replied, 'A hitherto undiscovered degree of affinity is the more usual.'

'Oh, well, if that's all! I'm sure, if we set our minds to it, that we could discover we had a great-great-grandfather or something in common. Would that do?'

'Gervase, really!' exclaimed his mother. 'If ever you paid attention, you would know that we carefully investigated the possibility of even the remotest kinship before the betrothal was arranged.'

Sir Guy felt it was time to intervene. 'Father Abbot,' he said, 'it should perhaps be made clear that the Lady Susanna would prefer not to marry Lord Gervase because she has a different husband in mind, and unless she can be released from this pre-contract such a marriage would not be valid in the eyes of Church or state.'

'That is certainly a consideration. May one enquire as to the identity of the "different husband"?'

Affably, Sir Guy replied, 'My son Piers.'

Abbot Ralph's eyes travelled from Guy to Gervase and back again. 'Ah, hmmm. And if she were to marry your son, would she be as well provided for as if she were to marry Lord Gervase?'

'He's got you there, Guy!' exclaimed Gervase cheerfully. He had come to a halt by one of the windows and was standing gazing back into the room with hands on hips.

Dame Constance let out a puff of exasperation. She would have left Gervase at home, but he had insisted on coming. Also, she was feeling exceedingly hot. 'Ralph, may I have my chair moved away from the fire?'

The abbot gestured to a lay brother standing in the corner of the room, waiting to make himself useful, and the chair was moved.

Fanning herself with one of Ralph's parchments, Dame Constance said, 'Guy?'

'The Lady Susanna would be comfortably, though not so grandly provided for if she married my son. I intend to make over my manor of Lanson to him.'

Gervase managed no more than a 'But', before Dame Constance snapped, 'That will do, Gervase!' Then she smiled winningly at Abbot Ralph and said, 'We have taken up too much of your time. But when the consistory court meets, I hope you may look kindly on Lady Susanna's suit.'

It was not quite a question, but the abbot, valiantly ignoring the twitching in his loins, relaxed his expression into something resembling a returning smile and said, 'Of course. It is always helpful to know more about the background of a case than is likely to emerge in court. Though I can make no promises, you understand.'

'I understand.'

3

And so everything was settled. Or almost everything. Or almost settled.

'I think I might change my occupation and become a *jongleur*,' said Dame Constance thoughtfully a few days later. 'I would never have dreamed it possible to juggle so many balls in the air at the same time. Perhaps I could give lessons.'

Gervase, tossing out the lure to his goshawk, remarked, 'Well, you bring it all on yourself. Why don't you let other people do things for a change?'

Coming from Gervase, this was altogether too much. 'Other people?' she echoed. 'Such as who?'

'Don't look at *me*. I think I should get back to Court as soon as possible. No, you've got old Walter and all the other household officers. And I'm sure Guy would be prepared to help out, if necessary. I've sometimes thought he has a bit of a soft spot for you.'

'Have you, indeed?'

'Which reminds me. When we were over at Stanwelle, you stopped me asking where he's going to live when he makes Lanson over to Piers and Susanna. But I suppose he has that other place over to the east, hasn't he?'

'Hervelock, you mean?'

'Do I?'

'Yes.' She took a deep breath. 'The problem, however, does not arise. He has asked me to marry him many times and I have finally agreed. He can come and live at Vine Regis.'

4

'Well, my dear?' Guy had said after their return from Stanwelle.

'Well, what?'

'Having wound Abbot Ralph round your little finger . . .'

'*That* would be an achievement!' she laughed.

'. . . and virtually ensured that he will permit the pre-marriage contract to be set aside, you have put Susanna and Piers in your debt forever. But what about me?'

'I had a dreadful moment,' she exclaimed, 'when I thought you were going to say something about us, and that Ralph would brandish the Table of Affinity at us and declare that it would be illegal for your son to marry *my* son's betrothed!'

'Don't try and divert me, you wicked woman. What about me? What about us?'

She needed him. She had been alone for too

long. Perhaps it was time to admit it—but not too readily.

'Us?'

'When will you marry me?'

She went quite still.

'Or, to put it another way,' he said, *'will* you marry me?'

He pulled her towards him and put his hand under her chin so that her eyes were forced up to meet his.

She closed them.

He shook her lightly and said again, *'Will you marry me?'*

There was mischief in her voice. 'If you insist.'

His gaze alight, 'I do.'

'Oh, well, if you choose to take that attitude . . .'

And, laughing together, as so often before, they had gone to bed and celebrated.

5

Now, Gervase dropped the hood over his goshawk's head so abruptly that the bird gave a faint mew of protest and shifted irritably on Gervase's gauntlet.

'You *what*?'

'I have agreed to marry him.'

'Oh.'

There was a protracted pause while he absorbed the information and considered its implications. 'Oh well, that's all right then. I won't have to worry about being away at Court for so much of the time. You two ought to manage, between you.'

Tempted, she agreed. 'I think so, though Vine

Regis will miss your—ah—lordly authority and interest in the estates.'

It went right over his head. 'Can't be helped. Anyway, if I make my name at Court it can only benefit the family. I mean, the king might well bestow some more lands and estates on me if he should happen to be feeling generous. Kings do, you know.'

'Yes, my dear. I do know.' She twitched on her reins. 'Now, let us get back. I have a number of people to see.'

It was only as they crossed the drawbridge that it occurred to him to say, 'I am pleased that you should marry again. Guy is a good man. I would congratulate you, but I believe it would be more correct of me to congratulate him rather than you?'

'Yes. To me, you should offer your good wishes.'

He went further than that. 'Good wishes, then, mother, and all happiness. You deserve it.'

She was too overcome to reply.

6

One of the people she had to see was M. Bernard, whom she found prowling around the building site watched suspiciously by Master Emile's remaining workers. He had brought Master Beke with him, who had apparently completed his work 'down Shaftesbury way' and might be prepared to consider taking over the Vine Regis project.

'Though I cannot be happy about taking over until I have carefully inspected the work already done,' said this gentleman. 'We would have to agree that I should not be held responsible for any flaws in the foundation work that might emerge in the future.'

'Of course not.' Dame Constance glanced at M. Bernard, who said, 'I would consider that as a reasonable proviso.' He paused. 'I have spoken to the Father Abbot about this, and he is content that I should ride over from time to time, in case Master Beke feels the need to consult me.'

'How kind. I must visit him and thank him.'

M. Bernard shook his head. 'He foresaw that and asked me to say that there is no need for it.'

Dame Constance surveyed him approvingly. M. Bernard had chosen his time well, and with only the most delicate prodding from her.

They had waited until the consistory court proceedings were over, when Abbot Ralph had achieved a compromise entirely satisfactory to himself by judging in Susanna's favour and thus pleasing Dame Constance, while gratifying his own sense of what was right and proper by admonishing the plaintiff for valuing her own selfish inclinations above her legal duty. So everyone—except William—was happy, with even Susanna conceding that the sanctimonious reprimand was a small price to pay for her freedom.

To Master Beke, Dame Constance said, 'Then may I ask you to consult with my treasurer about your contract?'

And that was another ball fewer to juggle with.

Sir Walter, once more instructed to act as superintendent of the works, reassured himself that Master Beke did not look like the kind of man who would permit rocks to be rained down on passersby such as himself, and Master Beke said no, indeed, that was not a practice of which he could approve.

Whereupon William, feeling that the new master mason—not, alas, a West Countryman—would benefit from knowing the fuller picture, spoke up. 'In case you should be wondering, Master Beke, I am William Burnell and I know a lot about the building works. I'll be happy to help and advise, if you need me.'

'How kind,' said Master Beke.

'William, go away,' said Susanna.

'No, stay,' squealed Blanche. 'I like having you to fight with!'

Dame Constance threw up her hands in despair and went off to discuss plans with Sir Guy.

7

A few problems remained. What was to be done about the children? Vine Regis was their family home, and they could not be transplanted to Lanson.

'Are you not going to be our mother after all?' Blanche had demanded of Susanna. 'What a pity, when we were just getting used to you.'

It was more than Susanna would have expected, if not as much as she would have wished.

'You can come and visit me often,' she said.

'All right. And Piers can teach us to ride. That would be good. But it's going to be queer with you gone, and Aunt Isabelle getting married too, and going away. Who's going to look after us?'

'You'll have to ask your grandmother.'

Dame Constance had no immediate answer.

'Who would you like to look after you? You'll still have Nurse.'

'We're too grown-up for Nurse,' Blanche declared, and Eleanor nodded a silent head. 'We ought to have proper gentlewomen, now.'

'Well, not quite yet, perhaps.' Dame Constance hid a smile. 'Would you like Alice to stay?'

Village girl or no village girl, Susanna's chamberer had caused none of the problems Dame Constance had anticipated, and had proved to be sensible as well as pretty and sweet-natured.

'Oh, yes. And Hamish likes her a lot.'

'Blanche!'

'Well, he does.'

Children could be appallingly observant, Dame Constance reflected as she sent them off to play.

8

Not wishing to overshadow Susanna's marriage to Piers, Dame Constance and Sir Guy decided to postpone their own marriage until later, and then hold it quietly in the chapel at Vine Regis, with no more celebration than a banquet for the household afterwards.

All the splendour was to be reserved for the younger couple.

Susanna having declared that never again, in her lifetime, would she travel by horse litter, she arrived at the village church on a wonderfully caparisoned palfrey, her saddlecloth embroidered in gold on white and gilt tassels everywhere. Master Nicholas had surpassed himself by creating a truly lovely kirtle and sleeveless surcoat for her in

340

the green she had almost begun to like, with more gold embroidery all over and an ermine trim round the deep armholes of the surcoat. The natural gold of her hair picked up an extra glow and sparkle from the embroidery and from the November sun, so that, to Piers, waiting at the church door, she appeared as a vision of loveliness.

She blushed a little as he moved forward to help her dismount, and then stood with him as he offered her, displayed on an open book, a number of gold coins as a symbol of her dower along with the ring that he would soon place on her finger.

They exchanged vows of love and honour before entering the church for prayers and to take Mass, and then to kneel under a canopy for a further blessing on their marriage and on the ring which represented the plighting of their troth. Susanna waited nervously for the new castle chaplain, Father Sebastian, who had supplanted Father Hoby for the occasion, to dip his asperser in the bowl of holy water and distribute it over the ring, but fortunately his aim with his aspersions proved to be better controlled than that of the village priest and everyone remained unsplashed.

Half the population from miles around had come to cheer the young couple—a wedding procession was always a welcome distraction from the dullness of everyday life—and to scramble for the coins tossed among them by the groom as he and his bride rode back to Vine Regis for the wedding feast.

It was a wonderful feast, with every exotic dish imaginable and many of them basted with a paste of saffron and egg yolks which made them glow like gold. There were peacocks and swans cooked

341

and re-encased in their plumage—too oily to eat with any pleasure, but lovely to look at. And all kinds of sweet things and spices to end with.

9

Afterwards, waving the happy couple off to their future home at Lanson, Dame Constance remarked to Sir Guy, 'What a relief. Only two, or perhaps three more weddings to go—Isabelle and Robert Salvin, our own, and just possibly Hamish and Alice. I will have nothing more to juggle with, apart from the building works. I won't know what to do with my time, will I?'

'You've forgotten something,' he said.

'Have I?'

'Gervase.'

She gave a faint moan. 'Oh-h-h-h, yes. I will have to start all over again, finding a wife for him.'

They had not been aware of Gervase standing close by until his voice said briskly, 'No, that's all right, mother. Don't trouble yourself. I am perfectly capable of finding a wife for myself.'

Dumbfounded, she turned and stared at him. And then she began to laugh, and laugh, as if she would never stop.

It was catching. Sir Guy soon joined her. And John. And William, soon to take his reluctant departure. And Isabelle, with her breathy little giggle, and Mr Salvin, who was not too sure what was amusing the others. And Hamish, who knew very well. Even Abbot Ralph managed a deep, rolling chuckle.

Gervase asked blankly, 'What is so funny?' but no one had the heart to tell him.